Champ

and

A Bit of Sunshine

A Cryptozoology & Craft Beer Adventure

Drink in the adventure
Mark J Trolly

Mark D. Trollinger

Abir Hasan (cover)

Copyright © 2018 Pensive Opossum Productions
Second printing
All rights reserved.

ISBN-13: 9781719960458

DEDICATION

I would like to dedicate this to my wife Susana, Karmina, Jorge, Lydia, my mom Linda, my grandma Jenny, Nan & Granddad, and Grandpa Ray. I don't know how Susana and the family puts up with all of my talk and interest in unknown monsters, but I am glad they tolerate it.

A special dedication to my friends Marsha (who loves New England and helped serve as a subject matter expert on this story) and Ronda. The three of us had some good travels around the country, including New England as "The Traveling Trio." They are not into beer, but next time we end up in Dover, NH together the Russelritas are on me (okay, just the first round)!

And also to my Dad. Even though my Dad drank crappy beer, he was a beer fan. I am a beer fan. Yet we only shared a beer one time. I imagine he would be reluctant to try new beers that are out today at first, but ultimately he would go for it. He loved music and he embraced hard rock and heavy metal bands when I was growing up. He wasn't afraid to try something new, and if he liked it he went for it, regardless of what others thought. We had the same birthday and I always find a Hamm's and have it in his honor on our day. I wrote and directed my first short film based on that idea. You should check it out on my YouTube page. The link is too hard to include in a printed book, but just go to YouTube and search Mark Trollinger ¡Salud!

CONTENTS

	Acknowledgments	i
1	Hickory	1
2	Shipping Up To Boston	4
3	Firebug	11
4	Salem	15
5	Portland	38
6	NH to Burlington	52
7	Late Night Snack	61
8	The 802	65
9	Film at Eleven	85
10	Bang a Uey	89
11	The Other Place	110
12	Does Champ Exist?	117
13	Sailing (Takes me Away)	155
14	Back on Land	168
15	Night Swim	176
16	An Inconvenient Truth	186
17	Fishes	203
18	Down Sella	206
19	Brattleboro	219
20	Back to Austin	226
	Beer List	229
	An Author's Tale	234
	About the Author	249

Trollinger

ACKNOWLEDGMENTS

A sip of Sunshine has been a well-sought after beer for several years now and is on the in search of (ISO) list of most craft beer traders around the country. I only joined the craft beer scene in 2012, and even in 2015, I was unfamiliar with this beer. While preparing to travel to Boothbay Harbor, ME over Labor Day to run the Boothbay Harbor Festival Half Marathon my friend and District Product Manager at World of Beer Tempe JP asked me if I could bring back Sip of Sunshine. (Even though it is gone I will continue to use its name. ¡Viva la World of Beer Tempe!). He knew I was driving all over New England and would be in Vermont. Without knowing what it was I agreed. Driving back from Burlington I searched on Untappd for it, found out Lawson's Finest Liquids made it in Wells, Vermont, so I drove there. After searching aimlessly down a few streets in the small town, I could not find a brewery for Lawson's. I happened upon the local general store, walked in, and asked an employee if she could tell me where Lawson's was located. I was looking for directions and was surprised her response was "down the aisle and on the floor." Say what? I followed her directions, and sure enough, there were several cases of Sip of Sunshine on the floor. I found some in the cooler too, but since I was not drinking it right away, the floor version would do fine. I bought eight cans and went on my way. I gave two cans to JP, traded one to my friend Katie also at World of Beer Tempe, for a Heady Topper, and I drank the other five. Amazing beer that I would not have experienced if I had not blindly accepted the request from my friend JP.

When it comes to New England, it is my favorite region of the country. My friend Marsha and I have been traveling there since I think 2002. I have been to all fifty states over the years, but number fifty for me was Vermont. If I could live anywhere in the country, Vermont or perhaps New Hampshire would be at the top of my list. I am from Yellow Springs, a small town in Ohio, and I love New

Hampshire and Vermont because of the small towns. I love the fall especially, so when I finished my first book which was set in summer, I immediately thought some time should pass, but not too much time. That lead into fall and when I think of fall I think New England. If my grandmother, Mary Lou, were still alive she would have thought of Gatlinburg, TN – but for me, it's always New England. Each time I travel there I try to make an effort to go to Burlington and Lake Champlain, mostly because of the legend of Champ, but also because it is beautiful. There is a parking lot and a trail that goes along the lake. A few park benches sit there, and I could sit and just watch the water for hours. There is a bike trail where I think I would regularly run if I lived there, and I teach at a university now, so I imagine working and teaching at the University of Vermont. I was happy to see on that trip over Labor Day that my wife, Susana, immediately fell in love with New England as well. She enjoyed walking that bike path, looking at the water and even having her photo with the Champ statue by the lake.

One thing I hope I do in these books, and it is a point of the research I put into them, is make it feel real. When I travel, it is about seeing sights along the way (often unusual sights), eating food, and drinking local beer. I want my characters to experience that as well, so they will try local restaurants and thanks to having traveled in the area many times, it be will loosely based on places I have eaten at, sights I have visited, and fun that I have had. Some might say that level of detail in a work of fiction makes it boring, or as one reviewer of my first book put it "my brain was numb, and my eyeballs were bleeding." Hopefully, I can avoid that degree of boredom for most others. My thought, and the thought of some others that I have asked is the detail provides texture to the story. I hope you'll agree.

The stories themselves are obviously based on fantasy, but that doesn't mean there cannot be realism along the way. If someone took this book and thought the meal Ty ate sounded pretty good and wished they could try that, or the beer Tegan drank sounds awesome, well visit and try them because those will always be real. If the group stops along the way somewhere like American Stonehenge or the Ben & Jerry's Flavor Graveyard, go there. It's real, and it's fun.

Books expand our mind with possibilities, and part of that is hopefully in these stories. But there is also a part that you can actually see, feel, taste, and drink. Go do those things. Get out and explore the country. Try new things. If anyone ever said they read a book by Mark Trollinger and it made them want to go check out San Antonio or Burlington or other towns for stories I have planned in the future, that would be so awesome. Too many times we stay near our home where we are comfortable. Break out from that and see what's out there. There are so many more things that are cool to see, good eats, or awesome beers than I include in these stories. I am always discovering too. Get out there and let me know what you found. I look forward to hearing about your experiences and the beers you enjoyed on your journey.

The book includes the use of trademarks for realism but there is no endorsement expressed or implied.

Drink in the adventure!

Trollinger

1 HICKORY

Friday, September 25, 2015

Daniel Richardson and his girlfriend Avery Fisher began to unload the back of Daniel's Nissan Armada and carry its contents into the rental house. Built in 1930, Blue Camp was one of the few remaining original Vermont camps; a three bedroom, one-bath seasonal camp on Malletts Bay. Daniel had been coming to Mallets Bay on Lake Champlain since he was a kid, but this was his opportunity to introduce his new girlfriend to the area. Originally from St. Joseph, Missouri she had only lived in Vermont for the past ten months.

Blue Camp was in an ideal location on the lake. It was located off of a quiet side street, yet within walking distance of a general store, ice cream stand, pizza place, and a friendly little pub. The Island Line bike trail and a drive-in movie theater were a short distance away. The rustic, charming cottage was right on the water, and the owner provided paddle boards, kayaks, a ping pong table, and bicycles to allow renters the ability to enjoy the lake. And enjoying the lake this weekend was something Daniel and Avery planned to do.

Today the weather was a little cooler sixty-five degrees – a full eight degrees cooler than on Wednesday. Despite the dip in temperature, the weather was still pleasant and offered perhaps the final opportunities to enjoy a warm weekend before the colder temperatures finally settled in New England. After two trips, the car was nearly unpacked. The only things that remained were Avery's Joy Mangano beauty case, Daniel's camera bag, and getting Hickory - Daniel's tan three-year-old Brussels Griffon from the back of the car.

Daniel opened the back door, and Hickory bounded from the vehicle, the rocks on the gravel driveway scattering while his human friends finished unloading the car.

Hickory scampered down the gravel driveway and out to the bike path sniffing the grass and fresh lake air. He was usually happy to play inside all day, but he did enjoy a daily walk around the neighborhood. This was a new place for Hickory, so he had to inspect every blade of grass and leaf along the bike path and eventually made his way down to the water's edge.

The grass was not too high, but for Hickory who was only ten inches tall and weighed about nine pounds, it tickled the underbelly of his rough, wiry coat. Despite the height of the grass, Daniel could see Hickory playing on the path and near the water. He whistled for him to come back to the cabin. Hickory stopped, looked at the man, but disinterested in joining his human companion turned and continued on his journey, displaying the stubbornness characteristic of the breed. Daniel stood on the steps of the cabin and watched the dog ignore his commands. He waited for a few seconds before deciding to give up and enter the house to drop the remaining bags.

Unaffected by his owner's calls, Hickory continued on his itinerary checking out the new environment and attempting to put his naturally suspicious personality at ease. He trotted to the water and stuck a foot it, retracted it, and shook it reacting to the lake's cold temperature. But he did enjoy swimming and decided to get in the lake and check out the area slowly.

Behind the cabin were a boat dock and a big yard. He could swim over there and hop out before walking up to the house and joining the humans inside. He was a good swimmer, despite his short legs and small size. Even though he loved to swim, he didn't usually venture too far out in the water. He liked the freedom of the water, but also the comfort of being close to the edge. As he swam toward the boat dock, a massive fallen log impeded his route, forcing him to swim a little further into the lake. He slowly paddled his way around the trunk and toward his destination, beginning to feel the cold from the lake. Looking forward to warming up in the cabin and enjoying his evening meal, Hickory continued.

Below the surface, a massive animal glided gracefully. It usually remained in the depths of the lake and avoided coming close to the inhabited areas, but it was hungry, and ripples in the water attracted it closer to the shore than it usually swam. It slowed down as it came closer to the source of the ripples. Able to swim much faster than the small animal above it, the big animal coasted silently awaiting its opportunity. Hickory was nearing the dock, unaware that just a few feet below him a hungry beast lurked, stalking him. He slowed his paddling slightly as fatigue began to set in.

The extra distance around the log was more than he anticipated, but before he could come up with a new plan, he felt the ripples pushing from below as the unseen creature swam closely beneath him to get a better look at the smaller animal. The sizeable underwater beast circled and approached the dog, who was now attempting to swim faster knowing something was below it. But he wouldn't make it much further as the massive animal darted quickly in the dog's direction from below. As the creature's head sprang from the water Hickory let out a yelp as the animal's massive jaws chomped on him, but anything further was lost as the monster took the small dog underwater.

Daniel stood on the porch of the cabin looking around for his dog but did not see him. He whistled for him again, but there was no response.

"I wonder where that dog wandered off to?" he said, scratching his head before returning inside the cabin. He assumed Hickory would paw at the front door any moment, but that moment on its signal never came.

2 SHIPPING UP TO BOSTON

Thursday, October 1, 2015

The light turbulence created a subtle rock-a-bye that kept many of the passengers comfortably asleep. That is until the Captain spoke over the intercom to announce JetBlue's flight 1038 with non-stop service from Austin's Bergstrom's International Airport (AUS) to Boston's General Edward Logan Airport (BOS) received clearance for its final approach. The flight left Austin, Texas at 6:30 p.m. and with local time currently 10:40 p.m. it estimations suggested the plane would land a few minutes before the projected 11:11 p.m. arrival time.

One of the cabin's sleepy passengers, Carson Quinn, pulled one end of his headphones to the side to better hear the announcement, then wearily replaced it knowing he had about twenty minutes before landing. Feeling it appropriate for flying into Boston he selected a custom playlist on his Google Play Music and hit play. It consisted of The Standells "Dirty Water," Neil Diamond's "Sweet Caroline," and Dropkick Murphy's "I'm Shipping Up to Boston." Also on the list, multiple songs by Boston groups The J. Geils Band, The Cars, Aerosmith, 'Til Tuesday, and his favorite disco artist, Donna Summer. He paused and his mind drifted distantly as the Cars "Moving in Stereo" played. Every time he heard that song he was instantly transported to being a teenager in 1982 and vividly remembering Phoebe Cates's infamous swimming pool scene in Fast Times at Ridgemont High. The song ended, and he returned to the present with a smile on his face and took a sip from the can of Coke Zero on his tray table as I'm Straight by one of his favorite Boston bands, Modern Lovers, played.

Turning to look out of the window to his right he couldn't see anything except the lights of Boston approaching. Having flown into Boston before he knew the airport sat right on the water and he always thought it was a refreshing sight. He remembered his first flight into the city as a teenager and thinking they were crashing into the water because of the proximity of the runway to Boston Inner Harbor. He was surprised to learn there are also water taxis that take passengers right to a Logan Dock at the airport.

Staring into the darkness, Carson felt that he was missing out on the thrill of seeing the water. With a sigh, he closed the window shade and sat back in his seat. Turning his head to the left, he saw his friend Tyson Carr still asleep. Across the aisle, Kareem Ortiz and Tegan Stone were awake and both reading paperbacks. Tegan had Where Legends Roam by Lee Murphy, and Kareem was nearing the end of Stephenie Meyer's Eclipse.

The past four months had been a whirlwind of activity since the group discovered the appearance of the naked hyena in San Antonio. Even though the specimen, unfortunately, had to be killed, tying it to the chupacabra legend brought a lot of media attention. Since the announcement of the discovery, the group was besieged by people wanting to meet them, conduct interviews, and hire them to locate other mysterious animals.

Carson did enjoy the attention, given that he was still between jobs. Tyson, Kareem, and Tegan had regular careers and found the constant attention somewhat distracting. This trip to New England was just what they needed to get away and relax for a week. There was no snow in the forecast, but the temperatures in the upper-50's to mid-60's would be a nice break from the still upper-80's to low-90's temperatures currently being experienced in Austin. A downside was the group would miss Austin's beer week - but the opportunity to see the fabled New England fall foliage and attend a few local Oktoberfests provided an excellent substitution.

"Thanks for forwarding the email about this flight sale," said Tyson as he began to stir. "I know I definitely could use the break. I'm sure Kareem and Tegan feel the same," he said to Carson.

"Yeah, it's been a crazy few months, hasn't it?" asked Carson. "I love the fall up here. I haven't been since I was in high school, but I'm looking forward to unwinding. Not to mention hunting down some of the New England hops people always talk about online, huh?" he said.

"No doubt! New England hops are always at the top of everyone's 'in search of' list," said Ty. Kareem finished his book and leaned over into the aisle.

"What are you guys talking about?" he asked.

"Just all of the New England hops we are about to encounter on this trip," said Carson.

"Do you guys know I packed an empty suitcase in my checked bag?" asked Kareem. "Like a set of Russian nesting dolls. I can check a bag much cheaper than shipping a box back home, and I don't want to miss out on the trade value up here. New England is a craft beer Mecca," he said.

"Definitely at the top of the list and still up-and-coming with new places all the time," added Ty. "I am just glad we can get some cooler weather, check out the leaves, relax for a week and drink some great beer. No killer prehistoric terror pigs, no jackalopes, no Bigfoot, and no Mongolian Death Worms. Just cold pints, bombers, and maybe a growler or two," continued Ty.

"This will all be new for me," said Tegan. "I have never been to this part of the country, so I am looking forward to seeing new things and trying the beer." Do we even have a plan for this trip?" asked Tegan.

"Tonight it is just getting the rental car and checking into the hotel. Tomorrow I thought we would drive up to Maine and hit some spots there. They have Acadia's Oktoberfest coming up, although that's next weekend and it is farther up than I planned on going. I thought we could go up to Portland. There are a lot of breweries in the Maine Beaches and Greater Portland area, then up to Lewiston. It isn't too far from Portland, and Baxter Brewing Company is there. Then we could head into New Hampshire and check that out, and then maybe end up in Burlington, Vermont. I think spending the majority of our time in Vermont will allow us to hit many of the well-sought beers," said Carson.

"As long as the trip includes beer and food, I'm good," said Ty.

The flight attendant interrupted the conversation with an announcement.

"Ladies and gentlemen, we are making our initial approach to Boston. Please stow your small electronics and return your seat to its upright and locked position. We will be on the ground momentarily," said the flight attendant.

Carson turned to Ty, "We have to ride a fairly long shuttle bus to the rental car center, but the hotel isn't too far from there. Since we are getting in late I just wanted to get a couple of beds close and rest up for the days ahead," he said.

The ground quickly approached, and the lights along the runaway passed rapidly, creating a blue blur in the darkness. A slight but sudden jolt followed by the immediate sound of the engines shifting into reverse thrust signaled their arrival. The pilot applied the wheel brakes as the flight attendant once again spoke.

"Ladies and Gentlemen, JetBlue welcomes you to Boston Logan with an arrival time of 11:02 p.m. As we taxi, please remain seated with your seatbelt fastened and items securely stowed until we are parked at the gate and the seatbelt light is turned off. Keep the aisles clear of all carry-on items and take a moment to check your seat back pocket for any personal items like tablets and cell phones. When you open the overhead compartment be careful as items may have moved in flight. You may now use your cell phones."

Carson stopped listening as the announcement moved into frequent flier program opportunities and returned to gazing out the window. The act of staring out of the window soon turned from finding out what was going on outside and into an exercise in discovering the contents of his own mind; a way to listen out for the quieter suggestions and perspectives of his deeper self. Memories from prior trips to the Boston area combined with memories from the past couple of years emerged. The struggles of losing his teaching job, the longs of depression that followed, the serendipitous run-in with Tyson Carr at Giddy Ups one night in June that began his transition back into healthy life - if you could call running through the woods hunting the legendary chupacabra normal. But that week in the woods of Elmendorf changed his life. He climbed out of a multi-year-long funk, made new friends, and discovered craft beer. Now he, Tyson, Kareem, and Tegan were best of friends and frequently spending time together discussing beer, watching sports, talking about their adventures, and how the notoriety and media attention affected each of them individually.

In many ways, the distance between his former and current selves felt like a lifetime, even though it was only four months. Plato suggested a metaphor for the mind: our ideas are like birds fluttering around in the aviary of our brains. But for the birds to settle, Plato understood that people needed periods of purpose-free calm, and that's exactly what this trip was intended to be: just four friends hanging out, drinking beer, peeping some leaves, and enjoying a purpose-free calm ten days in New England. The ding from the overhead communication system snapped Carson back to reality and served as the indication it was safe to move about the cabin.

The other passengers immediately stood up and started reaching for the overhead bin, but Carson and Ty remained seated, knowing it was going to be several minutes before they would have enough room to stand and begin exiting. They were in no hurry anyway. The ride to the rental car center would take several minutes, and they were only going to the hotel tonight. Finally, they were able to exit the plane. Since each member of the group checked a bag, baggage claim would be the next stop, following a trip to the restroom.

Once everyone retrieved their luggage, the group stood outside under the Blue Rental Car – Blue Line stop and enjoyed the night air. It was in the low 50's and a gentle freeze from the nearby harbor made for a pleasant evening. The airport's Line 33 Shuttle arrived to take passengers on the approximately six-minute journey from the airport to the rental car center. Even though it was late, several passengers from the flight stood in line waiting to board.

After a full day in Austin and a long flight, everyone was tired and ready to get to the hotel. The hybrid bus ride was smooth and gave the passengers a clear view not only of the airport but downtown Boston. The city was beautiful with the lights set against the night background. Windows extended down both sides of the bus allowing passengers to observe the full view of the town along the route.

The bus arrived at the rental car center – a one-hundred-twenty-thousand-square-foot customer service center and four-level garage operated by nine rental car companies. The center was recently built in 2013 and designed to reduce traffic congestion at the airport as well as improve the environmental footprint by reducing the number of diesel fuel buses and replacing them with fuel-efficient clean hybrid buses.

Despite the number of choices, Carson always rented from Alamo or National because they only held the price of the car on the credit card. Other companies routinely reserved an additional two hundred and fifty dollars or more deposit. With four people each with suitcases and the likelihood a lot of beer would be returning, a compact car would not be sufficient. Carson reserved a full-size SUV using an online discount website two weeks ago. The black Chevy Tahoe LT had a storage space, typically for two suitcases; however, the specifications stated it had seating for seven leaving plenty of room for their bags. The leather seats, LED lighting, and tinted windows provided all of the comforts that would be needed on the long road trip. The group loaded the suitcases, Tegan and Ty took the backseat, Kareem the passenger seat, and Carson drove.

Carson had pre-booked the trip hotels last week on Hotels.com and hoped that his daily estimations were accurate. It wouldn't be difficult to book a new hotel by using the mobile app, but if they had to cancel plans the same day, it would result in extra expenses. Day one was the Motel 6 Boston – Danvers. Just about seventeen miles from the airport it provided a short drive so they could check in and get to sleep quickly, but also was situated right off I-95, which was going to be the route for tomorrow. Motel 6 also was an inexpensive option and offered a standard room with two queen beds allowing for all four to share the room. In San Antonio they always had two rooms, but now everyone was comfortable enough with each other to share, and besides, the money saved could be spent on beer.

3 FIREBUG

Friday, October 2, 2015

The leaves had already started falling in Plattsburgh, NY, and in the yard of a stately 1918 Colonial home, a small heap of red and orange leaves began taking shape. The piles meant excitement and cheap entertainment to Alexa King's five-month-old yellow Labrador retriever, Firebug. Alexa didn't have to buy Firebug many toys. She was content playing with the leaves and sticks around the grounds of the historic brick home. That was fine with Alexa. More money for her and the farmer's markets when she made the two-hour drive up to Montreal. Especially her favorite market, La Moutonnière in the Jean-Talon Market.

It was a small, little creamery that offered semi-firm cheese made with a milk blend of Jersey cow and La Moutonnière's flock of ewes. She loved the cheeses; so rich and creamy with a subtle hint of acidity from the sheep's milk. But even with her attraction to cheese and the fantastic crepes, macaroons, and fresh flowers – especially lavender she found at the market, she always found time to bring Firebug a treat. She did spoil her, even if she wasn't interested in store-bought toys.

Even though she was still a puppy, Firebug was a medium-sized dog already. She ran from pile to pile jumping in the leaves, rolling on her back, and enjoying the lovely afternoon temperatures. The fresh air, the nearby lake, and the elevated lakefront deck where she liked to watch the boats go by were all part of an enjoyable day. She loved when Alexa brought her here, even though she had only been a few times in her young life. Alexa looked through the kitchen window to see Firebug having fun with the leaves, but thought the puppy might enjoy a little more activity.

She brought the tennis ball launcher from the mudroom and stuck it on the back porch. She had taught Firebug how to drop the mini tennis balls into the launcher so she could entertain herself while Alexa was working around the house or doing other things. Firebug barked and hopped excitedly as Alexa set up the device. She knew what it was and it would mean several minutes of fun running after the balls and the destruction of more leaf piles would undoubtedly be collateral damage. The launcher came with three standard-sized tennis balls, but Alexa had purchased the bonus pack of six because she knew some of them would quickly get lost. The device was capable of shooting the tennis balls either ten, twenty-five, or forty feet. She usually kept in on twenty-five because it was far enough to reach the yard, but not too far where it could get easily lost.

Alexa dropped the first ball into the machine to make sure it was working correctly. The ball shot from the device and Firebug immediately ran hoping to catch the ball. It shot twenty-five feet and landed just passed Firebug's reach. It took one bounce before being captured in the dog's mouth. She turned and ran back toward the porch feverishly wagging her tail. She dropped the ball back into the launcher by herself and again it fired the same distance. Repeatedly it was caught and returned by the puppy.

"That should entertain you for a while," said Alexa as she turned to head back into the house. Firebug barely noticed the human leave. Her focus was firmly entrenched on the ball and returning it home for another round of chasing. Each time she returned the ball she bumped the unit slightly causing it to turn fragments of an inch each time.

The change in trajectory was minuscule in the beginning, but eventually, it did affect the landing spot of the tennis balls. The next attempt saw the ball land on a rock and bounce off in a different direction. It landed in a pile of leaves, which Firebug scattered frantically looking for the ball. Eventually, it was located and once again returned.

The next drop also traveled twenty-five feet and hit the rock, but this time bounded in a different direction. The ball bounced toward the back of the lot and rolled quickly down the small hill leading to the lake. Firebug ran down the hill and retrieved the ball, but after several rounds of running was feeling tired. She walked along the lake, dropped the ball, took a long drink from the water, and picked the ball up in her mouth again. She continued to walk in the sandy dirt along the water, occasionally pausing to look out over the water and enjoy the weather. The waves rhythmically rolled in and washed back out, occasionally splashing her feet with cold water. When it did, she pulled her foot out of the water and shook it vigorously before continuing on her walk.

She heard a noise on the water that made her stop and turn, attempting to identify the source. It sounded like crashing water as if something sizeable breached the surface, but there was nothing there. She continued walking along the water's edge until she walked back up a small rise into a parking lot near the lake. The parking lot led to a sidewalk that continued to run along the lake, but also to a narrow pier that extended into the lake about fifty feet. Several birds landed on the end of the dock and caught the dog's eye.

Firebug barked excitedly at them and decided to give chase to the end of the pier, hoping to surprise one. She was unsuccessful in her quest as all of the birds returned to the air as the running dog approached. Despite the escape, she stayed on the pier barking toward the sky hoping at least one of the birds would return for her to grab. She sat on her hind legs and barked, but the birds continued toward a new destination. She let out a whine as she laid down with her head on her resting, extended paws. Even though no birds were remaining, the breeze was gentle and felt good against her short hair. Besides, birds were dirty maybe it was okay she didn't catch one. Instead, she could just lay in the sun and enjoy the fresh air coming off of the lake.

Her ears perked up, and she raised her head once again hearing the splash in the lake. It was louder than the standard splash of the waves against the shore, and this was coming from deeper in the lake. But just as before, she didn't see anything significant enough to generate such sound. This time she stood and walked around the pier looking around the water. She noticed a wake in the water about eighty feet from the dock but did not see the object causing the disturbance. The thing was coming toward the pier but had not fully surfaced. Whatever was in the water moved quickly and gracefully. About twenty feet from the edge of the dock a head emerged, then a long neck. Firebug barked at the unknown creature, but it continued toward the pier. No one was around to hear the dog's bark drawing attention to the beast.

The being in the water continued toward the pier, its flattened eyes allowed it, even underwater, to sharply see the animal above. The beast could not hear the barking dog well underwater, but it didn't matter as it primarily hunted visually and almost always ambushed prey from below rather than from above. With lightning fast quickness, the monster's head rose entirely out of the water and grabbed the dog in a single motion, like a killer whale snagging a seal on the beach. Firebug did not have time to react or make a sound as the large-mouthed animal engulfed her in a single bite then returned below the lake's surface.

4 SALEM

Friday, October 2, 2015

There was a chill in the air, but not too cold for an early October morning. Carson Quinn stood on the patio of the third floor of the motel drinking a cup of coffee and watching the sunrise. It was partly cloudy, but the sun attempted to break through as it slowly drifted up and to the right in the eastern sky.

The rosy horizon began to disappear as the sky appeared bright and golden. A light breeze began to blow, and Carson breathed profoundly allowing the fresh morning air to fill his lungs and clear his mind. He imaged the sunrise was even more beautiful along the waterfront. Even though his view was only an old partially filled parking lot, it was still a fantastic view.

Moments later, Kareem joined Carson on the patio.

"I can't get over how beautiful the trees are and how fresh the air is" he said as took a sip of coffee. "So, what's the plan for the day?" he inquired. Carson pointed to the left.

"That's I-95 right there. I thought we would take that up north into Maine today. It's different than driving back in Texas. Ever driven all day and you're still in Texas? Up here you can be in three states in a couple of hours. We can drive up to Portland. It's less than ninety miles up there, and there's plenty we can check out. We don't have to leave too early and can still be there before noon if we want, or we can take our time and see the sights along the way," said Carson.

"I've never been up here, some I'm cool taking in the sights," Kareem replied.

"Mornin', boys," said Tegan as she walked out onto the patio rubbing the sleep from her eyes.

"Good morning," both men said.

"Or, if we guys want we could take the Turnpike down to Salem. It's only about eight miles from here, and it's a cool little town. One of my favorite small towns in the country actually," continued Carson.

"Salem? Like from the witch trials?" asked Tegan.

"Yes, the same one," replied Carson.

"Is this patio going to hold all of us?" asked Ty as he joined everyone outside.

"Hey, Ty," replied Carson.

"I don't know about everyone else, but I've always wanted to go to Salem," said Ty.

"We could head down, grab some breakfast, and check out the local attractions if you want," suggested Carson.

After the group finished getting ready they loaded up the rental car and headed down to Salem. "There's a nice, local spot called Red's Sandwich Shop," said Carson. "We can grab breakfast there then walk around the town and check out the historical sites," he said. They parked behind the building at 15 Central Street and walked around to the front of the red Colonial-era building.

"This building is a part of historic Salem, dating back more than three hundred years," said Carson. "It's so old, the Sons of Liberty met here prior to the American Revolution. The building was built around 1698 in what at the time was the London Coffee House. It's become a local icon and has been named *Best Breakfast* for almost thirty years in a row," Carson reported.

"Ooh, I love the window boxes," said Kareem. "They're very charming!"

As soon as they entered the old building, the smells of bacon, cooked eggs, and an underlying musty smell of a Revolutionary War meeting house wafted through the air, enveloping the small interior. The décor was dated but that only added to the charm.

Carson was glad they came on Friday because there wasn't a line as they likely would encounter on a weekend morning. The hostess quickly showed them to a table for four, and the server appeared moments later. A petite lady with shoulder-length dark brown hair that curled at the ends arrived.

"I'm Jen, and I will be your server today," said the young, brown-eyed server. "What can I get yah to drink?" Ty ordered a coffee, Tegan the hot chocolate, Kareem the herbal tea, and Carson was happy to see chocolate milk available. "I will give yah a few minutes tah look at the menu," she said as she turned to get the drinks.

Looking over the menu, they found it difficult to make a selection. Tegan looked around at the plates of other customers who were already eating.

"Do you see the size of those pancakes?" she asked excitedly. "Big as your head!"

"I have no idea what to order," said Kareem.

"Being named as the top breakfast spot for three decades, we likely can't go wrong with any selection," suggested Ty.

"We are in New England," said Carson, "so I think I will have the lobster asparagus benedict with home fries."

"I'm good with the cinnamon French toast," said Kareem.

"Those blueberry pancakes caught my eye," admitted Tegan. "With a side of bacon," she added.

I will have the Red's steak bomb omelet with steak, mushroom, onions, peppers & cheese," finished Ty. "That should load me down for whatever we have in store for the day," he concluded. Jen returned with the drinks, took down the breakfast order, and disappeared again into the kitchen.

"When we finish with breakfast we can walk around," suggested Carson. "The witch history museum is just down the street, the old town hall just a few feet from there, and we have to hit up the Salem Witch House on the corner of Essex and North streets. That's the only structure still standing in Salem with direct ties to the Salem Witch Trials of 1692," Carson stated. "We can walk down to Salem Common which is just across from the historic Hawthorne Hotel. I also love to walk along the water near the old US Customs House. You might remember the customs house from the introduction of Nathaniel Hawthorn's Scarlet letter. Also at the pier is the Friendship of Salem – which is a reconstruction of a one-hundred-seventy-one-foot three-masted Salem East Indiaman built in 1797 and anchored at the Salem Maritime National Historic Site. An East Indiaman was the common name for any ship operating under charter or license to any of the East India Companies. The West India Goods Store is a cool building just down the street, built in 1804 and used initially as a warehouse for goods from around the world. And of course, the House of the Seven Gables is just down from that, from another classic Nathaniel Hawthorne novel," said Carson.

"I heard there is a town witch," added Tegan.

"Yes, there is," said Carson. "In the past witches were feared, but today Salem celebrates them, and of course it's a boost to local tourism. Laurie Cabot opened The Official Witch Shoppe in Salem in 1970, and it was the first 'witch shop' in the United States. She is a witchcraft high priestess, one of the most high-profile witches in the world, and one of the first people to popularize witchcraft in the United States. She also worked with special needs children and during the 1970's Massachusetts Governor Michael Dukakis named her *Official Witch of Salem, Massachusetts*," Carson informed.

As Carson continued with the verbal historical tour of Salem, Jen returned with the food. Tegan gasped as Jen presented the blueberry pancakes with pancakes larger than the plate it was on! The pancakes were bursting with a ton of blueberries, and she desperately wanted to get her hands on them. Carson's mouth began to water as he saw his dish. The lobster asparagus benedict was a pair of chilled lump lobster cakes each on an English muffin and topped with poached eggs and an abundance of Hollandaise sauce. The home fries filled the remainder of the plate.

The smell of cinnamon filled the air as Jen placed Kareem's plate before him. The cinnamon French toast also came with eggs, Canadian bacon, and home fried potatoes. Kareem's eyes grew large at the size of the portion and the gooey goodness of the French toast with thick maple syrup running down the edges of the bread. He immediately knew he would likely be unable to finish the plate. Ty was impressed looking at his omelet, but once he cut into it and took the first bite, he closed his eyes, leaned back in the chair, and a sense of enjoyment was seen on his face. The omelet used marinated steak tips instead of shaved steak commonly found in the popular North Shore sandwiches.

"How's everything lookin'?" Jen asked with an anticipatory smile.

"It all looks wonderful!" Ty spoke for the group.

During the meal, the friends didn't speak. All were focused on the large plate of food before them and enjoying the delicious tastes and smells causing a nostalgic sense of home. The restaurant remained busy during the whole meal with people coming and going, but the food made the group oblivious to its surroundings, placing each member in an acute sensory processing disorder. Finally, Ty threw in the towel.

"That about wraps it up," he said looking at his plate. Although an impressive attempt, he still had about one-fourth of the omelet remaining. "I can't do any more than that! We definitely will need to walk after this meal," he said while stretching back and rubbing his belly.

The other members of the group quickly followed suit, each unable to clear their plate, but given the uncertainty of the day each decided to forgo a to-go box. Noticing the line of people still awaiting a table, Carson motioned for Jen to bring the check.

Moments later they left the building and began walking the historic red brick cobblestone streets of Salem where witches, from cartoon witches to the characters of Hocus Pocus, were present in many souvenir stores that lined both sides of the closed-off walking path.

Continuing down Charter Street, the group turned and walked through the Old Burying Point Cemetery where old headstones dating back to 1637 provided a solemn reminder of the events that rocked the town just a few years before. Just past the cemetery, a small park contained a memorial of twenty granite benches created to remember the Witch Trial. The stones listed the name, a quote, and date of death for each of the victims who died during the events between July 10, 1692, and September 22, 1692.

Carson's favorite memorial in the park belonged to Giles Corey. Corey was different than others commemorated in the monument. The other markers listed the names of victims who were accused of witchcraft and died as a result of hanging. Giles Corey died in the unusual manner of being pressed to death. Corey was charged with witchcraft but did not enter a plea, choosing instead to stand mute. English law at the time ordered any prisoner who stood mute to be tortured in an attempt to force a plea out of the prisoner; a tactic called *peine forte et dure* which translated to "until he either answered or died."

The exact torture procedure consisted of stripping the prisoner naked, laying him on the ground and placing a board with heavy stones on top of him. The weight was slowly increased over the course of several days until the prisoner yielded. Sheriff Corwin used this method to torture Giles Corey in an empty field on Howard Street, next to the Salem jail where Corey was being kept, for two or three days in September of 1692. Although Corey had a checkered past with a prior trial for violence against a farmhand Jacob Goodale, and rumors that he paid for his freedom when the verdict was only a fine instead of jail time, the public was outraged at the treatment the eighty-one-year-old man received.

During the torture, Corey continued to refuse to submit, and the local stories state that he directed his tortures to add more weight. Because he did not submit a plea and did not give in the sheriff's torture techniques, Corey earned a place in local folklore and legend.

The legend rumored that Corey placed a curse on Salem and its sheriff during his torture by shouting "Damn you! I curse you and Salem!" at the sheriff before he died. Others claim to remember seeing Corey's ghost haunting the grounds where the torture occurred. Carson did wonder about the legend of Corey Giles and how much of it was true. Many unexpected circumstances occurred following his death including Sheriff Corwin's dying of a heart attack just four years later when the sheriff was only thirty years old.

The Great Salem Fire of 1914 and even the forced early retirement of Sheriff Robert Cahill in 1978 were attributed to the curse of Corey Giles. The sheriff's office was moved from Salem to a prison in Middleton in 1991, and many believe that broke the curse and spared the future sheriffs, as no further incidents had occurred.

"You really get a sense of the history of this town," said Tegan. "I could walk around here for hours."

"Yes, I could too," said Ty, "but right now this walking is making me thirsty. Look, there's Salem Beerworks up ahead!" he said.

"That's true," said Carson, "but just across Derby Street and down near the harbor is Notch Brewery and Tap Room. I did read online that Salem Beerworks has some good beer and excellent food, and they've been doing it since 1992, but I've heard some good things about Notch as well," said Carson.

"Well why not both?" suggest Kareem. "I mean, almost twenty-five years as a craft beer brewery is very rare and would be worth checking out," he reasoned.

"They are literally across the street, and it would be a shame to miss one of them," said Tegan.

"Sounds good to me," responded Carson. "We have plenty of time and Beerworks is right here."

Walking along the sidewalk to the front of the brick exterior of the building, the group headed to the main entrance. It was a small building, but the height and the angles of the façade made it appear larger. The front door was located in the small, flat section of the building, and the walls to the left and right jutted out at slight angles. One word appeared near the top of each part of the building and read "SALEM BEER WORKS."

The interior had a post-industrial modern look with exposed brick, abundant amber lighting, and steel bunting. The high ceilings soaring over a vast room with plenty of seating, brewery equipment near the entrance, and a large chalkboard along one of the walls to list all of the current beers on their many taps made the group feel comfortable. A large green neon broom-riding witch was affixed to the brick above the televisions and covered a space greater than three sets. Most of the seats at the bar were already occupied causing the group to decide on a leather-seated booth.

Soon after they took a seat a young lady in a low-cut black t-shirt, black jeans, and an unbuttoned flannel shirt with rolled-up sleeves approached. She had a large tattoo on her right wrist, and her straight, shoulder-length hair was a deep, almost black purple. She greeted the guest with a warm smile and a stack of beer menus.

"First time in the bah?" she asked.

"Yes, we're up from Austin, Texas for a week and thought we'd stop in and try the local beer," said Carson.

"Upta check the foliage and punkins? Well, I'm Cordelia, and I'll help ya out with tha menu. You stahvin or what?"

"No, we're good. Probably just a round before we head down the road," replied Ty.

"Well, I'll leave ya to the menu while I bring some watta."

When Cordelia returned, the group was ready with their order. "This is a nice place," said Carson. "How long have you been here?"

"Beerworks has been in Boston since 1992, first opening up near Fenway Park. This location in Salem opened in November 1996, so quite a while" said Cordelia.

"I like it. Very relaxed vibe," said Ty. Cordelia smiled.

"Do you know what you want?"

"I think I will have the REDeemer," said Ty. "That's a good choice. That is going to be our entry in the Great International Beer & Cider Competition later this month. I think it's on Friday, October 23 in Providence, Rhode Island if you are still up this way," suggested Cordelia.

"Good luck with the competition. But we'll be back in Austin by then. It would be nice to attend a large-scale competition like that sometime," said Ty.

Looking over the menu, Tegan selected Blue, a golden ale.

"That is definitely a local favorite. I have had people who moved away come back in and ask for that beer because it reminds them of Boston. And we add fresh Maine blueberries to the glass. Are you okay with that? Everyone comments on the blueberries in the glass" she said with a laugh.

"I will stick with the fruity theme," said Kareem as he ordered the Watermelon Ale.

"And we garnished that one with a wedge of fresh watermelon on the rim of the glass. We even put a slice on the rim on the tasters," Cordelia reported. Carson completed the order with a pint of Salem Pale Ale.

Soon Cordelia returned with the drinks. "Are you ready for some lunch too?"

"No, I think we are good for now. Just stopped in for a pint and to plan our drive up to Maine," replied Caron.

"Should be some good leaf-peepin' up there. Are you going up to Arcadia?" asked Cordelia.

"No, not that far up. Just up to Portland, then we are going to spend most of the week actually in Burlington. And we plan on taking in as many New England hops as we can along the way!" said Carson. Cordelia laughed.

"The past few years the hops have been almost as popular as the leaves, especially during the other parts of the year," she said.
Carson took a sip of the pale ale. It was a beautiful copper color with a light floral and cascade hop finish. Carson though it had a bit of an IPA bitterness, but lighter and smoother. "MMM, that's good," he said. Tegan was equally pleased with the Blue, a light and smooth golden ale with a nice blueberry aroma and taste. She thought the blueberries in the glass did give it a nice look.

"The presentation is very nice," she said. Ty took time to appreciate the REDeemer, a nice garnet color draft with a pretty smooth and creamy taste. It had a nice balance of malt, like toffee and chestnut, and a sweet mixture of floral and grapefruit.

"Wow, you might turn some heads in the festival with that one," he said. Kareem was the last with the Watermelon Ale. He smiled as he took a sip. A light, sweet, and refreshing ale, with subtle watermelon flavor.

"This would be a great beer on a summer day. Laying on the grass in the Common or another park taking in the water." He dipped the slice of watermelon into the beer for absorption and took a bite. His eyes widened as he spoke, "Now that's thirst-quenching!" Ty laughed.

"Isn't that a little like a hairy buffalo?"

"Yeah, 'cept I don't have rum, tequila, whiskey, and vodka!" he retorted.

"It's nice just to relax and enjoy the nice autumn weather," said Caron. "I bet that patio out there is killer on a spring afternoon with the wind off the lake."

"Probably pretty nice now" suggested Ty. "This definitely beats the heat of Texas right now," he said.

"After this, we are going to hit up another spot?" asked Tegan.

"Yes, just across the street is Notch Brewing. I thought we could have a pint there, then find something to eat before we head up north."

"It is nice just to have some down time after these crazy few months," said Kareem.

"It must be difficult for you guys. You all have regular jobs and with the increased attention from the chupacabra. I don't know how you do it," said Carson.

"It has been challenging," said Tegan. "A lot of phone calls, Facebook posts - it's crazy to see the number of notifications and direct messages on Twitter. Hell, even my Untappd is blowing up."

"It has been easier for me because I don't have a full-time job, but you're right – the calls, the requests for interviews is tough to manage," said Carson.

"Maybe we should look at opening an official agency," Ty said as he took a drink of his REDeemer. "At least we could have maybe someone to field the calls, schedule speaking arrangements, and whatever else for now. I am sure it will die down a little after the chupacabra discovery runs its course," he said.

"That reminds me. We should get back down there and check out the museum once they have it up and running," suggested Carson.

"It might not die down," said Tegan. "I have had some people call me saying they saw weird things in their area and asked if we could come out and take a look. It isn't out of the question to think this could be a thing if there are more unknown creatures out there," she said.

"They've got to be out there," said Kareem. "Look at really every culture and region on Earth has some type of legendary creature. They must be based on something," he said as he neared the end of his Watermelon Ale.

"I have enjoyed the attention. Kind of nice to be wanted after years of being unemployed," admitted Carson. "Maybe it warrants looking into?"

"We could come up with an acronym like the Ghost Hunters are TAPS and the Mountain Monster guys are AIMS. What would we be?" asked Kareem. "Hmm, something with cryptids. What works have a C? Or Austin – and A? Austin Cryptid...but what else?" brainstormed Carson.

"Maybe it could be a cryptid as an acronym. Like YETI," suggested Ty.

"YETI – I like it," said Tegan. "But what would it stand for? Texas for the T..." she followed up.

"Yeah, and maybe Investigation or Investigators," added Kareem.

"Nice suggestions. But the Y and the E are challenging – Enigma? Entity? Hell, I don't know," Carson said as he finished his beer. "You guys ready to go and hit the next spot?" he suggested as he stood up.

The group waved goodbye to Cordelia and left cash for the tab on the table. As they walked across the street, each person continued to think about the name they could call this would-be organization. They waited on the corner as a car drove past. Its windows were down, and the radio loudly played Jungle Love by Morris Day and the Time.

"That's it!" said Ty.

"What's it?" replied Carson.

"TIME...Texans Investigating Mysterious Entities," suggested Ty.

"Hey, that's not half bad!" replied Carson.

Walking up to Notch, the group again took notice of an outstanding patio.

"Let's sit outside this time. The patio is awesome, and with the light breeze it is very nice outside," suggested Tegan. Kareem raised his hand toward the bartender, a slim Caucasian man with long blonde hair in dreadlocks, a scruffy blonde beard, and sharp blue eyes. He wore a gray sleeveless tank top with a cartoon image of a barbigerous guy with a hat. The tank top revealed the colorful tattoos on both arms, as well as a hint of one on his upper chest peeking above the top of the shirt.

"Hey guys, I'm Bodhi. Take a seat anywhere here on the patio, and I'll be right with ya." He walked over to the table with the menus.

"Those are some nice tats, man," said Ty.

"Thanks. This one on my right arm is a girl at the beach because I'm originally from Oahu. The purple flowers on my left arm are Dendrobium orchids, one of the flowers they use in leis," Bodhi said.

Looking over the menu, Tegan decided to ask for recommendations. My favorite style is Berliner Weisse. Do you have anything similar?"

"Not on tap at the moment. I do have something in a bottle. A brew that we did last year and will probably have back in a few months. It's called Hootenanny, and it is a Berliner Weisse, but just in a bottle. When it's on tap, we do it up with either a raspberry (Himbeersirup) or a Woodruff (Waldmeistersirup) syrup shot like they do in Germany. We serve it in a bowl-shaped glass. I can fix it up like we do when we have it on draught if you want," he offered.

"Yeah, let's do it," she said. Kareem looked over the menu.

"I'm ready for an IPA. How about the Left of the Dial?" Carson selected the Dog and Pony Show.

"I'm really enjoying the lighter beers at the moment. I guess I am still living in the summer months," he said. Ty looked up from the menu,

"Well it is still feeling like summer back home, so it's probably all good. I am going to go with this Mule corn lager. I don't even know what that is and I am curious," said Ty.

"That one is a unique twist. But it gets a lot of pleasantly surprised feedback," said Bodhi.

As they awaited their drinks, they discussed the name of their group in more detail.

"So if we go with TIME, who is Morris Day and who is Jerome?" asked Ty.

"Don't you never say an unkind word about the Time!" said Carson quoting the beginning line from Jay and Silent Bob Strike Back. Bodhi returned with the drinks, giving the first one to Tegan.

"I brought the empty bottle too in case you wanted to see it," he said. She appreciated the appearance and presentation of the beer in the glass with the shot of Woodruff. Taking a sip she tried to place it. "Hmm. Soft and restrained, not too tart. Lemony and a little earthy. Kind of gives it a Lucky Charms taste," she said.

"It's one of our more popular beers when it is on tap. Since we have it in bottles now, it has increased the awareness of it too. It's a nice change from some of the other beers. A light and crisp option." Bodhi placed the rest of the drinks down, asked if he could get anything else, then returned to the bar.

"That Hootenanny is good," said Tegan.

"This Left of the Dial is also descent," said Kareem. "Not a New England hop, but a good IPA. It's a light floral hop aroma session IPA with tangerine, orange, and ruby red grapefruit. It gives it a touch of tropical flavors, maybe a little pine, and a pinch of earth. The low-medium bitterness finishes dry and clean." "How's that corn lager or whatever it was called, Ty?" asked Kareem.

"Man, this one is different. I kinda dig it. Smells a little earthy – I guess that's the corn. Tastes similar to a Pilsner with a rich body. A little lemony-corn flavor or that might be in my mind because of the suggestive marketing. Since it says corn, I probably look for the corn. I like the greenish straw color, and it is fairly complex and original." "Wow - this Dog and Pony Show. It may be my new favorite pale! It's creamy, sweet, floral, and grassy. Nice Citra makes it just a little hoppier than I expected, but not too much. Just the right amount of hops. Light body. I'm pleasantly surprised."

They returned to talking about their new organization and how they could use the new-found attention to not only research other animals by taking some of the requests people have been already asking, but they could use that attention to get speaking engagements.

"Ty still works in higher education. You might have some contacts that we could use to set up lectures in schools? Probably guest speakers in a classroom won't pay anything, but perhaps getting an engagement in a lecture hall might?" mentioned Carson.

"Worth checking out I suppose," Kareem said as he finished his beer. Within a couple of minutes, each finished the pint.

"It's about time to wrap it up," suggested Carson. "Let's hit up Boston Hot Dog Company before we go. We can catch the trolley then walk back to the car afterward," he added.

They waved to Bodhi as they exited and began walking to the trolley stop. "Right across the street from the Boston Hot Dog Company is the Lyceum Restaurant. You remember that from season Four of Ghost Adventures? The restaurant was built on the land of the first victim of the witch trials. Turner's Seafood moved into the location in November 2013, and many say they still feel a paranormal influence," reported Carson.

"I don't know if we have time for ghosts today," said Ty. "We catch this trolley, eat, and we still have a good couple of hours to get up to Portland. It will be evening by the time we get there."

The trolley arrived, and they each paid the fare as they entered and walked toward the middle of the vehicle. Overall the trolley was full, but they were fortunate to spot a couple of recently vacated seats.

Looking around the packed car, Ty noticed a young African-American woman a few rows back. He acknowledged her with a quick backward head nod. She smiled back.

"Do you know her?" asked Kareem.

"No, but there's not many of us up here if you know what I'm saying. The trolley continued toward the next stop. As the trolley began moving the young lady began coughing. She attempted to wave some fresh air toward her, but it wasn't working. She became sick in the aisle of the trolley, causing everyone to turn their attention toward her. The driver asked if she was okay. She asked if he could stop right there and she could get off. In a residential part of town, he stopped, and the lady exited. Carson and Ty looked at each other for a second, then out the window watching the lady as the trolley slowly pulled away. She hunched over a trash can and was sick again.

"Hope she's okay," said Tegan.

"Should we check on her?" asked Carson. Ty watched for a moment and noticed she was starting to walk around.

"Looks like she's okay. Probably just needed some air. These trolleys get kind of stuffy. She'll probably hop back on when it comes back around. If not, then we'll come back and help her out. 'We' gotta stick together," he said.

It was just a half mile further until the stop next to the Lyceum. They walked into a currently empty store. The owner came from the back wiping his hands on his apron. The store offered a large variety of hot dogs in natural or kosher casings but also had vegetarian hot dog options made of smoked apple and sage. Carson noticed the Cash Only sign and was happy to discover that he had some bills in his pocket. The owner was a quirky and authentic character that added to the charm of this favorite Salem establishment.

"What'll ya have?" he asked is a sharp and direct tone.

Carson ordered the Texas Dog with chili, sautéed onions, cheese sauce, bacon bits, and jalapenos. Kareem the Saturday Night dog with baked beans, sautéed onions, and bacon bits. Tegan followed with the New York City Dog – a hot dog topped with sauerkraut, Grey Poupon, chopped onion, sweet red pepper relish, and celery salt. Ty finished with the Southern Slaw dog made with homemade coleslaw, shredded cheddar, and according to the menu, award-winning chili. Each dog was under four dollars, and they took them to go since there was no seating in the restaurant. The owner fished the hot dogs out of a batch of warm water, grabbed the grilled butter rolls, and loaded them up. Carson handed him a twenty and told him to keep the change.

Eating the hot dogs as they walked back outside Ty looked around and no longer saw the lady from the trolley.

"She must have gotten back on," he said. "She's probably feeling better. Just needed to get some fresh air," he added. The walk to the car was not far from the restaurant. They made it to the car and did not see the lady around town as they drove through the historic downtown area one last time before getting on the highway headed north.

Continuing to drive up I-95 north the gang stared out the window at the fantastic scenery as they crossed into New Hampshire. It wasn't long, just about twenty miles before they were crossing the Piscataqua River Bridge between Portsmouth, NH, and Kittery, ME. Coming from Texas where they could drive almost an entire day and still be in the same state, the fact they could be in three within a thirty-minute drive was mind-blowing.

Carson briefly considered taking US-1 and heading out to Nubble Lighthouse, one of the most photographed spots in Maine. In fact, the Voyager spacecraft carries a photo of the lighthouse should any alien civilizations encountering the craft become curious about some of the prominent human-made structures of Earth. But Carson decided to continue driving and save that tourist stop for another time.

Not long after the passed the Ogunquit Playhouse, another place Carson would typically like to stop. The 1933 Playhouse joined the National Register of Historic Places in December 1995. He focused on making it to Portland, which was only just over an hour and a half from Salem, but he wanted to get settled for the day and look ahead to tomorrow's activities. He continued up the Turnpike passing Kennebunk and Kennebunkport, the summer home of former U.S. President and fellow Texan George H. W. Bush.

Passing the small town of Saco Carson decided they could spare a little time to make a stop at a location he heard positive things about online. Barreled Souls Brewing Company just opened in 2014, but was quickly gaining attention in the local beer community. Something that was adding to the appeal was the concept behind the brewery where all of the beer produced underwent primary fermentation in oak barrels. The fermentation system modeled a system used in the 1800's called the Burton Union system.

One of the benefits of the system was the oak being broken down by the beer during the fermentation process and releasing tannins that subtly but noticeable changed the beer. The barrels also affect the yeast due to the size and shape of the vessel. The rounded wall of the barrel helped the liquid churn and rotate during fermentation letting the yeast to more easily move around giving it better fermentation characteristics.

The primary purpose of using the Burton Union system was to allow for a means of re-capturing a healthy and active yeast crop to use for subsequent batches. As the beer fermented, yeast was driven up to the surface by the CO_2 created as it multiplied. The enzyme that rose to the top were the healthiest and most active yeast cells in the batch. By filling the barrels almost to the top, this top crop of yeast was pushed up and out of the barrels and into a catchment system that allowed the yeast to be captured and re-used in subsequent batches. Over generations, the yeast acclimated to the system resulting in a selectively bred strain the flourished.

The group was excited to try a newer place that was still off the current radar for many, but quickly growing in popularity, like discovering an underground hip-hop artist a couple of years before he blows up and everyone knows about his music. Just getting into the brewery was an experience. It was in an old house and appeared to be in the cellar of the home. Inside it was dark and rustic that presented a character as strong as the character the owners strive for in the beer.

"Everything is barrel-aged?" asked Ty.

"Yes, that's what the website says," confirmed Carson.

"Jesus...then I will have a flight so I can try as many as possible...and, wow," he said looking at the menu, "four in the flight for eight bucks. Not bad."

"I love the feel of this taproom," said Tegan. The cellar, the darkness, the barrels, plus the shuffleboard over there is cool."

The menu's offerings showed a good assortment of beers. Ty selected Paper Planes IPA as one choice and suddenly had the song by the same name from M.I.A. stuck in his head. He hummed the melody as he looked at the other selections. "Also, the Teotihuacán, the Mocha Grande, and the El Dorado," he said. Tegan selected the Stay Puft, Spring Tonic, and the Eat A Peach. Kareem the Quaker State, Half Nelson, Rosalita, and Golden Cucumber. Carson picked the Dark Matter, Cookie Monster, El Dorado, and the recently released ABCs.

"This place is charming," said Kareem as they took a seat, each with their flight boards. Of the selections Ty most enjoyed the Teotihuacán, an Imperial Stout made with raw cocoa nibs and oven-roasted habaneros. He imagined really would pair well with dark chocolate and made him think of Mexican mole.

For Tegan, the Stay Puft was her favorite; an Imperial Stout made with roasted marshmallows and graham crackers. It had chocolate, cotton candy, and vanilla aromatics with flavors of charred marshmallow and dark chocolate.

Kareem liked the straight-forward approach on Quaker State, a traditional Oatmeal Stout with roasted barley and caramelized malts. Carson loved the Dark Matter, but the ABCs took a slight edge because of the season. Closing in on Halloween the fermented apples and hints of cinnamon captured the spirit of the holidays.

"Well we won't have too much further to go tonight," Carson said as he finished the El Dorado taster. There is another spot I want to check out, but it's just an attraction. Nothing to drink there, and then the hotel won't be too far after that."

"We should probably head up the road though," suggested Ty. They left the flight board on the table, waved to the server, and headed back to the car to return to the highway for a few more miles.

Carson pulled over near the boardwalk in Old Orchard Beach deciding it was time to pull over and fine-tune his navigations to the hotel. He pulled off of the Broadturn Road exit, and onto US-1 before pulling up in front of Lin Libby's Candy Shop.

"This is as good a place as any to stop and search the GPS. Plus we can stretch our legs and pick up some candy," Carson said.

Getting out of the rental car, each member of the group stretched and enjoyed the fresh air. "Let's check out the store and see if they have a restroom" suggested Kareem. Inside the door, the smell of chocolate invaded their nostrils. It was a pleasant assault and one they willingly succumbed to. Pushing their way through the invisible clouds of chocolate they came face-to-face to another legendary animal, the infamous life-size chocolate moose, Lenny.

Lenny was made of seventeen hundred pounds of milk chocolate and stood in a pool of white chocolate tinted with food coloring. Lenny debuted in July 1997 and had been drawing crowds ever since. The group took the opportunity to take a group photo with Lenny as well as individual selfies with the chocolate beast. "The TIME crew with another animal find!" said Kareem.

He then headed to the restroom while the rest of the group walked through aisles of salt water taffy, Maine blueberries, seasonal fudge, and ever-popular maple sugar candy. There were large chocolate Lenny Mooses, similar to a chocolate Easter bunny but instead it was a moose, cherry cordials, and truffles that caught the group's eye. In the end, they returned to the car with just a few samples of fudge and one small Lenny Moose chocolate candy.

Carson reviewed his Hotels.com reservation to see how far they were from the hotel. The La Quinta Inn & Suites Portland was just nine miles away. Carson had two rooms reserved because the room with two double beds might be a little too cozy. A double bed would be fine individually, and each room did have a refrigerator and microwave, which was always important.

The hotel was just twenty miles from Freeport, which is where some of tomorrow's adventures would begin, and for tonight it was only about five miles away from Allagash Brewing Company on Industrial Way. About fifteen minutes after leaving Lenny the Chocolate Moose, Carson pulled into the La Quinta parking lot, just down the street from the Portland Sea Dogs stadium.

"That would be nice to see a game there if it were still baseball season," said Ty.

"So many things already, we will have to come back," suggested Kareem.

"I'm down. We are just getting a taste of these states on this trip. I thought it would be nice to see some things on the way to Vermont, but we have a lot to explore if we come back on another trip," replied Carson.

Checking into the hotel was easy. Ty, Tegan, and Kareem lingered around the self-serve snack section while Carson checked in for the two rooms and rejoined the group with the keys.

"This one's for you," he said as he handed one to Tegan, "and one for us. Let's hit the room, freshen up, and rejoin in the hallway in, what? Twenty minutes? Then we can hit that up that brewery. It's just about ten minutes from here."

Tegan and Kareem met up with Carson and Ty in the hotel lobby. Carson looked through the collection of brochures from local attractions while he and Ty were waiting.

"Hey guys, check this out," he said as he held up one of the brochures. "International Cryptozoology Museum! We have GOT to check that out tomorrow! It's on Avon Street which is less than two miles from the hotel. It has exhibits, samples, and stories about a wide variety of mysterious creatures" revealed Carson.

"Yeah, maybe we can find that elusive jackalope," teased Ty. Carson smacked Ty's chest with the brochure as they headed out to the car. "I am familiar with Allagash, at least a little bit," said Kareem. "They specialize in Belgian-inspired beers. I received a Black in a trade. It was delicious from what I remember. Kind of like cryptozoology's mysterious animals, technically there isn't a Belgian stout, but they create one. That's where the "Belgian-inspired" comes from I guess."

"Sounds interesting, and I'm ready for a nightcap, so let's see what they've got," said Tegan.

Carson pulled into the driveway in front of a large blue and white warehouse-style building. The walk to the brewery from the parking lot was beautiful, even in the darkness of night. Small lights reflected up along the concrete sidewalk. The scent of fresh night air and lupines filled the air as the group walked past dozens of the purple flowers lining each side of the walk under wooden pergolas. The smell reminded Carson of home. The bluebonnet, state flower of Texas found in abundance around the state and the parking lot of Giddy Ups was also a lupine.

Inside the smells of malt, barley, and the bready aroma of wort revealed that it recently had been brewing day. Some people dislike the smell of brew day, but Carson enjoyed it immensely. Since discovering the joys of craft beer just a few months ago, it was a smell that instantly attracted him. He turned to see his partners stopping to take in the scent as well, and he could see they all viewed brew day as a favorable experience.

A young man with a large frame and round belly approach. He wore a light blue t-shirt and a black baseball cap, but his thick red beard and mustache stood out to the visitors.

"Thanks for dropping in this evening," said the man. "My name is Flannery. Take a seat wherever you can find a spot. First come first served." The large open room was full and showed this was a popular Friday night spot in town. In the far corner of the long wooden bar, Tegan secured a portion with enough seating for all four. Flannery soon joined them from behind the bar with menus in hand. "I will give you a chance to look those over. Let me know if you have any questions."

"I've had Black, and I like that, but I think I will try something new," said Kareem.

"How's the White?"

"White is excellent," said Flannery. "It's our best seller. More than half of our total sales are from that beer, and it helps us spread out into some of the wilder varieties."

"I'm sold," replied Kareem.

"Well, the Black sounded good from what Kareem told us" responded Carson. "I will go with that one."

36

"If you guys like dark beers, we have one that we just produced and are getting ready to release on a larger scale. Right now we are just calling it House Beer, but we will probably do some Halloween theme with it. It comes in at 6.66% ABV, and it is inspired by Porters. We talked about calling it Haunted House or something. Right now it's not on the menu, but I can pour one if you like," Flannery added.

"That's right up my alley. Let me get one of those," said Ty.

"And for me..." Tegan paused as she looked over the menu, "the Confluence," she determined.

"I don't know about you guys, but I am thinking about picking up a couple of bottles to pack back home," suggested Kareem.

Flannery returned with the drinks and sat them in front of the team. "Is it possible to get beer to go?" asked Kareem.

"Definitely! We have a large selection of bottles for carry-out," responded Flannery.

"I already know I want the James Bean, the 20th anniversary Fluxus, and the Ghoulschip since it's almost Halloween," ordered Kareem." "Awesome. I will go ahead and bag those up. Anyone else?" said Flannery.

"How about a bottle of Farm To Face and one Uncommon Crow for me?" asked Tegan. Flannery headed to be back to get the bottles while leaving them to enjoy their pints and enjoy the final hours of the evening.

5 PORTLAND

Saturday, October 3, 2015

The next morning the crew woke up around 10:00 a.m. The day would be spent in Portland and a little further up the coast to Freeport, but nothing too stressful. It was a vacation after all. After getting ready, they met up in the lobby for bagels and coffee. By the time they arrived breakfast hours in the lobby were technically over and they only found a couple of plain bagels and some white bread for toasting. The chairs were pushed in every direction from the prior guests.

"Looks like our options are limited," said Ty.

"I am sure we will get something around town later," replied Kareem.

Carson arrived last and walked in adjusting his Astros hat.

"What's the plan for today?" asked Ty.

"I want to check out the cryptozoology museum this morning. It opens at eleven, and I figured we could spend time there then drive up the coast a bit."

"Sounds nice. I'm still learning about cryptozoology, so I am a little excited to see the museum," said Tegan.

"Yeah, me too. I can't wait to see some of these things you and Ty talk about," responded Kareem.

"Well we do a lot of talking," said Ty, "but we have seen too much…yet!"

Champ and A Bit of Sunshine

"We saw the chupacabra," added Carson.

"That's true. And who knows what else is out there or in our future," said Tegan.

"Another place I planned on checking out this morning is just about a half hour past the museum, and that's Maine Beer Company up in Freeport. We can hang out in that town as well. That's the town where L.L. Bean is from, and they have a huge outlet we can explore," said Carson.

Carson looked over the rack of brochures that he studied the night before, looking for more attractions to add to the itinerary. "And just because I make suggestions it doesn't mean we have to do those things" added Carson. "All plans are soft!"

"It's cool with me," said Kareem. "I've never been here, so I don't know what there is to see. I just know I want to bring some hops back to Texas and expand my trade market."

"I have been here, but it's been so many years it is like it is new to me also," replied Carson. "Anything you guys see or want to check out just holler, and we're there."

He picked up a brochure on Freeport, one about lobster rolls, and an Ogunquit Playhouse playbill for Saturday Night Fever that apparently a fellow hotel guest stuck in one of the display slots. "Huh, this show is playing until October 25," he said as he turned to sit down at the table. He pushed a Fingerhut catalog to the side as he sat down.

"I do love a good musical," said Kareem.

The bagels and toast were just okay. Enough to stave off starvation, but not enough to satisfy. At least the orange juice was good. Carson grabbed the playbill and finished off the juice.

"Let's get rolling and see what we see," he said as he threw the cup into the trashcan. Exiting the hotel lobby, they were a little surprised that the morning air was a chilly fifty degrees. At least crisp to a group of Texans not used to the autumn days of New England. But the colder temperature also brought a crispness to the air that reminded them of what a stereotypical New England fall morning was supposed to feel. The sun shone through the leaves creating a magical feel to the yellow and orange leaves that sprinkled the town. Tegan grabbed a light sweater from the trunk of the car as they prepared to get in.

Driving up Park Street and turning on Congress Street, the museum was about a mile and a half away. Parking around back, they walked around the side of the building searching for an entrance. "Are you sure this is the place?" asked Tegan. "That's the address on the brochure. Maybe it is on the other side?" replied Carson. Walking around the building, they eventually made their way to a door marked as the museum entrance. They slowly walked in, and the floor creaked as they took the first steps inside.

The group walked through the door and made their way to the counter, where a man with a white beard awaited. Their eyes darted around the large open room as they prepared to pay the fee. Carson reached into his wallet and paid forty dollars in cash to cover entrance all four. The man rang in the transaction and joined Carson as he started to explore the first area.

"Woah, Bigfoot!" exclaimed Kareem.

"Yes, that's one of our more popular attractions in the museum," said the man.

"Not to act like a total tourist, but I want a selfie with him," said Tegan.

"We should get a group shot too," suggested Carson.

"He likes to hide amongst the trees even in the museum," said Ty, commenting on the two large faux trees on either side of the giant creature.

"We try to depict its natural surroundings," replied the museum's operator. "We have not only the life-sized Bigfoot, but we have footprint casts, actual hair samples of Abominable Snowmen, Bigfoot, Yowie, and Orang Pendek, fecal matter from a small Yeti, and even a Sasquatch baby "reborn" doll. Some of our artifacts have appeared in many documentary programs," he added.

"So this is the place for Bigfoot?" asked Kareem.

"It is a unique museum that contains many documented artifacts not only from Bigfoot, but other cryptids from around the globe. The Dover Demon, the Montauk Monster, the Jersey Devil, and others are here. We just recently updated our lake monster exhibition," the curator added. Ty pointed to the far corner of the room at a head mounted on a trophy plaque.

"Hey Carson, there's our jackalope," he jested.

"Very funny. We might have to go back to looking for it now that we have a larger team," snarked Carson.

"You might try looking in South Dakota or Wyoming where it was first introduced in the 1930s," suggested the man.

"See, that's what we were doing wrong. We were in Texas," laughed Ty.

"Texas – you all do look familiar. I've seen you in the newspapers from San Antonio. You found the chupacabra, right?" the man asked.

"That's right," replied Carson. "Earlier this year we were called down to San Antonio to investigate the death of some cattle in the area." Carson continued to talk as the man joined them on their walk through the museum, eventually stopping at a chupacabra display.

"One thing we were interested in was the difference in descriptions between the Puerto Rican chupacabra and what we frequently see in Texas when people talk about chupacabras. That almost unknown and forgotten breed of hyena with its strong back legs and ability to walk on two or four legs split that gap," said Carson.

"Yes, cryptozoology is the study of hidden animals, so that includes animals that are extinct, animals whose existence has yet to be proven, and animals discovered far from where they should be geographically. Your forgotten species of hyena fits the bill," said the curator. "So what's next for your chupacabra?"

"The one we captured is still with the taxidermist, but it should be ready for display soon. The town has been working on building a small museum there that will house the animal when completed. I think there are others out there, but that one was making its presence known and attacking the local livestock. We haven't heard of any more reports of incidents since that one that was killed," said Carson. "Things have been hectic for us since then with a flood of calls for interviews and requests to search for other cryptids, but right now we are trying to relax a bit and get away. We are spending the week up here just to enjoy the leaves and local beer."

"It will be difficult to escape since your discovery," suggested the man. "Where are you headed to this week?"

"We were going to head over to the Burlington area and enjoy the lake for a few days," said Ty. "Burlington? Well maybe you will run into Champ while you're there," suggested the curator.

"Champ?" questioned Tegan.

"Yes, Champ is the sea serpent in Lake Champlain. Similar to the Loch Ness Monster in Scotland. Many reports since the days of the Iroquois suggest something is there" responded the man.

"Hopefully he will lay low while we are here. We are on vacation!" said Kareem.

The man showed the group around the displays in the museum. A life-size bronze sculpture of a thylacine —the largest known carnivorous marsupial of modern times was on display, as well as newspaper articles, artist drawings, and other depictions of the chupacabra.

"I saved some newspaper clippings from your expedition and was planning on adding them to the exhibit to update it with the newest developments," said the man. "Do you mind if I take a group photo that could be added as well?" he asked.

"Not at all! It would be an honor to be included in this museum. It's one of the coolest places I have ever been," stated Carson. "It like my childhood dream in full display!"

The curator sat up a tripod and set the camera on a timer so he could join the group in the photo. The camera snapped the picture which was quickly reviewed and approved by everyone.

Champ and A Bit of Sunshine

"Nice! We can print it here on the color printer. Maybe you all would be willing to autograph it?" the man asked.

"Who would have thought just a few months ago when I met you in that brewery in Austin that less than six months later I would be signing autographs and considered a cryptozoologist," marveled Tegan.

"Right – I didn't even really know what a cryptozoologist was then," replied Kareem. "Now, apparently I am one!" he laughed.

The group continued its walk around the museum looking at mermaids, yetis, the Dover Demon, the Minnesota Iceman exhibit, and stopping finally in the gift shop area. "I'm thrilled you guys stopped by today. Feel free to come in again anytime."

"We will be in touch," said Carson. "I'm going to sign up with the International Cryptozoology Society and maybe hit up the ICS Conference."

"Maybe we could get you all down there as a presenter? It's coming up in January – the 4th through the 6th in St. Augustine, Florida," suggested the man.

"That would be great. We will be in contact." The man handed Carson a business card as the group exited the museum. "Thanks for the tour," said Ty as they shook hands before they left the building. As they walked back to the car, Ty and Carson were star-struck.

"That was so cool! Do you guys know that man is one of the country's foremost cryptozoology experts, and we just met him! I am stoked!" Ty said excitedly.

"Not only that, but we just got added to the museum display!" said Carson. "I can't even...Who is ready for lunch?" asked Carson.

"I'm starting to get a little hungry, but not quite there yet," responded Ty. "Okay... well, how about a drink?".

"That's just my game!" said Kareem.

Just about twenty minutes up 295 was Maine Beer Company located just south of Freeport.

"We can hit it up, then get some lunch in town afterward," suggested Carson. "One cool thing about them, in addition to some good, well-sought after beer is their position of giving back. They have a motto of Do what's right and give one percent of all sales to environmental non-profit groups," reported Carson.

"That's really cool. Let's check it out," replied Tegan.

The parking lot was full, but the lot was spacious enough to accommodate the increased traffic they had experienced in recent years as the popularity of the beer increased.

"I'm glad we are stopping here," said Kareem. "I already scouted out the website hoping we would visit and saw they have bottles to go. They have a such a good trade value I am planning on getting a few to go."

The large solar panels on the side of the building indicated they arrived at the correct place. A large, white building gave off a welcoming vibe as they approached. Inside, they looked around and even though it was bustling, the space was spotless and the taproom well-lit. A window into the brewery allowed for the ability to watch the early stage of the beer-making process. The number of people in the brewery and number of bottles leaving the door was impressive for a small, although well-established brewery. The staff was polite and helpful, even though the counter was slammed with people.

There were more seating options outside in addition to a large porch and yard that created a very chill and relaxed vibe that screamed "Maine!" There wasn't much room inside to sit due to the large crowd, but Carson envisioned it would be more enjoyable to sit outside and drink while taking in the charm of the state with the beautiful background of fall foliage.

"Let's order at the counter and sit outside. If you guys know what you want, Ty and I can order for you if you two grab us a table," he suggested to Kareem and Tegan.

"I wanted to try Dinner, but it looks like it doesn't release until October 24," Ty said as he noticed a flyer on the wall.

"Man, just a few weeks too early!" said Carson.

"They have an 'All in flight' of five ounces of each of their eighteen beers on tap for eighteen dollars," read Ty. "But I don't know if I can do all of that. Might be worth a share. Otherwise, I will just get a pint. Who knows where else we might stop today," he said.

"Yeah, I think I will just do a pint as well," replied Carson. "Maybe the Peeper Ale for me. That's the one that really got them started and has been a staple since the brewery opened."

"It is lunchtime, so I will go with Lunch. That is an excellent IPA from what I have heard," said Ty as he looked over the menu. He looked down at his phone.

"Tegan says she wants A Tiny Beautiful Something and Kareem will also have a Lunch. We can pick out the to-go bottles when we are ready to leave," he suggested.

They ordered and paid at the counter, each carrying two pints to the table on the porch where their friends awaited.

"I've been searching my phone while you guys were ordering," said Tegan.

"I need to try a lobster roll while we are up here, and I read there is a good spot for lunch just down the road at Harraseeket Lunch and Lobster Company on Main Street in Freemont. The reviews say they have one of the best lobster rolls in town" she said. "That works for me. We can have these drinks, pick up bottles to go, then head there for the lobstah rolls. After that maybe hit up the L.L. Bean Outlet to walk off the lunch and beers?" proposed Carson.

"Not only that, but it is a little cooler than I expected so I might need to pick up some warmer clothes," said Ty.

"We can hook you up with the white boy uniform – cargo shorts, a fleece pullover, and some boat shoes... or some Nantucket Red?" suggested Carson.

"Um...I'm good. Maybe just a sweater or a light jacket" responded Ty.

"Say whatever you like, but I am going to buy some duck boots," said Kareem.

"Maybe some cute flannel shirts," Tegan thought aloud. The time spent on the porch drinking beer and talking with friends about the events of the day was as nice as Carson imagined it would be and he felt as if Maine got it right with the slogan "The Way Life Should Be."

Finishing the pints, Kareem walked inside to pick up some bottles. "Six dollars each isn't bad," he thought as he looked at the options.

He selected King Titus American Porter, Mean Old Tom American Stout, a Peeper Ale, and a Lunch IPA. He planned on securing a nice cache not only for trading but having a bottle share with some of his other friends following his beer adventures vicariously on Facebook. He placed the bottles in the trunk with his earlier finds. Now sufficiently hungry, his attention turned to lunch and his first experience with a lobster roll.

The group gasped with excitement as Carson pulled into the parking lot of Harraseeket Lunch and Lobster Company. A large red building with a big blue tent overlooked the water and plenty of red picnic tables. The air was fresh coming off the water, but the smell with its combination of seaweed, mud, water, and seafood attracted the group to the outside tables. They ordered the food at the lunch counter where all four ordered a fifteen dollar lobster roll. Carson also ordered the half pint of fried clams for eighteen dollars suggesting that they all share it. Between the lobster and clams, it was a taste of Maine they all craved.

The only thing missing now was a bowl of chowdah, but there was dinner yet later that night, and Carson expected he would soon check that off his Maine food bucket list. They sat at a table that overlooked the water and watched the boats and the bait barrels on along the lobstering wharf.

The seagulls circling overhead watching for small fish to surface near the lobster boats provided the music. The weather, the conversation, and the end of the pint glass of brought enjoyment to everyone's mind. They were glad to be in a place with friends, away from the hounding media attention, and just taking in the relaxing natural and beautiful setting.

"These lobster rolls are to die for," said Tegan. "I could eat these every day!"

Following lunch, the next stop was a short drive into town where the group stopped at the L.L. Bean factory outlet. Another photo op awaited right in front of the store.

"Hey, Kareem – there's your duck boot," Carson said as he pointed to the giant sixteen and a half foot tall by seven and a half foot wide representation of an L.L. Bean's signature, waterproof Maine hunting shoe – also known as the duck boot. It was an homage to the boot Leon Leonwood Bean created in 1912 that put the company on the map.

"That one is a little too big for my feet, Carson!" Kareem said snarkily. Walking inside the first sight was a giant fish tank with an observation bubble. Inside the tank, four species of trout swam with plenty of room. While they are common fish, it was relaxing and enjoyable to watch them swim. In the hallway was a beautiful display of hundreds of L.L. Bean catalog covers, spanning decades.

"Wow, this is cool just to see and realize the history of the store and the importance it brings to this town," said Tegan. "It's entertaining walking around here," said Kareem. "I am not into hunting, fishing, or camping, but this place is cool. With the fountains, ponds, and the fish tank it seems like a large lodge, and I almost want to buy a canoe to go with my duck boots" he continued.

Being Saturday, the store was busy, but it was still a pleasant experience. Before they knew it, two hours had passed just roaming the aisles. They decided it was time to check out. Tegan with a couple of flannel shirts, Kareem with the duck boots, and Ty with a fleece pullover.

After checking out, they wandered the streets of Freeport looking at other outlets, a McDonalds that also served lobster rolls, and Wicked Woolies' for a whoopie pie – another item on the Maine food bucket list. Returning to the car they enjoyed a short drive down to Wolfe's Neck State Park where they took in a beautiful view of the ocean and small islands.

The water from the sea was cold but still enjoyable. Living in Austin, it was more than three hours to the nearest beach in Galveston and a drive that none in the group regularly made. This was nice – to connect with nature and just enough an autumn afternoon with the seagulls, the fresh ocean air, and the gentle lapping of the waves against the shore.

The park was busy with people – some active and enjoying the lovely Saturday afternoon, and a few loitersacke gentleman just lounging on the side. Carson marveled at the ocean and what it brought to the surface – everything from seashells to a tin watering can. He briefly wondered about the watering can. It seemed out of place. Where did it come from and how did it end up on the shores of Freeport, Maine?

As the sun lowered in the sky, the group decided it was time to head back toward the hotel, and as inconceivable as it was, their thoughts turned toward dinner.

"I know it seems like we just ate, but those lobster rolls don't last long. I mean it's basically the size of a hot dog, right? Let's hit up that restaurant we passed in Yarmouth coming up here, the Muddy Rudder I think it was. It looked nice, and it will be a good spot for our last taste of Maine. Tomorrow I think we drive across New Hampshire and make it to Vermont," suggested Carson.

"It's kind of a shame we aren't there now. In Exeter, NH today is the Exeter Powder Keg Beer & Chili Festival, and in South Burlington, it's the Oktoberfest 4 to benefit Vermont Foodbank, but both will be over by the time we get there tomorrow," said Carson. "We should be able to hit up some breweries, but most of the bigger ones are a little more south than we are going. We can probably hit them up on the way back to Boston next weekend."

It was just nine miles to the restaurant. The large building sided in gray shingles with multiple white bay windows overlooking the parking lot announced the name Muddy Rudder with a large blue sign and yellow text. Inside, the live piano player added to the ambiance. It took about ten minutes to be seated, which wasn't bad considering the crowd. The hostess sat them in a covered dining room providing a beautiful view of the marshy waterfront as the sun set and the sky glowed with a bright orangish-red. "I know I want a cup of clam chowder, said Carson to the group, ticking off the final food bucket list item.

"The lobster bisque is speaking to me," Ty replied as he continued to look over the menu. Kareem and Tegan also ordered a cup of chowder. For dinner, Carson ordered the lobster mac 'n cheese, Kareem the seared scallops, Tegan the seafood scampi, and Ty the barramundi, each just under twenty-five dollars. A glass of water for each rounded out the order as they decided they would save their final evening drink for a brewery close to the hotel.

The conversation continued until the server returned with the soup. The creamy clam chowder itself made the stop worthwhile. The bisque was equally impressive, totally blowing Ty's mind, with large chunks of lobster swimming around in the bowl.

"This is exactly what I was craving," he said. When the main dishes arrived, the group's eyes popped. Carson's mac n cheese dish came with a quarter pound of fresh-picked lobster meat, a blend of three kinds of cheese, and cavatappi pasta.

The scallops paired with a sweet potato puree, grilled asparagus, prosciutto crisp, and micro arugula. Ty's barramundi included seared seabass, baby bok choy, and local mushrooms in a miso broth. Finally, Tegan's seafood scampi featured shrimp, scallops, and mussels, oven-roasted tomatoes, linguine and scampi butter.

The smell of butter and seafood made each mouth water and was a scent they considered representative of what they thought Maine would smell. The taste equaled and even exceeded the anticipation delivered by the smell. The meal was pricey, but an excellent, classic seafood dish. Something they felt was needed to have at least once when visiting New England. Kareem motioned for the server, and everyone threw cash in the middle of the table while Kareem wrangled it in a neat pile with an included tip.

"One more stop before we hit the hotel, and the night is getting starting to get late. We have a long drive tomorrow so we should turn in soon. There is Sebago Brewing Company just down from the hotel. It's about fifteen minutes from here. Are you all good with a nightcap then calling it an evening?" asked Carson.

"I thought there was another one close by," asked Tegan. It was on Anderson Street I think."

"That's Bunker Brewing. I have read good things about them as well. Lots of great beers here in Portland. We could almost make just this town a beer-cation," replied Carson.

"Well seems a shame to miss it since we are so close," suggested Ty. "Right you are my good man!" Carson said as he typed the address into the GPS.

They pulled up first to Bunker Brewing, a small brewery housed in an old brick scrapyard building in the East Bayside neighborhood focusing on small-batch ales and lagers. It was a little hard to find, but that added to the charm once they did. Inside it had a casual, homey vibe and despite everyone else in town has to go back to work in the morning, the crowd was still larger than Carson expected. They each ordered one pint and paid to close out with the order. Carson ordered a Machine Czech Pilz; a Czech Pilsner brewed right there in Maine. A mixture of German malt and Saaz hops, the server spoke about the rave reviews the beer has been receiving. Tegan ordered a Weekend At Burniez, a limited collaboration between Other Half and Bunker Brewing. It was described as a wheat India pale lager brewed with lactose.

"Enjoy that one," the server said. "It's a one-time only brew and won't last much longer." Kareem ordered the Beast Coast IPA and Ty the Cypher Pale Lager.

Following Bunker, the group drove just down the road to Sebago Brewing Company to close down the evening. The brewery was on the bottom floor of a building with a Hampton Inn above it. "If we stayed here we'd be home for the night," said Ty.

"Bissell Brothers is hitting it out of the park with their delicious hazy New England-style IPAs. I wonder if we can pick any up at a local package store before we leave town?" wondered Kareem.

"We can see what's open tomorrow, although we will probably be up and out before most are open. We might be able to hit some at the edge of the state though," suggested Carson.

Looking over the menu the group again decided to pay for a pint and close out. "I want something light and easy drinking," said Tegan as she selected the Saddleback Ale.

"What the hell? We're going to the hotel next, right?" asked Ty. "Give me the bourbon barrel aged Lake Trout Stout."

Kareem ordered the Royal Tar Imperial Stout, an Imperial Stout that was smooth like a milk stout. Carson rounded out the order with a Hefeweizen.

As the car pulled into the hotel parking lot, everyone was tired and ready to fall asleep. They knew it would be a long day tomorrow, but looked forward to the drive over the Vermont where they could spend a couple of days just relaxing around the lake.

6 NH TO BURLINGTON

Sunday, October 4, 2015

The vibration of the cellphone against the wooden nightstand caused Tegan to awake. It was a series of texts from Carson reading "Up and at 'em! Early day today. Picking up McDonald's before we hit the road. What do you want?" She stretched and rubbed the sleep from her eyes. She looked over at the other bed and saw Kareem was also stirring.

"Hey – what do you want from McDonald's? Carson says we have to get on the road and he is picking up breakfast," she said sleepily to her roommate.

"Coffee and a sausage McMuffin with egg," he responded. Tegan replied with Kareem's order and a sausage McGriddle for herself.

"Do you want in the shower first?" asked Kareem.

"No, you can go ahead. I am going to lay here for a couple more minutes," Tegan replied.

"Any idea what we are in for today?" asked Kareem.

"I think driving across New Hampshire and getting to the lake tonight." Kareem walked over to the door and opened it, walking out onto the porch in his pajama pants and no shirt.

"Woo – that air is crisp this morning. Definitely a flannel shirt day!" he reported to Tegan. "I love the freshness of the air up here, even if it is cool," he said. Tegan turned on her side to face him and glimpse a peek of the outside world through the open door.

Kareem turned back inside, closed the door, and searched through his suitcase to pick out the clothes for the day.

"Back in a jiffy," he said as he entered the bathroom and turned on the water in the shower. Twenty minutes later he emerged in a white terrycloth robe and a white hotel towel wrapped around his head like Ferris Buehler in Ferris Buehler's Day Off. Tegan headed to the shower while Kareem got dressed – a red and black flannel shirt, faded blue jeans, and the newly acquired duck boots. Ty and Carson knocked at the door. Kareem walked outside to join them while Tegan finished getting ready.

When she joined the guys, she was also wearing flannel and jeans. She turned her head to the side and ran a hairbrush through her shoulder-length red hair as she talked.

"We ready to do this?"

"Yes. I wanted to get on the road a little early because it's going to be about six hours – but we have some stops along the way to stretch and of course lunch. We are going to head through central New Hampshire, and we should get some great views of the leaves in the White Mountain region. We will be just below it. I was planning on stopping at Squam Lake, which is about two hours from here," revealed Carson. "Ty and I already checked out and have the car loaded. You guys need help carrying things down?"

"No, we are good," said Kareem. I will just grab my suitcase and I'm set." Tegan returned to the room, put her brush in the carry-on, and grabbed the hotel shampoos and soaps.

"Ready, Freddy!" she said as she grabbed her purse and suitcase.

As they left town, the traffic was light. It was early, and it was Sunday morning. Many of the locals were likely in church. Congress Street turned in ME-25W, and they were on their way to the next adventure – whatever that was. As they continued further inland and onto the ME-112 then the ME-25, the trees transformed from green to a kaleidoscope of colors; a speckled mass of vibrant orange, red, and yellow covered the landscape. Having seen photos online before the group knew what to expect, but seeing it in person was breathtaking. The scenic country roads and the occasional backdrop of a red barn or a white steeple church felt like a postcard-ready image everywhere they looked.

It was an excellent week to travel, even though most considered Columbus Day weekend to be the best time to visit for the best foliage color, arriving just a week earlier gave a good look at near-peak leaves without the bigger crowds that would likely come next week. Much of the car ride was silent as everyone inside stared out of the windows and marveled at the natural beauty.

Crossing into New Hampshire, the impressive views continued. Carson slowed entering the town of Center Ossipee with its winding country road through a small cluster of buildings with rusted tin roofs. There was still several green trees due to the number of pines in the area. But it was still beautiful with the quaint small town feel, the landscape speckled with orange, and Ossipee Lake in the background. Carson pulled into a driveway when he saw a building for Sap House Meadery, but the taproom was only open from 1-5 on Saturday and Sunday.

"Looks like we will have to skip that one," he said as he pulled back onto the road as the NH-25W and NH-16W intermingled.

Eventually, the NH-16 split off, but the NH-25W was then joined with NH-113 for a few miles, passing through the town of Sandwich. He briefly stopped at the foot of Wentworth Hill in front of a small wooden farm stand for Chestnut Meadow Farm selling fresh organic produce and farm-raised eggs. Carson consulted the atlas while parked in front of the building.

"Looks like just a few more miles until our first stop," he said. "How's everyone doing? Anyone need a bathroom break or are you good for a few more minutes?" All agreed they were fine for now and Carson resumed driving.

Just down the road from Sandwich began the Squam Lake region of New Hampshire. The car's occupants gasped at the beauty of the beautiful lake, surrounded by mountains appeared with still a cast of morning fog hanging above the pine trees. The lake was calm, clean, clear, filled with interesting coves and canoeing crevices, islands, and wildlife. Many signs along the road advertised for cabin and boat rentals.

"Right before we get to the town of Holderness there is the Squam Lakes Natural Science Center. We'll stop there and stretch. They have some nature trails we can get out and walk a bit," said Carson. "If you are familiar with the movie On Golden Pond, Squam Lake is Golden Pond from the movie."

"The loons! The loons! They're welcoming us back!" quipped Kareem. Walking into the Center Ty picked up a pamphlet describing the center, the trails, and some of the native New Hampshire wildlife along the way.

"Hmm. The exhibits house bald eagles, red-tailed hawks, otters, mountain lions, and black bears," Ty said as he read through the brochure.

"We do have a pontoon boat ride that is available to learn all about loons and local wildlife if you are interested," said the center's employee.

"That sounds wonderful, but I don't think we will have time for that today," replied Carson.

"Let's start on the trail and see the animals," suggested Tegan. "I want to see the black bears!" They headed back outside and began walking the nature trails, stopping to look at the exhibits that showcased the animals in their natural habitats and to read the interactive displays with facts about the wildlife presented. The markers described the animals as ambassadors of their species, most being orphaned, injured, or otherwise unable to survive in the wild. The exhibits gave people a chance to see the animals in a natural setting and interact with them to have a deeper understanding of them.

Continuing on the gravel trail running through the middle of the woods, the walk was one mile all the way around a nature trail. The path included a dozen or more buildings and animal enclosures. Just as depicted in the movie On Golden Pond, the loons were out and filled the air with their song. As they walked through the woods, they noticed the air smelled of balsam fir with just a whiff of boiling malt from a brewery.

"Is there a brewery around here?" questioned Ty.

"Yes, actually there is one just down the road - Squam Brewing," replied Carson.

"Are we stopping there?" asked Kareem.

"Well, it's just a small, three barrel nano brewery, so they don't have a taproom. They brew beer and sell it around the lakes region in twenty-two-ounce bottles. We can buy the bottles in town at the Squam Lake Marketplace." They finished up the hike around nature trail and returned to the center.

"We should buy one of those CDs for the car with sounds of the loons" suggested Tegan. "Might be relaxing!" The others walked outside to the car while Kareem purchased a CD at the gift store.

The Squam Lake Marketplace was a blue and beige large house that was very spacious inside. The wooden floors and large shelves gave it a comfortable, homey feel. The smells of bacon and lunch meats combined with coffee and brownies. The store was clean and the shelves well stocked with everything from snacks, T-shirts, and souvenirs, to local wines and of course the sought-after large selection of Squam Brewing beers.

"I might grab a sandwich or something to go. I'm a little hungry after that walk," said Ty. Looking over the menu board, he noticed a section that read *Breakfast Served All Day*. "I know we had 'breakfast' but check out that breakfast burrito – eggs, cheddar, spinach, avocado, salsa, and either ham, sausage, or bacon. Put me down for bacon!"

Kareem spoke up, "Um, that says 'breakfast wrap.' Ty looked back at Kareem.

"What the hell is the difference between a wrap and a burrito? It's the same thing. Just different words." A young man in his early twenties wearing black jeans, a white V-neck t-shirt under an unbuttoned denim shirt, and orange toboggan overheard and interjected.

"No, they're different. It's all about how you feel at the end," the young man said.

"Excuse me? What do you mean?" asked Ty.

"A burrito, you feel too full and sleepy. After a wrap, you want to hang out," the man responded. Another young man behind him spoke up.

"A burrito is Mexican. I'm racist, I'm sorry. A wrap is healthy because people like to use words to make them feel better about things."

Kareem responded, "Really? What makes a wrap healthier than a burrito?" The second man replied

"It's not. It's just people using words." Apparently satisfied with the responses Kareem and Ty nodded their heads. Ty ordered.

"Let me get the breakfast wrap, with bacon." He turned to Kareem and the two men. "I went with the wrap because I might want to hang out later, you know?"

Perusing the beer section, Carson picked up a few bottles. Within a few minutes, the rest of the group joined him and added additional bottles to the collective basket. They came away with The Camp Barleywine, Golden IPA, Halcyon Steamer Stout, Ice Harvester Porter, Imperial Loon Stout, Rattlesnake Rye-PA, and Moose Ale.

"That should last us for a couple of hours anyway," said Ty.

"There are a couple of other breweries right around here, but some of them are not open to the public either. But there is one in Portsmouth, NH I planned on stopping. The brewery itself isn't open, but Sublime Brewing Company has taps at a place called The Last Chair," said Carson. "The menu is limited, but I was planning on stopping for a late lunch a bit later. We could pull up, sit at the picnic tables outside with a lovely view out over the mountains, and have some beers," he suggested.

They sat at a picnic table, and each looked over a menu. "Although…" hesitated Carson, "that brick-oven maple apple bacon pizza sounds amazing!"

"Hey, I won't judge," said Ty. "I just ate a burrito!"

"A wrap…" interjected Kareem. Ty looked at him skeptically.

"No, I will wait for food," Carson said ignoring the bantering of the burrito versus wrap debate. "They have just a few beers, but if you like something they do have growlers to go," Carson added.

A young man with messy brown hair and a long, full beard approached.

"I'm Zayn, and I'll take your order. A few brews for you?" he asked.

"Let me get the Sublime Double IPA," responded Carson.

"The Plymouth Pale Ale for me," said Kareem.

"I'll do the Blonde Ale," added Tegan.

"This Grissette sounds interesting," said Ty.

"That one is interesting," said Zayn. "It's a European-born beer, a light, slightly saison feel to it."

"I am not familiar with the term," replied Ty.

"The history on that is a little vague. Kind of lost in time because early European brewers were a bit indifferent to record keeping. But what some speculate is that it was originally brewed for miners in Belgium's Hainaut province. The word "grisette" refers to the color gray, and some theories suggest this beer was made in a region with a lot of stone quarries, and it would quench the thirst of those workers who came back covered with gray dust. Since New Hampshire is the granite state, it seemed fitting to apply it here" Zayn said.

"The lunch stop is about two hours away yet if that's okay," said Carson.

"That's about two o'clock. I can make it," said Tegan.

"Good. I thought we would stop for lunch, then not too far after that we can stop for ice cream," Carson responded.

"Ice cream? It's like forty-five degrees," Ty gasped.

"Trust me; it's worth it" proclaimed Carson. Zayn brought the drinks and distributed each to its requestor.

"I love these little rimless pint glasses," said Kareem.

"Me too," said Ty. "I think they call it the craft beer can glass because it's kind of shaped like a can."

"Whatever they call it I would love to put a couple in my purse," suggested Tegan.

"We should probably hit the road if we still have a couple of hours today," suggested Kareem.

"I don't know if we will see the lake tonight, but I would like to get up there and check out the town," he said. Ty motioned for Zayn to bring the check.

Back on the road, it was a two-hour ride through mainly rural areas of Vermont. The group was glad the rental car had Sirius radio because the local options were limited and frequently faded in the sparse countryside. By the time they arrived in Warren, Vermont they were beginning to get tired and once again hungry. Carson pulled up to a rustic barn style of the building.

"This is The Common Man restaurant. There is a chain across Vermont and New Hampshire that specializes in comfort food, and it bears the same name; however, this one is not related, although it has the same name and also serves comfort food.

Inside it was very spacious with a soaring ceiling and a roaring fire was already in place. It was getting late in the afternoon, and the fire felt useful in keeping the chillier evening weather at bay. The hostess greeted them and walked them to a table in the back of the restaurant and close to the fireplace almost immediately.

"Enjoy your dinner," she said as she left. "Wow this place is great," Ty said as he looked around searching out intricate objects stashed in almost every corner of the restaurant.

"It's very comfortable here," commented Kareem. The wooden floors, wooden beans, thick wooden tables, solid hand-crafted chairs filled the vast space, and a thick wooden bar created a nice bar area. The smell from the fireplace and the sound of the crackling embers was something they didn't often experience in Austin. Between the time on the road and the relaxing atmosphere of the restaurant, the group became quiet and enjoyed the meal and company. The server suggested the chilled pea soup and mentioned the special of the day was halibut on a bed of rice and a butternut squash sauce. Tegan ordered both. Kareem ordered the black sea bass and Carson the house-made lamb sausage with mashed potatoes.

Ty studied the men, "I'll be adventurous and order the octopus."

"That's an excellent dish," said the server. "One of our most popular dishes."

"I think after this we will head to Burlington and get the hotel," suggested Carson. "I thought about stopping for ice cream, but we can do that tomorrow. It is just about thirty minutes from here, but I don't know they will still be open, and we won't have the time to explore it tonight."

"That's fine with me," said Ty, "I am getting tired, and we have plenty of time to see the sights around town."

"We can be in Burlington in about an hour," Carson said as he looked at the GPS on his phone and searched for a hotel. He found a cheap hotel and booked for two nights, deciding they could check out Tuesday and plan their next step from there. They remained at The Common Man for a while longer, finishing the meal and talking about their plans for Burlington over the next couple of days. They were looking forward to relaxing by the lake and drinking some of the local beer without worrying about itineraries or unseen creatures.

7 LATE NIGHT SNACK

Sunday, October 4, 2015

Just southwest of Kingsland Bay State Park where Otter Creek flowed into Lake Champlain small groups of people were enjoying one of the final weekends when swimming was still possible. Sixteen-year-old Alayna, fourteen-year-old Kelsey, and ten-year-old Emma prepared to enter the water while their family stayed back at the park enjoying a late-season picnic and fishing. Hopefully the girls' dad, Michael, would catch a couple bass or walleye that could become the family's dinner later that evening.

The swimming season typically lasted from July to September, but the water temperature was still lovely at sixty-three degrees Fahrenheit, even slightly warmer than the air temperature of in the mid-fifties. Historically the water temperature showed a steady decrease by ten degrees by the end of October. But today was excellent in the water and out with the sun lightly filtered by thin high clouds and light, variable wind between five and fifteen miles per hour from the southeast.

The girls wadded along the beach around Porter Bay with wind surfboards and stand up paddle boards. The beach was strewn with natural debris suggesting better, wetter days in the recent past. Lake Champlain had receded enough to leave a broad section of the beach dry and leave the distributed tree branches, plastic bottles, and other trash from the lake.

There was an unusual round object that appeared to be a burlap sack that caught the girls' attention. Kelsey poked it with a stick, and it appeared to be a bag of wool. Alayna guessed it was probably from a nearby farm and it washed away in an earlier summer rain. She told her sisters it probably floated down Otter Creek and into the bay, but dried up with the recent lack of rain and growing dry beach. The lake's lowest season was typically September and October where water levels were just almost ninety-five feet above sea level, but this year it dipped below ninety-four feet back in mid-September and remained there.

It was an enjoyable afternoon with smells of hamburgers from the distant grills in the park, sounds of seagulls, and general activity from people enjoying the day before the colder autumn months, and eventually, harsh winter hit the area. The girls left the boards on the sandy beach and jumped in the water. They knew not to swim out too far. Their dad talked with them about how when they swim in the shallow areas, it feels nice and warm, but swimming out a little bit deeper, and it gets colder. He previously warned the first couple of feet they'd probably be fine, but once they hit three or four feet, they could get cold water shock and have trouble swimming.

Alayna pushed her board out into the deeper water until the fin was clear of the bottom and maneuvered the board so that the sail was downwind of the board. Resting on her knees, she grabbed the uphaul, and slowly rose to her feet while rocking back and forth. Taking hold of the mast with both hands she began tilting the mast and caught a stronger the wind that propelled her slowly. She leaned back pulling with her back hand and accelerated in the water. Kelsey was practicing too but was not as skilled yet as her older sister.

Emma mostly watched, straddling the board and laying the paddle on the front edge of the board. Using her hands, she paddled further into the water and watched as her sisters were catching big breezes pushing them further away from the shore. Emma decided to stand up and paddle out to where she could continue to watch her older sisters.

The water was clear and mostly calm, with barely more than a ripple on the surface. The breeze and the wake behind her sisters caused a little disturbance, but by the time the water rings reached her they were of no significance. Suddenly the water began making swirling waves that broke with a white foam. She continued to paddle through the water but was a little unbalanced with her footing. The waves increased in intensity, and it felt like something hit the board from underneath, causing her to fall off the board. As she fell into the water, she reached for the board and was able to grab it to prevent her from falling completely in the lake. She rested there for a second with her arms draped across the board and legs dangling in the water. She planned to pull herself to her knees on the board and paddle back to shore, but something brushed against her thigh. Uncertain what was below the surface she let out a scream, causing her sisters further along the coast to stop and look back at the younger sister.

The underwater creature felt rough against her bare legs and feet. Then she could feel her foot in its mouth. She frantically kicked the beast with her other foot. It was enough to cause the animal to release her foot, and in one motion she pushed back onto the board, sitting on her knees, and began paddling wildly toward the marina. The animal descended back into the water and swam around to get another shot at the small girl. Her sisters now back on land could only watch as the girl continued paddling toward the dock, but they could not see what was chasing her.

She stood upright on the paddleboat she was close enough to jump to the edge of the pier. The animal was underwater and closing in on the girl. Just as she leaped, the beast's head surfaced and chomped down on the surfboard, but she was clear. She hung on the edge of the dock and had just enough strength to pull herself to safety. She rolled over on her back; her blonde hair was wet and matted from the water. She laid there breathing hard thinking about the narrow escape until her sisters ran to her at the end of the dock. Hysterical at the near-tragic events, they collapsed on the pier and held the younger girl. They noticed her legs were bloody with several lacerations; some of them down to the bone.

Her father had heard the screams and ran toward the dock while her mom signaled park rangers to notify paramedics of the emergency. Michael arrived at the pier where the girls told him what happened. The older sisters reported their father they saw a creature with a dark and long snake-like body with a roundish head when it surfaced to attack the surfboard. Michael turned toward the water and saw Emma's paddleboard was floating split in half with a long serrated break between the two pieces. He then turned and looked toward the lake for the creature, but saw nothing. The lake was once again calm with just a slight ripple.

Sirens blared as the ambulance arrived at the end of the dock. Two men rushed down to the girl, one draping her in large warm towels to prevent shock from the water and the other examining the lacerations on her legs. She had suffered more than two dozen cuts to her foot and leg. Paramedics told her father she would likely have to undergo surgery to repair a tendon in her foot, but she should be able to make a full recovery. The paramedics placed her gently on a stretcher and carried her to the back of the ambulance before transporting her with her father riding along to Porter Medical Center.

8 THE 802

Monday, October 5, 2015

The overnight temperatures dipped to thirty-five degrees, giving the group another reminder they were not in Texas. It hadn't felt too chilly in the afternoons, typically in the low to mid-sixties each day, but the mornings were much colder than they experienced in Austin. Thick, dark gray clouds blanketed the sky, although the forecast did not call for any precipitation.

"Look, I can see my breath," said Kareem as he blew hot air from his lungs into the chilly morning air. "I can't do that back home," he said.

Carson looked down at his phone, "You're right – this morning in Austin it is almost seventy now with a high this afternoon of eighty-five." They stood on the balcony of the Travelodge South Burlington looking down at the busy road in front of them.

"I can see a Burger King from here if you want a quick breakfast, or we can explore the area a bit for something a little fancier," said Carson. "We are booked here today and nothing really on the agenda. I thought we could hit the town and lake today, and then tomorrow we can head south into Massachusetts or explore more of central Vermont. Whatever you guys want. I'm open for anything," he concluded.

"I would love to see the lake," said Ty. "I am not too hungry. A Croissan'wich would do me just fine."

"That's good with me too," said Tegan, "Let me run in and grab my jacket. It's probably a little colder around the lake."

"I was checking out the area on the map, and it looks like there is a nice spot just a couple of miles down the road. There is a parking lot off King Street where we can park, then get out and walk along the lake on the bike trail," suggested Carson.

After a quick run through the Burger King drive-thru that netted three ham, egg, and cheese Croissan'wiches, the new addition Fully Loaded Croissan'wich, four hash browns, and four large cokes, the group drove down US-7 to St. Paul Street before turning left onto King Street.

The road took them across Battery Street, over the train tracks, and into a white-gravel parking lot beside the King Street Dock. The Ferry Dock Marina was located right in downtown Burlington, Vermont within walking distance to the Burlington waterfront, restaurants, hotels, and the Church Street Marketplace. Being early Monday morning, the parking lot was empty. Carson parked the car in the first spot facing the lake. That early in the morning, the ticket booth wasn't open either, nor was the small shop located in the gray stone building. It was peaceful, with no one around, a gentle breeze coming off the lake, and the sound of seagulls searching for a morning meal.

Walking across the paved road the group walked toward the gray building to get a better look at the Burlington Shipyard, and down to the docked ferry, and Breakwaters Café & Grill located at the end of the dock. As they walked down the dock road, Ty pointed toward the shop after spotting a sizeable green sculpture.

"Hey, isn't that Champ?" he asked.

"Yes, it is!" replied Carson, "looks like we have a sighting!" He yelled toward the sculpture, "Hey, Champ! We're on vacation! No time for monsters!"

"I like that one," said Tegan, "it doesn't bite!"

Kareem walked over to the sculpture with his cell phone in hand, "Selfie time!" The rest of the group joined him, and more photos collectively and individually followed. After the photos, they stood looking at the sculpture.

"So that's the creature the guy at the museum told us about, right?" asked Tegan.

"That's right," answered Carson. "If you ask any person on the street to name a cryptid – but first you probably have to tell them what a cryptid is – after they get it they will probably say Bigfoot first, the Loch Ness Monster because those are both well-known and transcend just those interested in cryptozoology…but Champ would probably be their third response. Up here in New England Champ might be the first name mentioned because it is everywhere. The sightings have been happening since the Iroquois and Abenaki lived here. You have statues like this one and one down in Brattleboro plus other monuments around the lake, and they even named the minor league baseball team after Champ," he concluded.

Ty picked up where Carson left off, "Even Samuel de Champlain for whom the lake is named was said to have seen Champ back in 1609."

"That's a lot of sightings," said Kareem.

"There is some question about what Champlain saw. The Champ legend was attributed to him saying he saw something twenty feet long that was thick and had a horse-like head, but his diary describes something closer to five feet and a mouth with rows of sharp teeth. Many people believe what he saw was a garfish," reported Ty.

"But speaking of the number of sightings, down in Port Henry there is a billboard with Champ sightings over the years," said Carson.

They turned and walked down the dock and looked out over the lake. "It certainly is a large lake. Plenty of places to hide," said Tegan.

"Yes, it's over one hundred twenty miles and runs between New York, Vermont, and up to Quebec," said Carson.

"Amazing views too," Kareem said. "I bet the fishing is excellent up here."

"It is a freshwater lake and is known for great bass fishing," said Ty. "But I don't know about a lake monster. It makes for a good story and is a big boost to the local economy, but a lake monster over hundreds of years? It's a closed lake now. The animal would have to have entered when the region was open and have enough population to allow for breeding, then remain after the lake closed off. Not to mention remaining hidden except for the occasional sighting. It seems very unlikely," theorized Ty.

"You are probably right," said Tegan, "but it does make a good story." "Whatever makes a better story, as one of my old friends used to say," said Carson.

"Let's check out the trail," suggested Kareem.

They walked back toward the car and through the gravel parking lot into another paved parking lot that opened into a grassy area and a small children's playground. The bike path ran alongside the yard and disappeared into the distance amid a collection of trees speckled with yellow and orange. The trail continued to Roundhouse Park where a small granite stone called Monument to a Lake Monster included the engraved image of Champ in the lake and the inscription "Dedicated to Champ," dated July 29, 1984. Just behind the monument, a wooden bench provided a nice resting spot overlooking the lake. "I think I could sit on that bench and stare out at the lake for hours," said Kareem.

Tegan walked passed the bench and climbed down onto the beach noting dozens of odd objects in the rocky beachline.

"What the heck are those?" she asked.

"Those are cairns," said Ty.

"What is a cairn?" asked Kareem.

"They are human-made markers. Basically, a pile of stones heaped up as a landmark. They are seen throughout North America. Sometimes they are boundary markers, sometimes memorials, possibly indicators marking the way somewhere, or here they could be art. There is a large artist community in Burlington," Ty noted.

Tegan turned and looked at the scattered stacks and began counting. She counted more than a hundred stone cairns standing on the rocky shore between the park and the observation deck on the boardwalk. Some cairns were made from massive slabs of granite, tilted at an angle, some incorporated metal or driftwood.

"I wonder where they came from?" asked Tegan.

"Some say it's an ancient spirit that occurs spontaneously all over the world," said Carson. "They are both beautiful and mysterious along the lake," he said.

"I know it's going to be crazy cold, but I wanna dip my feet in it," said Tegan as she bent over and untied her shoes. After removing her shoes and socks, she placed the socks inside the shoe and carried them in her left hand as she walked down to the water's edge. Then she gently placed her right foot near the water, hovering at first, then after a pre-emptive gasp to get ready, she quickly sank her foot into the chilly water to the wavy sand below.

"Shit! Shit! Shit! That's cold!" she exclaimed. After quickly retracting her foot she mustered up enough courage to return it to the water. She stood on one foot trying to get used to the temperature, then bravely put the other foot in the lake. The water was only ankle deep, and after the initial pins and needles sensation, she got used to the temperature.

She walked along in the lake's edge while the boys stayed on the path. Seaweed and twigs scattered along the water's edge, gently moving as each wave splashed softly on the shore. Birds and ducks also sat on the side of the lake watching the humans as they passed. Some sections of the beach had high concentrations of large rocks, making it challenging to walk. Others had large chunks of granite, with carved images depicting various things from monsters to mermaids and King Neptune.

"That's about enough of that," she said walking back to the beach, shaking her foot as dry as she could, and placing each foot back into the warmth of the sock and finally back into the shoe. Walking along the Burlington Bikeway, they came to an arched wooden bridge with brown rails. The rails, painted with red, orange, and yellow leaves added to the fall foliage colors. Smaller docks with sailboats, pontoon boats, and kayaks provided a picturesque view of the lake. A cloudy morning reduced visibility on the lake and made for a nice backdrop to the small marina.

"We should probably head back" suggested Carson. This path runs fourteen miles from Burlington to Colchester. We can go back to the car and check out other spots in town. Maybe see if the sun comes out and burns off some of the haze," he suggested.

As they walked back toward the car, Tegan studied her phone. "Hey, if we can make one more stop before we go, something interesting is just on the opposite side of the Lake Monsters store. It's within walking distance down the bikeway," she said.

"We need to check out that Shanty on the Shore restaurant before we leave town," suggested Kareem.

Passing the Lake Monsters store at the King Street Dock, the group came up to a brown brick building with a green roof. An erected flag stood at in the center peak of the roof, and strange steel figures appeared on both sides.

"What are we looking at here?" asked Carson.

"This is One Main, and those steel sculptures are flying monkeys," revealed Tegan.

"Flying monkeys? Like the Wizard of Oz?" questioned Ty.

"Exactly!" said Tegan. "Says here that they were created back in the 1970s when there was an old local waterbed store called Emerald City. As you might guess from the name they had a Wizard of Oz theme and those monkeys were on the roof, but when the business went under the sculptures spent about twenty years moving around the city before they ended up here. The monkeys were so popular that after the large one arrived here, the sculptor installed another pair of flying monkeys, this time baby-sized, atop the same building. There is another pair of adult flying monkeys on the Lake and

College building right over there," she said as she pointed to a building adjacent to the One Main building.

"Those are pretty impressive," said Carson. "Hidden monsters within the city. That's cool! Good find!"

Leaving the King Street Dock Carson turned right onto Pine Street. "What the heck is that?" Ty asked, pointing toward a small green house near 240 Pine Street that had a sign reading "Vintage inspired lifestyle marketplace."

The oddity was the life-sized rhino head crashing through the upstairs wall, its head projecting to the street below. Just beside the building was a gold, red, and green building for Conant Metal and Lights. In front of the store's entrance, a life-sized metal giraffe guarded the door.

"Looks like we found the artistic part of town" observed Kareem as they continued driving. "Either that or the former corporate headquarters of the old Vanilla Rhinos CDFL football team!"
"Another hidden animal in town," said Carson.

Just on the side of the road at 208 Flynn Ave stood a Burlington artistic landmark. A nice photo-op, the world's tallest filing cabinet was a roadside attraction that was thirty-eight feet tall and made with real file cabinets welded on top of each other into a skinny, towering pile. Built in 2002, it was now a little rusty. Some of the higher-up drawers were left partly open, and the number of birds flying in and out of them suggested that they were now used for nests. They watched as occasionally a squirrel popped out of a drawer.

"Switchback Brewing Company is just a couple of blocks away, but they aren't open yet," said Carson. "We can come back to that later because it's not far from the hotel."

Even though the road was technically a highway, in town, it was just a city street with two lanes on each side and a turning lane in the middle. The city of Burlington was awake now that it was mid-day and the roads were teeming with students and families. The University of Vermont wasn't too far away. The town was a delightful mixture of a college town with a postcard-pretty downtown and an artistic feel to the South End. Driving around town it was evident that it was a great place for foodies and craft beer enthusiasts. The sidewalks were lined with political yard signs for favorite politicians from local, state, and the upcoming federal elections.

"Man, this town loves Bernie Sanders," said Ty. "

Yes, Bernie is their guy. He used to be mayor here and is a state and local icon," said Kareem. Ty looked out the window as Carson continued to drive through town. "This presidential election is crazy," Ty said. Turning to Carson, he asked, "Who ya got?" Carson turned toward his friend and shook his head.

"I'm not into politics. I'll stick to monsters. They're less scary!"

"Speaking of state and local icons, how about a little music?" Carson said as he plugged the aux cord into the car stereo and found Phish on his phone. Weekapaug Groove played as Carson drove through the town.

"I never understood the connection between Phish and the Grateful Dead," said Ty.

"I'm not sure either, but both have a huge cult following. I imagine it has to do with the jam-session style of play on stage, but I only really know a few songs from each band," Carson admitted.

Tegan's phone vibrated, and she paused to look at the notification. She stared at the message, and her index finger began working rapidly.

"Um, guys…?" she continued to search the internet while she spoke, "do we have dinner plans?"

"Not really," said Carson, "Just planned on playing it by ear, why?"

"I just received a notification on my phone from Untappd. Heady Topper is available at Pascolo Ristorante! It's an Italian restaurant located on Church Street…that's the good news. The bad news is they are not open for lunch, so we have to wait until 5 p.m. when they open."

"Holy hell!" exclaimed Kareem. "That's on my beer bucket list. We have to get there. It's difficult to find. They produce it in

Waterbury, but the cannery isn't open to the public. They have a list online that shows the deliveries around the area, and people stalk the trucks because it's so difficult to locate."

"Sounds like we know where we are going to eat tonight!" said Carson.

"The other bad news is we will have to drink it there and can't get a few cans to go," Tegan acknowledged.

"Yes, and I love my trading partners," replied Kareem, 'but I come first, and if that's the only way we can try it on this trip, that's what's going to happen."

"Nice, so we have a few hours to kill. We can grab some lunch or hang out at the lake," suggested Carson.

"I vote for both," said Ty. "We can go back to the dock and grab lunch at Shanty on the Shore overlooking the lake."

"The lake has a big place in American history, and not just for the stories about Champ," responded Carson. "Back in 1776, the lake was the site of the first naval battle between the British Navy and America's first Navy. That was called the Battle of Valcour Island. The American fleet had fifteen ships, and the British had even more. It was amazing because there were so many ships in such a small area. Ultimately, the Americans fell in defeat during the battle. Most of the American ships were captured or destroyed, but the commander of the fleet, Benedict Arnold did get past the British and retreated to Crown Point. There is a monument on the island marking the battle."

"Really? I don't remember hearing about that in school," remarked Kareem.

"True. The only thing we remember about Benedict Arnold is the word 'traitor' because he returned to London and eventually returned to lead the British army in battle against the men whom he once commanded," replied Carson.

Still on her phone, Tegan interjected, "Looking online it says the Port Kent crossing from Burlington to Port Kent, New York is already closed for the season. Looks like we will have to find something else to do."

"Instead of driving all over town, let's hit up Switchback Brewing. It's right down the street and will give us time to relax before heading to our early dinner," said Carson. He pulled into the parking lot, and they walked to the front of the brewery; a clean, modern-looking facility. The front of the building was a combination of beige colored wood, cedar-colored wood, and dark tinted glass panels. The entrance was a framed aluminum and glass portico.

The bar was made from wood that looked like stacks of light-colored railroad ties and a thick granite counter top. The wood behind the bar was also light color with a chalkboard hanging. The lights hung from what appeared to be a similarly colored wooden pergola. It was open, and ample light from the sizeable tinted glass panels – the perfect place to enjoy a noon-time beer. There were a couple of black wooden chairs empty at the bar, but the group chose to sit at a wooden table just in front of the bar seating. Two men walked in behind the group, and they sat in the empty bar chairs directly front and center of the chalkboard.

Watching the guys who came in behind them, Carson thought they appeared to be new to craft beer. They were asking several questions, and the bartender was pouring small samples of various beers, giving them background, talking comparisons, and getting a feel for what they liked. The men sometimes made faces after the sip and other times projected a pleased reaction.

Carson looked over at them, then turned to Ty.

"I remember it wasn't long ago I was like those guys," he said. "Do you usually jump in and talk to guys about beer? Get them on the road to enjoying craft?" he asked.

"No, not usually. Sometimes when I am hanging out by myself, I overhear a table next to me full of men talking about random stuff. Sometimes it's local high school football, sometimes it's politics, and others they delve into craft beer. I hear them, and I might listen in. Maybe even at times I want to be a part of it. Maybe go over and say,

'I couldn't help but overhear you guys talking about beer! What have you tried recently that you love?' and just geek out for a while. But I never do…usually, never do," he said.

"Why not?" asked Ty, "You did with me."

"You were an exception – I knew you, but ordinarily I don't go up to randos," Ty recalled.

"You know what it is? I don't want to sound like a dick. I don't want to come off as that person who thinks they know more than you. I don't want to sound braggy, and I don't want to be one-uppity. When I'm out in public, I usually have a beer in hand and can check myself lest I wreck myself. I can gauge the level of interest others have in what I'm saying. I can see the opportunity to make a recommendation and know when to keep myself out. I can quickly assess how deep into the rabbit hole I want to go with my love for craft beer. But if I am somewhere with no beer in hand to break the ice, then no," he commented.

"Well, I have run into a few of what they call beer snobs out there. I guess I am not really a fan of them," replied Carson.

Ty continued, "If there's one thing that I absolutely hate about the craft beer community, it's the snobbish one-uppity dicks that you can't even carry a normal conversation with them. Is there anything worse than 'that guy' that can't just let you enjoy your beer without the 'yeah but Heady is still better' sneer? It makes me cringe, gives me douche chills, and I know I'm not alone. Am I right?" he asked looking at Kareem and Tegan.

"Yes, I hate them too," replied Kareem. "Those guys that loved Goose Island but now that they are owned by InBev they make dickhead comments about 'fancy Budweiser' and turn their faces at it, even though they probably secretly buy it because they still like it," continued Kareem.

Interrupting the conversation, a young man approached with the menus.

"Good afternoon, my name is Huck, and I'll be taking care of you this afternoon. Any water to get you started? Here is our beer menu.

We have Switchback Ale which brewed all year long while we have seven rotating specials which are brewed once a year. We also have our limited releases which are small batch brews typically only available in the tap room for a short period. We also have twenty-two ounce and twelve-ounce bottles available for sale. Or, we have five beers currently, and I can do a flight of four."

"I am down for a flight – what's on it?" asked Kareem. The Switchback Ale is one we always include since it's our year-round staple. We also have a Thai Lime Gose right now, the Citra-Pils Killer Bier, a smoky Märzen, and the Export Stout. The board they are served on is cool too. It's made out of snowboard and in the shape of the state of Vermont." Kareem and Tegan chose to eliminate the Märzen while Ty and Carson eliminated the gose from their selection.

Ty continued his rant. "And, we're not the only ones who do this. I've also seen some of the weirdest wine snobs out in public who can't help but scoff at your basic wine choice and can't stop their stories of rare wines and 'how this one tastes so much more like slate than granite' from pouring out of their mouths like toxic sludge. Knowing and learning how to talk about something without sounding like a dick takes time, practice, and the desire to even want to do so in the first place. I stay out unless invited in because I don't want to be 'that person'. I prefer to sit back, relax either by myself or with company, and enjoy the beer. I will comment when it really stands out, and I might say this has a nice whatever flavor, but not to the extent of some of these guys," he concluded.

"Beer used to be about hanging out and having fun with your friends. That's what I still try to do, and yes most of my friends are like Tegan and Kareem here and enjoy craft beer also, but we don't exclude people who like other beer."

Kareem joined in, "When they get too snobby it ruins the vibe. I agree it should be about having a good time with your buddies. Relaxing after a long day or week of work, celebrating a big sale or an upcoming trip, or just chillin'. A guy would walk into a bar and say 'gimme a beer' — any kind would do. There was no discussion of 'mouth feel.' He did not take notes on what he was drinking. I don't take notes per se, but I do regularly check in Untappd and leave a few comments. More for my future-self than being snobby. If I have a beer now and don't have it again for a year later, I like to remember what I thought about it. Might affect my decision to buy it," he said.

Huck returned the four flight boards of the selected beers.

"Hope you enjoy!" he said, returning to talk to the bartender assisting the other customers.

"Life is too short to drink crappy beer," Tegan said, jumping back into the on-going conversation. "I have heard people come into breweries and freak out about the price. I heard one guy say that beer should be two dollars and he was shocked at most of them being around six bucks. When I was in college, I used to drink cheap beer, and the focus was on the price. I would drink anything, even if I didn't like it. Buy now I am not really distraught if I have a fifteen dollars bottle of beer. If I don't like it I will pour it in the sink; price be damned. In college no matter what I wouldn't even consider a drain pour, and if it were expensive... Well, I never knew expensive then, but I think I would have drunk it. Now I just think I have a job and I bring home a decent check. If I don't like it I am not going to force myself to drink it just because of the price," she said.

They dug into the beers on the snowboard.

"Damn, I know I always order it when available, but I love a smoked beer," said Ty. "This one smells like wood and ham or bacon with a gentle medium-caramelish malt base. It's just the right amount as less wouldn't quite be bright enough, and more might be too much" he said.

"I think this gose is great" revealed Tegan. "It's got that lip puckering goodness I love with a little salty and a little funk." Carson enjoyed the keller bier the most.

"Tastes like a good Pilsner with a little lemon citrus. I could drink this all day" he said.

Kareem added his two cents, "I like the gose also, but since you all chose a different one, I like the stout. It's very flavorful with a roasted coffee, hazelnut, and bittersweet chocolate taste."

"Now see, we were all on the same page there and not being snobby dicks. When the conversation is like that it's okay to talk about aromas and hints of flavor," acknowledged Ty.

Carson turned back and looked at the guys at the bar. The bartender was still talking to them about choices and narrowing down their preferences.

"Bartenders are underappreciated," he said. "Most take a lot of time to talk to customers, especially newbies, and they have so much beer knowledge. It isn't just pouring a handle and handing someone a glass," he observed.

"Bartenders often have to be especially good listeners. They often have to deal with people's emotional crisis, and they also have to be nonjudgmental and careful with their advice. They have always been America's sounding board in any establishment. People sit at the bar to forget their problems and often tell those problems to the bartender. Heck, if you pick up Men's Health magazine, there is an advice column where Jimmy the Bartender offers advice on women, work, and other stuff that screws up men's lives. Same thing that has been happening around the country since the 1700s I imagine," said Ty.

With each person on the final half of their last taster, Carson raised a glass.

"Here's to not becoming douchy, dicky beer snobs!"

The others raised their tasters and met with a clank, "Here! Here!" Carson looked down at his smartphone and noticed it was nearing time for the restaurant to open. By the time we check out, drive over to the parking lot, and walk to the restaurant it will be open," he said.

Kareem motioned for Huck to come over and close out the tab.

Finding street parking just down the road, Carson pulled into a lot and the group walked down Church Street with anticipation. Church Street was known for the famed marketplace with its unique and wonderful shops, but the friends were searching for something even more magical and unique to the local area – one of the commonly listed whales for craft beer lovers, especially Hop Heads, Heady Topper. Or as the locals usually called it, "Heady."

The afternoon air was magnificent, and it was a great afternoon to dine al fresco. As they approached Pascolo Ristorante, they were pleased to find an expansive patio as a dining option. Not so much a terrace as it was a bricked and closed-off street where people could enjoy walking from shop to shop, bar to bar, or restaurant to restaurant, and all combinations in between without the worry of oncoming traffic.

They approached the outdoor hostess podium and asked for a table. The restaurant was just opening, so there wasn't a wait, and they had their choice of seating locations. It was a little earlier than usual for dinner, but the primary focus was the Heady. Now that they located it on the Untappd app they were not about to let it get out of their sights.

The hostess sat the group at a table outside just off the sidewalk next to the terracotta and gray interlocking brick road.

"This is beautiful," said Tegan as they sat down. Looking around, she added, "The streetscape is picturesque. Everything is absolutely beautiful and kind of reminiscent of Europe. I love that it is pedestrian only and that it's brick-lined!" she said with a smile.

Soon, the server approached and interrupted. She was a short, young lady with close-cut black hair and full eye well-manicured eyebrows. She wore the standard black dress pants and white long-sleeve dress shirt as other servers. The top two buttons were undone and revealed an upper chest tattoo of a deck of cards showing the three of hearts on top, giving her an aura of being a tomboy and perhaps a little edgy. She leaned across the table and poured water for everyone while introducing herself.

"My name is Maisie. Are you ready for dinner or just in for some drinks?" she asked as she finished pouring the water.

"Kind of an unusual question first," started Carson, "but rumor is you have some Heady Topper?" She smiled as it was already a popular question.

Yes, we just received a delivery of Heady yesterday and have some cans left. They are seven-fifty a can, but we have some in the cooler ready to go," she revealed.

Carson looked in the eyes of his friends, "I believe we will begin with four of those," he said.

"Coming right up," she said, "I will leave you some time with the menu. Do you guys want a glass or drink it from the can?"

"Just the can is fine with me," said Ty.

She went inside, ran downstairs, and returned moments later with four cold cans.

"It does say 'Drink from the can' right on the can," she said, "so that's a good choice!"

Maisie sat the cold, silver aluminum cans down in front of her guests. They each starred at the can for a moment, then Carson picked it up to marvel at the artwork and check out the details before actually opening it. It was a long-awaited prize, and each wanted to bask in the glory of having acquired it, soak in the detail, and enjoy the moment before actually tasting it.

"I think I am going to order first before taking a sip," said Carson. "Plus I have to get my Untappd ready!" Looking over the menu Carson quickly settled on the Adams Farm chicken parmigiana – one of his favorite dishes. Tegan ordered next; the Italian sausage and mushroom hand-rolled gnocchi. Kareem selected the Polpette house meatball linguini, and Ty continued to study the menu.

"I think I am going to be a little different and order a pizza," he said. "I will stay simple and have the Margherita…one of the world's classics," he said sitting his menu in the middle of the table on the pile of others.

Maisie collected them all, "Sounds great. They shouldn't take too long since you are one of the first customers." She disappeared back into the building while the team returned to staring at the silver cans in front of them. Carson pulled up his cellphone, searched for Heady Topper on his Untappd app, and snapped a photo.

"That should make the home folk jealous," he said. "If you had taken this trip by yourself as you originally were planning and I saw that on your timeline and me sitting alone on the couch, you would have had an ass-whoopin' awaitin' you when you got home," said Ty.

"That's right," interjected Tegan. "You'd have to catch these hands!"

"Damn! You too?!" replied Carson.

"Stop talking and get to drinking!" suggested Kareem. "This is literally the first whale I added to my want list, and I am stoked to have a can in my hand finally." Kareem attempted to sniff the beer through the hole in the can but didn't get much through the narrow opening. He took a sip directly from the can and closed his eyes. Watching his reaction, the others joined in and enjoyed the floral, grapefruit, a not too strong, but ever so slight bitterness and overall great hop profile right from the first taste.

"This lives up to the hype," said Ty.

"Sweet mother of Jesus, that's good and dank," said Carson.

"This is what they mean when they talk about New England hops. This is the standard," said Tegan.

"I am so glad you set up the notifications on your app for this," replied Carson. "Definitely a highlight of the trip."

Maisie returned with the food. The smell of roasted tomatoes, sautéed mushrooms, and chicken parm filled the air, and the group's mouths began to water. Great food and a highly anticipated beer living up to their lofty expectations made the evening nearly perfect. As the sun started to set and early evening approached, more people began milling about the street at Church Street came to life. A young kid set up an open suitcase on the corner across from the restaurant and started playing the violin.

Tegan said, "See, just like being in Italy!" The pasta was fresh, and the sauce clung to Kareem's linguini. It was the perfect mixture of tomato, meatball, pasta, and herbs in one bite.

"Maybe we should just move here," suggested Kareem. Each person finished their plate and Carson reclined reflecting on a wonderful dining experience. Maisie returned and looked over the carnage on the table.

"I'd say you enjoyed your meal?" she said rhetorically.

"Indeed. I don't know of anything that could make this a better night," replied Carson.

"Well…we have a special dessert tonight: Jimmy Carter ice cream sundae with peanut brittle. What do you say?"

Ty threw down his napkin and looked up at Maisie, "You twisted my arm!"

"Me too," said Tegan. Kareem raised a finger adding his name to the list.

"Might as well bring four I guess. Round it out" said Carson.

The bill arrived, and they all chipped in with cash, plus a generous tip for Maisie. "Say, Maisie. What's good to do around here in the evening? We definitely need to walk and work off this meal," said Ty.

"Well, Church Street is great. You can walk down the street and explore all of the shops. Some really cool ones. My favorite is Cody's Emporium. It's just a few stores down from the restaurant, and it has some unique things from around the world. It's kind of funky and eclectic. Definitely one of a kind items there. I love it," she promoted.

"You haven't steered us wrong yet," said Kareem. "Let's check it out!"

"I was hoping we could sail the lake today, but the ferry has closed for the season," said Carson.

"Yes, they close down at the beginning of October, but you can always find some guys to take you on the lake if you really want. There are people at the docks who will do it," she suggested.

"Thanks for the tip," replied Tegan.

Having the table right on the edge of the brick-lined street, it was a short walk to join in with the growing number of people enjoying the evening walking one of the city's most popular shopping streets.

The streets lined with trees and bustling with window shoppers along Banks Street and Church Street provided a pleasant evening experience. A dark green façade marked the entrance to Cody's Emporium, on the opposite side of the street from the restaurant.

"Let's check it out," Tegan suggested. Maisie said it was cool, and from the looks from the street they have a lot of stuff."

Ty opened the door open while the others entered. The store had a dusty, piney smell from the collection of items, but also a hint of freshness from a lovely line of body products named The Handsome Goat Bath Co. It was a fantastic bazaar-like shop, filled with finely made local products, charming vintage, and antique items, as well as unique clothes and beautiful accessories from around the world. Music played overhead that for some reason Carson thought appeared to be traditional Peruvian music.

Walking around the store, they stumbled upon a section of Peruvian crafts including small mini hand-crafted white llamas made from genuine alpaca wool, hand-carved wooden flutes, and small pottery items. In another aisle, they found local Burlington items including miniature wood carvings of Champ, painted to resemble the local legend. There were also drawings, necklaces, and plush toys of the creature.

Other things from the local aisle included blown glass items, paintings, woven fabrics, and a hand-crafted pool cue with ornate inlay. A shelf of t-shirts also included mention of the town. Another aisle contained Native American items from the American southwest. Pottery, jewelry – including an extensive collection of turquoise objects, paintings, and toys from the Hopi, Navajo, and other Native American nations.

Carson's eye was drawn to a carving from the Salt River Pima-Maricopa Indian Community in Arizona. It depicted what appeared to be a centaur – a creature half man and half horse, although the animal didn't look exactly like a horse.

"This is interesting," he said picking up the item as a curious and confused look crossed his face. "Usually Native artwork depicts things in their surrounding that they experience themselves. I guess this is a centaur, but that seems to be more of a work of fantasy and unusual for them to portray in their work. I wonder what the story is with it?"

He sat the animal back on the shelf and continued browsing at the interesting and unique items.

"I really like this type of stuff," said Kareem. "I appreciate the global village and the oneness with people around the world. Despite the borders and differences, we have a lot of commonalities."

The group continued to explore the shops along Banks and Church streets for another hour until it was getting late.

"Hey, what do you say we grab a drink and call it a night?" suggested Ty.

"Yes, I'm tired and ready to wrap it up. I thought we should check out in the morning and head either east a little or down south. See what else we can find in the way of New England hops," suggested Carson.

"Sounds fine to me. I need to fill my suitcase with beer," reminded Kareem.

"We can just find a local pub here in the area and have a drink since we are here," suggested Ty.

9 FILM AT ELEVEN

Monday, October 5, 2015

Just a few blocks walking distance from Cody's Emporium the crew stumbled upon The Vermont Pub & Brewery. It was late, and they were tired but decided to have one more local drink before calling it a night and heading to a new part of the region tomorrow. A wooden sign in front of the row of shops showed a crow in a coat, monocle, and pocket watch perched atop a sign reading "The Vermont Pub and Brewery, Est. 1988." "This looks like a good spot. Let's check it out," suggested Ty.

Inside the bar was dim with lots of wooden accents and what felt like mid-1980s décor. Even though it was night outside, it felt even darker inside, something like a subterranean grotto. The drop ceiling with its white tiles, a large, thick wooden bar, and small tables with little oil-fired lamps and candles gave it a dive bar atmosphere; unusual for a brewery.

"This is cool," said Ty. "It feels like a dive bar, which are places I still love to go, but it's a brewery. A unique mixture that you don't see every day. I like it!"

Another group of people was leaving, and Carson sat at their table after they got up – the lone empty table remaining in the brewery. It was big enough for all four of them and was in front of the one hanging big screen TV. A recap of yesterday's baseball game between the Baltimore Orioles and New York Yankees showed highlights of two home runs hit by Chris Davis to give Baltimore the win as the regular season closed.

A young lady approached with newspaper-style menus in hand.

"Here's our menu. Let me know if you want anything to eat. The kitchen is still open for a bit," she said as she handed the menus and left to check on the other tables.

"I think we are just going to have a drink tonight," said Kareem, "And I think I will have the Vermont Maple Lager."

"The Lake Champlain Chocolate Stout for me," ordered Carson.

"Vermont Smoked Porter," said Ty, and Tegan concluded the round of drinks with Handsome Mick's Irish Stout.

"That's one of our classics," said the server.

The drinks arrived, and the group began discussing the plans for tomorrow. "So we are checking out in the morning?" asked Kareem.

"Yes, I haven't booked a hotel anywhere yet, so the rest of the trip is kind of open. What would you guys like to do?"

The group quietly thought about the options for the upcoming days. The television returned from commercial break and caught the attention of Carson. The local news was showing a man nailing "Missing Dog" posters on telephone poles in his neighborhood. A young brunette held a microphone while discussing the local story.

"Dozens of dogs have been reported missing over the past few weeks along the shores of Lake Champlain," she said. "We're here with Daniel Richardson who reported his dog Hickory missing nearly two weeks ago. Daniel, what can you tell us?"

"My girlfriend and I arrived at our cabin for a nice weekend and Hickory was playing outside while we unpacked, but he ran off down the bikeway and hasn't been seen since," Daniel reported.

"Daniel's story is one that is increasing in occurrence. Just over the past three weeks, there have been more than twenty-five dogs reported as missing on both sides of the lake," she said.

As the camera panned the area near the reporter dozens of homemade posters with photos of the missing dogs lined the streets on telephone poles and community center bulletin boards.

"Many of the dogs were last seen swimming in the lake causing some to wonder if Champ is to blame."

Carson looked back down at the others, "Hey guys, you hear this? They are talking about Champ on the television."

The reporter continued, "In the past Champ has never attacked dogs on the lake, but the sudden spike in incidents have caused people to speculate. I'm also here with Michael Stokley who was spending this past weekend on the lake with his family when something attacked his youngest daughter Emma. The ten-year-old suffered dozens of lacerations on her legs and just had surgery on a torn tendon suffered during the attack." "

The other girls said they saw some kind of creature in the lake. It had a round head and a long snake-like body," Michael said. "She's lucky she just had the cuts and the tendon injury. Whatever it was chomped the paddleboard clean in half. That could have easily been her leg, or worse" the father said nervously.

"There you have it – missing dogs, an attack on a child, and a neighborhood on edge, hesitant to return to the water following the unknown circumstances. We will continue to update this story as we learn more. Back to you, Jeff" concluded the reporter.

"Champ?" inquired Ty. "Seems a bit unusual. They talk about it as if it is a known creature rather than a local legend," he said. "And if it were a known creature, at least based on what the theories are about it and other sea monsters, those usually have diets of plants and small fish. Not dogs and humans. But it does seem to be odd that they say there has been a sudden spike in the number of animals disappearing," said Carson.

"That attack on the girl – sounds kind of like a shark-type of attack, but that also wouldn't happen in a freshwater lake," theorized Tegan. "I doubt it's a sea monster," said Kareem. "I mean the chupacabra is one thing – a lost breed of common animal, but dinosaurs? And a freshwater lake? That's a stretch. But I do hope they find the true culprit. I imagine it will have a negative impact tourism, and for towns like this, tourism is critical."

Carson slapped his knees with the palm of his hands, "Welp, we better hit the road if we are going to get up on back on the road in the morning."

"Yes, time to call it an evening," suggested Tegan.

10 BANG A UEY

Tuesday, October 6, 2015

Carson finished checking out of the hotel and jogged to the car where the others were already waiting for him. It was a little chilly, but ten degrees warmer than yesterday morning. With the humidity and clouds, it didn't feel bad.

"Who's ready?" asked Carson.

"I'm ret ta go," said Ty in his best Jamie Foxx as Wanda on In Living Color impersonation. When the line didn't get a reaction Ty pursed his lips and said, "Heeey," again imitating Wanda.

"Get in the car, Wanda," said Carson. "I thought we would work on hitting up some more Vermont sights today, and by sights I mean beer. A couple of other places, but mostly beer."

"I like beer," Kareem said from the backseat, "Where are we going? These twisted rocky, dirt roads aren't a good sign. Are we lost?"

"The green trees and cows also make it seem like we are lost," commented Tegan.

"No, we're not lost - I put it in the GPS. I thought we would get the farthest one out of the way first. It will take a little more than an hour to get there, but the beers are extremely limited, and I am sure you will all be pleased," Carson vaguely identified. "We will pass by a couple of places that we will hit on the way back. I was thinking we would head to these places, then hit up southern Vermont, but in doing so we will backtrack a little," he stated.

"Hey, I'm just along for the ride and enjoying time off work," replied Tegan.

"Me too!" said Ty. "We have a new classroom system that just rolled out at the start of the school year, and the questions still come in hot and heavy. Getting away for a bit is a huge relief!"

Carson took 89-S to VT-100N and eventually in the town of Hyde Park took VT-100E into to Greensboro Bend.

"Here we are," he said as they pulled into a gravel driveway leading to what looked like a huge house with a full wrap-around porch and a couple of work buildings. A small wooden sign hanging from a wooden post out front said "Hill Farmstead Brewery."

"Oh. My. God! Are you kidding me? We are here?! YES!" exclaimed Kareem. "I was hoping we would find it, but I wasn't exactly sure where it was located. This is huge! I have so wanted to try their beers, but I can never get them! If there is a flight available, well, come to daddy because that's what I am having! This is a top-notch destination for craft beer drinkers on their pilgrimage for farmhouse and IPA redemption!" he said excitedly.

Everyone exited the vehicle, walked to the still lush grass and just looked. Looked at the green grass, the thick pine trees in the distance, the mountains, the beautiful open sky filled with puffy white clouds, and the big house in front of them that they knew contained a trove of well-sought after goodies. It was like a postcard from paradise!

"I knew not to miss this place," said Carson. "Since they opened in 2010 they have been a destination spot for this part of the state."

"Wow! I would say it is a destination spot. This parking lot is full. Even a few buses," said Tegan.

"They are only a few years old, but in 2013 and again this year they won the RateBeer.com award for Best Brewer in the World," said Ty.

"This is one of the most popular tourist times of the year, and we are getting close to the foliage hitting peak probably in another week to ten days," said Carson. "Busloads of tourists along the road and popular attractions are frequent, and with the increased attention on craft beer in general, and especially from this region, these places are on a lot of tourism lists. It's been harder reserving hotel rooms as well. A couple of times the hotel has filled up while I was looking at it on the app, and the list of available rooms has been far shorter than normal. Most of the cheaper rooms have already been scooped up, and just the more expensive ones remain with a few rooms."

The group looked at the crowd in front of them and decided to stick it out.

"Still, it's worth the wait, and there is plenty of seating outside so even if the inside of the building is packed, we can likely have a spot to enjoy it," said Kareem.

The retail shop opened at noon, but there were already many people waiting outside. The line was long but moved at a steady pace once the shop opened. Within forty minutes they were near the entrance to the brewery and could get a peek inside. The line continued to the counter, but Carson couldn't tell how many were in front of them. He saw t-shirts hanging on the wall behind the bar and rows of wooden barrels stacked four high to the left of the line. Wine and whiskey barrels age some beers at the brewery and the air flowing outside from inside the brewery's open door smelled of wood, whiskey, yeast, and malt. All in the group closed their eyes and took in a deep whiff, anxiously awaiting the opportunity to set foot inside the door where they presumed the smells amplified.

Finally, it was their turn to enter. Once instead the smells did not disappoint. There was a loud continuous level of chatter as the people in line talked with their friends while awaiting their turn at the counter.

"Dude, I could just chill here all day," said Ty.

"With that awesome wrap-around porch we just might," responded Carson.

"We should grab a ticket for a growler fill," suggested Ty. We can buy the growler here and drink it back at the hotel. I have seen their growlers, and the design is cool."

"That's a good idea," replied Carson. "The growler fills are over in the other building, but we should definitely. In this building, they have some merch as well as bottles for sale in addition to the beers on tap."

"Yes, we need to get some of those bottles home with us. This is the only place where you can buy bottles of Hill Farmstead and take home. All other beer in the market is sold to restaurants and bars where it is only served on tap," reported Ty.

"I think that is also what makes it special," said Kareem. "You can't just buy the beer at the local gas station or packie. You have to come to this place, and it's a bit of an adventure."

Finally, they reached the counter. Waiting in line had given them an opportunity to scout out the board of available beers before arriving at the counter. When their number was called, they were ready to order when it was their turn. Most of the customers were there for growler fills or to pick up bottles to go, but they did have a flight of samples- four two ounces pours for five dollars. Or, thanks to the expansion earlier in the year, the beautiful taproom was open and allowed for customers to pop a bottle or two and relax while staring at the beautiful mountains in the background.

While watching the prior customers in line, they noticed a peculiar thing regarding the tasters was that they only got one at a time. The brewery did not have enough glasses to give out five beer flights to fifty people on any given day, plus the brewery laws in Vermont didn't allow them to pour more than that one tasting flight.

"Do you know what you would like?" asked the lady behind the counter.

"Yes, we are ready." Carson looked back at his group of friends. "We would like to get a bottle of the Civil Disobedience to share here," he said. "And I would like a flight of Edward, Legitimacy,

Abner, and Susan." He turned again toward the group, and each nodded to him. "Actually, each of us would like a flight of the same beers," he added.

"Great," said the young lady behind the counter. "We can pour the flight beers one at a time and can open the bottle when you are finished with the last one. That way you can relax while waiting for your growler number to be called."

She poured each person in the group a taste of Edward, the first beer the brewery made and the first one they brewed on a regular basis. The beers all had an intriguing backstory as each bore the name of one of the owner's ancestors. Named after the owner's grandfather, Edward was a just over five percent American pale ale. It had proven to be so popular that in the early days of the brewery that its sales alone allowed ownership the opportunity to be creative and explore other beers and collaborations.

As the server poured the beer into the glass, the beer had a hazy, golden color with almost an orangish-blush and a creamy head of white foam. While it was listed as a pale ale, the aromas were similar to an IPA. Each member of the group enjoyed hops, and this was definitely a brewery to visit. The owner mastered the use of hops in a way that showed a great variety of flavor and aroma similar to a renowned artist using his paints.

Ty tasted it first and was impressed. While it smelled like an IPA, it didn't have as strong of a hops taste, but rather a more fruity, mainly grapefruit and citrus. It was very crisp and refreshing, something Ty pictured would be an excellent beer for those hot Texas summers. "What I like about this is the body," Ty said. "A lot of times with pale ales you can get an all water and bitter taste with no body, but I think the hops really give it that body that stands up and makes this an exceptional beer. Truly a great homage to the owner's grandfather."

The second beer in the flight was Legitimacy, a six percent IPA brewed under the Grassroots Brewing label. The craze for New England IPAs was already at a high level, but this beer was brewed with 2-row malted barley, oats, and citrusy hops from the Pacific Northwest. Kareem picked up his glass and was surprised that it was very pale and hazy with a nice thick head. The smell definitely had tropical fruit notes, but a mixture of citrus too, green grass, and light pine.

"Just the smell sets the mouthwatering," said Kareem. "Wow, it doesn't disappoint in the taste. Tangerine, papaya - then a more piney and earthy follow up. This is really full flavored without being a hop-hammer."

Third came Abner, an eight percent imperial pale ale named after the owner's great-grandfather. Abner lived on the land that is now the home of the brewery, and the beer was made using water from Abner's well, like all of the other beers at the brewery. The beer was unfiltered and dry hopped and poured with a nice, thick foamy head. This one has become almost the flagship double IPA of the brewery with subtle citrus and maybe just a touch of tropical notes in the aroma.

"Wow! That's fantastic!" Carson said as he swirled the glass and took a sip. "It actually tastes more tropical than it smelled, but the orange, tangerine, papaya, and mango with a lingering bitterness on the end."

"It's sticky – a nice malt sweetness, but not malty. It mostly sticks in the background. This for me is what a double IPA should be – big, hardy, and hoppy with a malt background." He paused to smell again. "I was blown away right from the aroma, but the flavor of this beer? My God!" concluded Ty.

Finally, Susan a six percent IPA and named after the owner's grandfather's sister. As soon as the beer hit the tasting glasses, the aroma of tropical nectar with a bit of pine jumped out. In the glass, it was a little hazy due to the unfiltered nature and potentially the volume of hops. Carson's anticipation grew as he swirled the beer around the glass. Tegan didn't wait and was the first to take a sip.

"Nice clean taste. A dry finish to it. A little bit of malt to balance it out and even though it has that hop bitterness, it is subtle," she remarked.

"I could totally drink this with like an herb-roasted chicken," said Kareem. "It would pair very well."

"Damn, someone's hungry I think," said Carson. "But, I think you are right. Almost like a honey-orange flavor in the background. Definitely something you could drink a whole pint of and just enjoy."

The group's number had not yet been called for the growler fill, so they proceeded to the bottle. Carson was given a glass for each of them, and he took it outside to pour. The Civil Disobedience #5 was a single wine barrel from 2012, a blend of Ann, Art, and Flora.

"Oh wow," remarked Ty. "A touch of plum. Slightly sour. Soft. Delicious. This is remarkable."

Finally, their number was called! Heading back inside the building they made their selection. The new two-liter growler was ten bucks but definitely worth it. Carson picked up two growlers for the hotel later. One was filled with Edward for another fifteen bucks. The second one the group selected Abner, but it only could only be purchased in the 750ml growler for ten dollars, plus three additional dollars for the cost of the growler.

The brewery boxed up the bottled beers in two large cardboard boxes.

"I am not sure how we will get these back on the plane," said Carson.

"We will figure that out when we get there. Remember, I have an extra suitcase," replied Kareem.

"Right, but remember you already bought some beers, and we have a more places yet to see on the trip," reminded Carson.

The bottles selected for the trip back home contained a mixture of several beers available. Dorothy, a Citra Brett wheat farmstead ale was a revised recipe this year based on prior customer reviews from the 2010 batch. The Society and Solitude #4, one of the best double IPAs the brewery offered. According to beer review ratings, it was basically Double Galaxy and Double Citra and was said to be a fantastic beer.

The Hill Farmstead Anna was a honey saison brewed with Vermont wildflower honey. The Clara was a beer named after the owner's grandfather's sister and brewed with Vermont Organic Wheat, Nordic Saison was a collaboration beer between Hill Farmstead, Kissmeyer Beer & Brewing, and Cambridge Brewing Company that included honey, heather, rose hips, rhubarb, and wheat. The Florence, Brother Soigné under the Grassroots Brewing label was a saison brewed with lime, hibiscus, and blood orange. The final bottle was Vera Mae was named after the owner's grandfather's eldest sister and blended with Vermont organic spelt, American hops, Vermont wildflower honey, and dandelion flowers from the brewery's fields. All totaled, the group bought twelve bottles to take back to Texas, and the two growlers to enjoy over the next couple of evenings.

"Besides the naming of the beers after his family, I like that the brewery stays true to the farm grounds and local Vermont ingredients. Those dandelions in the Vera Mae come from the farm, and the water used in the beer comes from the well water on the premises. It is a throwback to when people lived off the land they farmed, and I think it's an inspiration," said Tegan.

"I can appreciate that the owner keeps his business on his family's property. That and the fact that he names his beers after his ancestors shows how much pride he takes in his craft. You're not going to make a crappy beer and name it after your grandmother," said Ty.

"This place is as awesome as I expected it to be," said Kareem.

"I could stay out here and enjoy this beautiful scenery all day, but we probably should get the car loaded up with our haul and get going. There are a few other things on today's itinerary," suggested Carson.

"This was a good couple of hours spent in the country, and I'm excited to be able to cross another spot off my brewery bucket list," Kareem said as he carried one of the boxes toward the car's trunk.

"These should be just fine back here," said Ty as Tegan added the two growlers around between the boxes and wrapped them in sweaters left in the car from earlier in the trip.

This time Kareem took the shotgun position while Ty sat in the back with Tegan.

"What's up next? Are we going to check out that Five Mile Long Tasting Trail I heard someone in the brewery talk about?"

"No, that's down in Middlebury, which is on the other side of the state. The next stop will be closer," said Carson. "But that would be great to do some time. A lot of good food and beer options there. Maybe we can do it later this trip? Everything is still basically open and just spending time enjoying the sights. Let's pencil that into the itinerary," he suggested.

"Might as well. All plans are soft," responded Kareem.

"We are going to backtrack about an hour, but I think you will like the next place. You are all familiar with the story, but you might not realize it is here. You might also not realize there is a brewery with it," revealed Carson.

"Hey, I am ready for round two," responded Ty.

The roads remained small and the area lush with green grass, speckled in the autumn colors, and fresh air as they journeyed back toward Stowe, turning off on Cape Cod Road, and eventually Luce Hill Road. The small two-lane road was quiet now, even though it was afternoon. The crew got the impression they were lost as the Luce Hill Road began to climb up the large hill. The number of trees along the road increased while the number of cars decreased to non-existent, further anchoring the perception they were lost. Except for Carson who trusted the reliability of the GPS app on his phone. Remarkably his phone showed no signal, yet the app continued to monitor the progress and indicated their destination was just ahead. The forest seems to close in on them now, with trees and grass on both sides of the road and little signs of life around. Carson continued ascending the hill.

Driveways occasionally appeared on either side of the road, then disappeared into the seclusion of the woods, the houses unseen from the road. The road continued to twist and turn and climb.

"Well it must come out somewhere," replied Tegan. Eventually, another road emerged, and Carson turned left onto Trapp Hill Road. A small orange creek ran along the side of the road. The minimal water flowed over rocks and cut through the green grass and continued downhill. There was small wooden structure along the side of the road. It appeared to be two posts with a roof overhead, and stacked rocks created an area where caretakers had planted flowers. The sign read *Trapp Family Lodge* and *Welcome* with an arrow point up the road ahead.

"Not far now," indicated Carson as he turned on the new road and continued to ascend. Soon the trees broke away as if pages opening in a book. The road continued to climb, but it was open now, and the car's passengers could see a widespread landscape overlooking the countryside below and the surrounding mountaintops. The trees were a magical blend of red, yellow, orange, and green. A road appeared on the left, but Carson continued up the hill.

"I think that's the road we need to turn on, but I want to go just a little further up to show the main building. Then after a quick look around we can come back here," Carson said. Just past the road, another area opened up with a large lodge on the right and a gravel parking lot on the left. "We're here," said Carson as he pulled into an empty place in the parking lot.

The onlookers could not help but gasp a collective "Wow!" as they finally reached the top of the hill and saw the expansive views in front of the parking lot area.

"This is the Trapp Family Lodge, or von Trapp as you may remember from the Sound of Music," said Carson.

"You mean the actors from the movie live here?" asked Tegan.

"No, the movie is based on real-life people and events, with some Hollywood liberties. But there is a von Trapp family, and they did have a musical group that toured the world. In the early 1940s, the von Trapp family toured the United States as the Trapp Family Singers, and they decided to settle in Stowe, Vermont because it reminded them of their home in Austria. This place opened up as a resort in the summer of 1950. Maria Augusta Kutschera was a real person born in 1905, she really did dedicate her life to the convent. And she really was assigned to the home of retired naval captain, George von Trapp. It wasn't to care for all of the kids like the movie showed, but she was assigned to the home to care for one of the Captain's daughters who had rheumatic fever. But she actually did marry him in 1927, and they did have a musical group that toured around the world singing," replied Carson.

"That's so cool. I love that movie," said Kareem.

"Does she live here?"

"No, she died a few years ago in 1987, but she is buried here on the property," said Carson. "One reason I wanted to come up here is not just because it is cool and I also like the movie, but earlier this year they expanded and now have an on-site brewery, von Trapp Brewing. They started brewing in 2010, but the expansion offers more to the public."

"That building didn't look too big. They can't have a large production area, can they?" asked Ty.

"From what I read, Johannes von Trapp first had the idea to brew beer about ten years ago. We all know how good the Austrian beer is and he wanted to replicate that lager with a similar American version. He was able to produce two-thousand barrels per year here. Now with the new expansion that is much larger. They aren't out near us, but they can distribute to Vermont, New Hampshire, Massachusetts, Maine, Rhode Island, New York, Connecticut, New Jersey, and Pennsylvania," he stated.

They spent time walking around the grounds, and inside the resort building. "Wow, this building is impressive," said Ty looking at the expansive wooden construction serving as the family lodge.

"They have a pool up there on the deck that overlooks these mountains behind us, as well as a hot tub. I saw them online, but I bet it would be amazing to just chill in the hot tub and have some nice beers while looking at the mountains and the green grass," said Carson.

"I have to say, this is a very relaxing and wonderful trip so far," replied Tegan. "Great leaves, wonderful beer, nice views all-around. I am sure in the dead of winter it is tough, but right now I would say let's move!" she replied with a grin.

"I don't know – if you're into skiing, this may be just the place even in winter. Tons of skiing in Vermont and New Hampshire. The lodge here even has skiing a few miles up the road," replied Carson.

The von Trapp Brewery and Bierhall was a recent addition, replacing the old Austrian tea and tap room. They passed it on the way in and even though it was just a ten-minute walk from the main lodge Carson decided to drive it and then head out from there. Walking in, the bierhall was impressive. The atmosphere was unmistakably beer hall, with views of lawns and hills out the many windows, long tables, benches, and soaring space overhead. It was a bit noisy, but it was the sound of everyone having a good time.

"They always have a Helles, a Dunkel, a Pilsner, and a Vienna lager on tap and there is usually a seasonal too. This time it was an Oktoberfest beer," reported Carson. "Hmm, I am not sure which one I want to try," said Carson. "The name and family history, of course, attracts people here, but they have been receiving great reviews on their beer in a crowded beer market."

"It looks like a nice representation of German/Austrian lagers," said Ty as he reviewed the menu.

"I don't think I have had many Dunkel bocks. I am not even quite sure that it is," replied Carson.

"You see they have a Helles here, that's a Helles bock or sometimes called a Maibock or heller bock. It means pale bock. Dunkel bock is a dark bock. So you have a lager beer style typically from southern Germany, and one is pale – the Helles, and one is dark – the Dunkel," replied Ty.

"Oh, I got it. My German is rusty. So what's bock mean? Beer?" asked Carson.

"No, bock refers to where the beer originated. In the 14th-15th century beer was being brewed in a German town called Einbecker. Actual written evidence showed the export of Einbecker beer dates back to 1351. Einbeck joined the Hanseatic League, or the Hanse, in 1368. That was a commercial and defensive confederation of merchant guilds and their market towns. The league was created to protect the guilds' economic interests and diplomatic privileges in their affiliated cities and countries.

That helped to broaden the distribution area which allowed the beer to be reached from Antwerp in the west to Riga in the east and from Stockholm in the north to Munich in the south. Just like here in the US, different regions of the country have varying dialects and accents. In Munich, the name Einbeck was mispronounced as "ein bock," which means a billy goat. Because the Bavarian treasury was empty again, the Duke needed his own brewery to save money. When the ducal brewhouse, or Duke's brewhouse, copied the style, the name was shortened from "ein bock" to just "bock." The Dunkle bock is the older beer. Back in the 1600s, there wasn't pale malt. Everything was dark and smoky malt. We didn't get the pale malts until around the 1800s. But the pale malts are very light and crisp. It is difficult to hide imperfections there, where the darker beer can mask it a little more. To make a good Helles it must be perfect," said Ty.

"Sounds nice. I think I will go with the pale and order the Helles," said Carson.

"I like that rich malty profile, so lemme have a Dunkel," Ty said to the server.

"When I think of European beers I think Pilsner," replied Kareem. "And for me, I will have the seasonal Oktoberfest," added

Tegan. The server poured the four draughts, and each person took the glass and walked toward the large windows to check out the view.

"This is probably a pretty nice spot to sit and watch it snow in the winter time," said Tegan.

"Heck yeah, a little skiing then relaxing here in the bierhall with a couple of nice Old-World lagers?" added Kareem.

"This is a nice place to relax. The bierhall isn't that old, and I think it makes a nice addition to the overall resort," said Carson.

"Where are we staying tonight?" Tegan asked. "I haven't booked anything yet, but from here we have one more quick stop, then a one that is a little more involved. But that's the last thing on my agenda today. So, we might end up in Waterbury if I find a place," Carson said.

"How far is that from here?' asked Kareem. "Not far. Maybe thirty minutes," replied Carson. Finishing up the drinks, Carson and Tegan returned the glasses to the bar and headed back to the car. "This next stop is about fifteen minutes from here, and it is a quick stop," added Carson.

Back in the car, they returned to the road, this time heading down the large hill. Once they reached the main road again, it was a short drive to the next location. Carson eventually pulled over to the side of the road. Just ahead stood a single-lane, fifty-foot-long bridge, its wooden frame dark and weathered.

"What's this? There are a lot of covered bridges in Vermont," said Ty. "Yes, there are, but not quite like this one," Carson responded. "This one was built in 1844 and is called the Covered Bridge Road over Gold Brook to many, but to others, 'Emily's Bridge.' They say that in the 1920s a girl named Emily was supposed to meet up with her boyfriend and run off to elope. But he didn't show up. She was so heartbroken, she hanged herself from the rafters of this covered bridge. As the legend goes, she's still pretty pissed off and takes that out on the visitors to this bridge. Some reports say witnesses have seen claw-like gouges down the sides of cars passing through the bridge and even bloody scratches down the backs of pedestrian crossers. They also say there is the sound of loosely dragging feet on the roofs of cars or the noise of strange voices emanating from inside the short tunnel," Carson reported. "The locals don't really like the attention the bridge now brings because ghost hunters come here late at night and there a lot of partiers who come and are an annoyance. So much so that the Stowe Police Department has upped nightly patrols in the area, so we shouldn't stick around too long. But much of it is lost to urban legend and speculation."

"There are many versions of the story. In another version when Emily's man didn't show up at church for the wedding the heartbroken bride sped away by carriage and accidentally plummeted to her death in the rocky brook by the bridge. More modern variations the vehicle was a car instead of a carriage. But only a few wealthy families in Stowe would have owned a car in the 1920s. Some others say she just jumped off the bridge. But not only are the details uncertain, but the timing of the supposed event as well. Some claim the ghost began to appear in the 1930s while others say it started in the 1970s. There was even a 1968 high school paper written by a student who said that he communicated with a spirit who identified herself as 'Emily' while he was using an Ouija board on the bridge," Carson continued.

"The historical society has no known record of a woman named Emily killed here, and ghost hunters have for years haven't found anything in the records. But Emily's story continues to be one of Stowe's claims to fame. While there isn't a record of 'Emily,' there is an old graveyard located within Stowe village, and in it, there is an unassuming headstone with the words 'Little Emeline' inscribed on it. Maybe that's her?" he concluded.

Carson slowly drove the car through the bridge with all windows down, and the radio turned off. The wooden floor of the deck was firm and did not creak as the vehicle rolled across. Listening intently, there were no screams, no scrapping on the roof, or any visual apparitions.

"Guess we're good. Let's roll," said Ty. "One more stop and we will find a hotel afterward for the evening," replied Carson.

The next stop was only about twenty minutes from the bridge. "I hope you guys are as excited about this as I am," revealed Carson. "This is a must-see for anyone coming to Vermont," he said as he pulled off the main road and into a gravel driveway where a man stood outside directing traffic. The others saw the large sign beside the road announcing "Ben & Jerry's."

"What's this? The headquarters?" asked Tegan.

"Yes – this is where they make the ice cream. They have factory tours, tastings, a gift shop, and just all-around cool stuff," said Carson. "I don't know if we can take the tour because it's usually busy and it is late in the afternoon now. Probably missed the final running – but we can still walk around as much as you want, and the ice cream shop is open up that steep hill. But another thing that is cool is they have a graveyard!" he said.

"A graveyard?" repeated Ty in a surprised tone.

"Well, a flavor graveyard. It is to honor the flavors that are no longer in production. They have died and moved on," Carson said.

From the parking lot, they walked across the street to a large white building with a green roof. There were cows in a pasture along the walk and a small wooded area with a path on the other side. The hill was steep and curved around taking the breath out of them slightly as they finally reached the top.

"So we can buy a cone or something from the shop and walk around the cemetery?" asked Tegan.

"Yes, that's probably the best plan since we can't take the tour – but the tour is cool. We should do that another time," Carson added. At the top of the hill were many activities, including a brightly painted Ben & Jerry's bus, wooden plank cut-outs to stick their head and take photos, a tent to make tie-dye t-shirts, another for kids to do arts and crafts, and an ice cream counter to order the ice cream. The line for the ice cream counter was incredibly long but moved quicker than they expected.

Champ and A Bit of Sunshine

Once in the line each of them ordered a waffle cone. Sea salt caramel blonde for Tegan and the sweet cream and cookies for Kareem. Carson selected the spectacular Speculoos – dark caramel and vanilla ice cream with Speculoos cookies and Speculoos cookie butter core. Ty concluded with The Tonight Dough – a blend of caramel and chocolate ice creams with chocolate cookie swirls and gobs of chocolate chip cookie dough and peanut butter cookie dough.

"I thought about getting that Vermonster, but I didn't want to embarrass you all," said Ty as he took a bite from his cone.

"Are you kidding?!" asked Tegan. "That's a twenty scoop sundae that comes served in a bucket. And's it's like fifty bucks!"

"Like I said, I didn't want to embarrass you and break out my competitive eater skills," responded Ty.

They walked back down the sidewalk toward the parking lot, then up the hill to the Flavor Graveyard. Under the trees, the graveyard consisted of dozens of faux tombstones for people to pay their respects and mourn their favorite discontinued ice cream flavors. Each monument showed the name, the production dates, and had a funny poem about the flavor's demise. It was peaceful in the graveyard and the trees sheltering it from the sun provided what was undoubtedly a welcome relief in the summertime. Varieties such as Sugar Plum, Bovinity Divinity, Crème Brûlée, Economic Crunch, and Wavy Gravy were among the casualties.

"Maybe we should try to head south tonight and go over to Brattleboro or maybe down in Massachusetts?" wondered Carson. As they leisurely strolled through the cedar mulch covered graveyard eating their cones, Carson's cell vibrated in his pocket. He moved the cone from his left hand to his right and reached into the pocket of his jeans. "Hello?"

"Hi? Carson?" the female voice on the phone replied.

"Yes, this is him."

"Hey, Carson. It's Maisie. We met the other day. Well, I work at Pascolo Ristorante, and you guys stopped in," she said."

105

"Oh, yeah. I remember. Did I leave something?" he asked confused. "No, nothing like that…it's kind of long story. But you looked familiar the other day and then later that night I remembered seeing you on the news a few months ago. About that chupacabra in Texas?"

"Yes…," Carson said speculatively wondering what the call was about and how she got his phone number.

"Well I didn't know your name, but I remembered your face from the news…and I'm a student at the University of Vermont. I take classes in the day and work at the restaurant at night…anyway, I had something weird happen over the weekend, and I was talking to my anthropology professor about it. When I mentioned what I saw he mentioned something about the chupacabra and I remembered seeing you. I told him that I just saw you in the restaurant and he knew your name. He was surprised you were in the area and said that he saw you at some conference a few years ago. He gave me your number," she said filling in the details of the mystery.

"Professor? Hmm. The only one I can recall from Vermont is Millard Howard; I think it was," Carson said searching his memory.

"Yes! Dr. Howard, that's him!" Maisie said. "Well, with what you did with the chupacabra I think I need to see you and discuss this. It is something that I think you can help with and I don't know anyone who else can help. Can you do it? Can you meet up with me?" she asked.

"Um, well we are in Waterbury at the moment, but yeah…I guess we could come back to Burlington. It's not too far away, and if you think it's something I can help with…does it have anything to do with the stuff on the news yesterday about the girl?" he asked.

"Yes! I was at the lake Sunday night, and I saw it. I saw the whole thing! And well, I told the police about it, but they didn't believe me and just brushed it off. They said they don't investigate monsters or urban legends," she said.

Champ and A Bit of Sunshine

"Hmm, well that doesn't sound too good. Are you sure you saw something? I mean if the police weren't even interested, maybe it was nothing?" he said.

"No, it was something! It was Champ!" she said excitedly.

"Champ? You mean the sea monster?"

"Yes, that's him! He's usually peaceful, but lately, there have been weird happenings in the lake. You gotta come and check it out!" she said pleadingly.

"Well, um...," uncertain what to say. "Yeah. Yeah, we can come and check it out. Where do you want to meet? And give us about forty-five minutes or so to get back to town," he added.

"Great – meet me at The Other Place – it's a little dive bar in Burlington on Winooski Avenue, not far from the college."

"Okay, see ya there. I've got your number now and will call when we get close," Carson said as he hung up the phone and walked back over to the group.

He gave Ty a single slap on the back of his shoulder, "How'd you all like to head back to Burlington and spend a few more days?" he asked.

"Heading back to Burlington? What's up? Something wrong?" asked Kareem.

"We are about to find out. That call was from the server we had at the Italian restaurant the other day," Carson said.

"Italian restaurant?" Ty asked.

"Where we had the Heady Topper," said Carson.

Everyone responded, "Oh, the Heady! Yeah!"

"Now I remember," said Kareem. "That was some good beer..."

"Yes, well she wasn't calling about beer. She said she saw something in the lake Sunday and needs to talk to us about Champ!" he said. "Time for T.I.M.E. to get on the case!" Carson said.

"Another monster?! This could be a great opportunity to get our name further out there and introduce the T.I.M.E. crew to the world," said Ty.

Carson drove back toward Burlington a little quicker than he left.

107

"This could be a great opportunity, and since the trip itinerary is soft, we are not missing too much. I mean I did want to go to Alchemist and try to find more Heady and maybe Focal Banger, but they operate out of a cannery in Waterbury that isn't open to the public. Rumor is they are planning to build a large brewery and visitor's center in Stowe, but that won't be opening until next year," Carson said.

The rest of this part of Vermont is mostly yard art and maybe some maple pipelines near sugar houses.

"What is a sugar house or a maple pipeline?" asked Tegan.

"It goes by many names – sugar house, sugar shack, sugar shanty, sugar cabin, or sap house. It is a small cabin or groups of cabins where sap is collected from sugar maple trees and then boiled into maple syrup. The maple pipelines are tubing methods for sap collection used in large maple sugaring operations. Farmers who own a sugarbush – that's a woods full of sugar maples - drill small holes in the trees and collect the sap as it drips or 'runs' out of the holes. These pipelines move water, food, and sap up and down the tree. Basically the sap is collected in the spring around February and March when the weather begins to warm up a bit. Spring thawing and freezing creates positive pressure in the sap flowing through a maple tree's pipeline system. This means that sap presses against the walls of the tiny pipes," said Carson. "Maple is huge up here. Not only maple syrup, but maple cream, maple bread, maple cookies, and a popular treat - sugar on snow," added Carson.

"You sound a little like Bubba from Forest Gump," added Ty.

"What is sugar on snow? Doesn't sound healthy," said Kareem.

"That's dessert. They save snow in chests and serve, basically like shaved ice, but it's actually snow. And it's drizzled with maple syrup," responded Carson. "Some places serve it with a side of plain donuts, saltine crackers, or even sour pickles so that it cuts that sharp sweetness down," he said.

"Where are we going to meet Maisie, and did she say anything about what she saw?" asked Ty.

"She didn't say too much. Just that she saw something and told the police. I think it has something to do with the kid we saw on the news yesterday," Carson responded. "We are going to meet her at a little dive bar in Burlington and see what she knows."

11 THE OTHER PLACE

Tuesday, October 6, 2015

Carson pulled up in front of a row of businesses along Winooski Avenue and noticed the green storefront labeled "The Other Place." It appeared to have a garage door front, but it was rolled up allowing the night air to provide a gentle fresh breeze into the building and those in the front to people watch as folks walked down the sidewalk.

"Oh, this is just a couple of blocks from the restaurant Maisie works at," recognized Carson. "Must be why she hangs out here." He pulled into a parking lot just down from the backside of the bar. Once parked he texted Maisie to let her know they arrived. His phone soon vibrated with a message stating she was already inside and sitting at a table in the back.

The night air was cold but refreshing. Carson took a deep breath as they walked down the sidewalk and to the small, neighborhood bar. An older man with his elbows propped up on the bar looking outside appeared to be already suffering from the woofits, perhaps attempting to take in the fresh air to perk himself up. Other than him the bar seemed to be filled with mostly college kids, even though it was a "school night."

As they walked inside, the bar was very dark. Carson noticed the bar appeared to have a tin ceiling, which he thought was unusual. A red neon sign reading "The OP" hung on a mirror over a fully stocked bar. Posters on the walls promoted well-priced drink specials for every day of the week and free popcorn. The place reminded him of his old stomping grounds Giddy Ups with a well-worn pool table, slightly sketch bathrooms downstairs, and a few color TVs were showing sports.

Further inside they found the crowd to be more diverse and a strong candidate for a fun people watching spot. But they weren't there to watch people tonight. They were there for one particular person. The pool table dominated the small space, and it was reasonably crowded, but the group pushed past and found Maisie sitting at a wooden table with slightly wobbly legs in a dark corner. Her white dress shirt was wadded up and sitting on the table. She was wearing a white tank top that exposed the tattoos on both arms, her neck, and upper chest. She ran her hand through her short dark hair as they approached.

She looked up from her cell phone and greeted them with a slight smile. "Hey, thanks for coming. Want a drink?" she asked. Maisie already had a pint of Allagash Brewing Company Black in front of her. Carson looked around at the other tables with people mostly drinking pitchers of PBR or Bud Light, cans of Rolling Rock, and wait…what?

"They have Heady Topper here?!" he asked surprisingly.

"Yes, they do have it, and it's cheaper than some other places. They also have Focal Banger too. This place has a nice selection of cheap beer but also Vermont beer," she said.

He looked at his group of friends, "What'd ya say? Focal Banger?" he asked.

"Let's start with that," suggested Ty. "Might have to have another Heady afterward. I mean, since we're here, and it's here…" Carson pointed at Ty.

"Good call! I'll be right back!" he said before walking up to the bar and squeezing into a small gap between a couple of people.

Trollinger

One man was at the bar and closing his tab. The bartender put the receipt on the bar while the man dug through his pockets. "Four Focal Bangers," Carson spoke up.

The man beside him reached his whole hand into his pocket and returned it to the surface of the bar, emptying its contents. Carson stared down at the miscellaneous pile while awaiting the bartender to return. The collection contained some wadded up fives, ones, and perhaps a ten. Some random denominations of change sat on top of the bills, as did a bent paperclip, five hard candies, and a loose orange bill of what appeared to be the male enhancement pill Vydox. Carson turned and looked at the man, "Right then," he said as the bartender returned with the cans. Carson handed him a credit card.

"Keep it open?" asked the bartender. Carson nodded in agreement and returned to the table where Maisie and the gang were chit-chatting about the bar, Burlington, and the current semester at college.

"So what's up? It's nice to see you again and in a more comfortable atmosphere," said Carson. "You too. This is my place to get away after work. A non-pretentious crowd. Pretty chill overall and the music varies depending on who is working. Anything from rock, country, hip-hop, punk, you name it," she said.

"You said you saw something this weekend?" asked Tegan.

"Yes, I was at the lake enjoying a rare Sunday off work. It was afternoon and just soaking up some sun and reading a book on my Kindle. I happened to look up and saw the head of a large animal emerge. It was a large, flat head on a long snake-like neck. I couldn't see its body, but from the size of the wake behind it, the animal was long. It was swimming quickly, but silently in the water. Then, I saw the three girls. The animal's head went back underwater, then reemerged closer to the younger girl. She was on the paddleboard, and I saw the head snap down at her. The animal missed her but tore the board in half. She screamed, and the animal returned underwater and disappeared. But it was there – it was Champ!" she said anxiously.

Maisie was visibly shaken as she thought about the event witnessed just a few days ago. She leaned to one side, reached into her front jeans pocket, and pulled out a slender black vaporizer. Even though the governor signed into law a statewide vaping ban for all indoor places where smoking was prohibited, including bars and restaurants just a few days ago, she rebelliously put the vape to her lips and inhaled. An aroma of cotton candy hung in the air as she blew white vapor through her mouth and nostrils.

"Champ? So you think it's a real animal?" asked Kareem.

"Yes! Of course – lots of people have seen Champ even going back to the time of the earliest settlers in the area. I had never seen it myself, but I know people who have, and I tell you, that was Champ. Something attacked the poor girl, and I know what I saw," she said as she grew more excited.

"And the police?" asked Ty.

"They brushed it off. They said they didn't have time for monster stories and they thought the girl got too close to someone's boat or maybe hit some rocks close to the shore. Even though the board was broken in half. I haven't seen a rock do that!" she said.

"What happened next?" asked Kareem.

"Next was chaos. The kids were screaming, the dad running over the hill, and the paramedics and police arriving on the scene," she recalled.

"And the creature in the lake?" continued Kareem.

"Gone. Just like that," she said as she took another puff.

"I'm still hung up on the lake monster," said Tegan. "You're sure that's what you saw? I know there have been sightings, but it's just not likely something can live in an area where people are around every day and not be seen regularly," she said.

"It has been seen regularly. More than three hundred times and dating back to the early explorers of the region," Maisie said. "Champ is one of the more well-known of the cryptids and lake monsters around the world," she said with another exhale of vapor. "But…it is a local attraction, and until now it hasn't really attacked people, so that's unusual. Something's different with it lately," she concluded.

"Even with the sightings it's hard to imagine it exists," replied Tegan.

"Like the chupacabra?" Maisie responded, effectively ending the string of questions. Tegan's looked down at her now empty can and her thoughts drifted to her experience months ago with the chupacabra and how nervous and frightened she felt seeing it first-hand.

"Um…I'm getting another round. Anyone want in?" asked Tegan as she stood ready to go to the bar. Everyone including Maisie nodded.

After she left Maisie continued, "Look. I know what I saw and the police ain't gonna do shit about it. This type of thing is up your alley, and I think you can help. I mean just to find out what's different and how it can be stopped. I don't want to see another kid get attacked. There are families out here on the lake all the time in the spring through fall. It could easily eat someone's dog or a small child like the girl Sunday. She's lucky," said Maisie.

"Dog…," said Carson thinking back. "Ty, remember the news story we saw talked about the girl, but before that, they talked about a large increase in missing dogs."

"That's right!" remembered Ty. "I bet those things are connected. First, it starts eating small animals like dogs and then something a little larger like a small child. The report said all of those incidents were in different towns, but they were all along the lake!"

"We came up here to get away from the monsters and the crazy people and reporters calling us all of the time," said Kareem.

"This will put us right back into the fold."

"Yes, you're right, but we talked about doing this type of investigation work and presentations at conferences or universities. We've proven there can be truth behind sightings. We saw that in San Antonio. Sure, there are also crazies out there who are making up shit but think about how many people around the world see some unknown creature. That many people cannot be crazy and many times their stories are similar and span across different countries and cultures. I mean look at Bigfoot – how many legends are there of that guy? From the US to the Wendigo in Canada, the Yeti in Nepal, to that story in Russia. That's a similar animal around the world that science just hasn't caught up with yet. Maisie's right –the number of people who can help with this type of investigation are few, and four of them are sitting at this dark, wobbly table," said Carson.

Tegan returned with the next round, a mixture of Focal Banger and Heady Topper. She looked around at the table.

"What'd I miss? We are going to look for the creature, aren't we?" Tegan asked. She made eye contact with Kareem, and he too remembered the terror he felt back in June, but both realized they made it through that event and now knew a little more what to expect. "So what's the next step?" asked Tegan.

Carson stroked his chin with his index finger and thumb while he thought.

"I guess we start putting together what we know about Champ. I had heard of him before, but never really reached the sightings. We need to find out first if this creature does exist and next, as Maisie said, figure out what is causing it to become aggressive suddenly. Then we need to talk to people and see what they've seen or heard. Put that together and see what we're dealing with," Carson suggested.

"Do we want to split up? Maybe two hit the library and two talk to people?" suggested Ty.

"That could work. Save time by splitting up, then regroup and share what we found," thought Carson.

Maisie added, "You guys should speak to my anthropology professor. He's been here for a while, and he would be a good source for local research."

"Good call, Maisie!" added Tegan. "I don't mind staying back and hitting the library," said Tegan.

"Yeah, me too," Kareem added.

"That would be great. I wouldn't mind catching up with Dr. Howard," said Carson.

"I thought he might stop by here tonight, but I guess he is working late," said Maisie.

"Oh, does he hang out here often?" asked Ty.

"Yes…well sometimes. We like to come here to get off campus and away from prying eyes. Even though this is close to campus people don't care about us or what we do here," Maisie said.

"Um…Alrighty then… Tomorrow morning? You guys hit the library while me and Ty talk to the professor. It will be nice to see him again," Carson said.

The evening wound down with another round, a discussion about the upcoming hockey season, and classes at the university. While they chatted, Carson searched his cellphone to find a nearby hotel for the next couple evenings since it appeared they would be spending at least the next few nights in town. With that task completed, he returned to the conversation and enjoyed learning about the local area from Maisie.

12 DOES CHAMP EXIST?

Wednesday, October 7, 2015

The group left the hotel early in the morning and headed to Muddy Waters for coffee and a light breakfast before heading to the university to start researching Champ. Walking into the café they were instantly drawn to the warm atmosphere. It felt like a secret, upscale treehouse, complete with art on the walls. The low timbers and freeform plants gave it a cozy, earthy feel. A few over-stuffed, comfy chairs were scattered, and being close to opening they were available. Ty and Kareem secured two while Carson and Tegan went up to place the order. They breathed in the warm, amazing coffee bean smell that filled the café.

"Just the smell of coffee gets me going," said Carson.

"It's a little chilly this morning and when I am cold there's nothing like hot chocolate. I'm going to have the white hot chocolate with whip cream," said Tegan as she studied the menu board.

"Oh, and a soy latte for Kareem." Carson ordered the Bianca with a double shot of espresso for him and a Maté Latte for Ty.

"What?" Carson said as they awaited their drinks. "They also have craft beer on tap and cocktails? Damn, this is a sweet place!" he said. "We might have to come back here in the evening and recap our findings," he suggested.

Rejoining the others, Carson and Ty returned with the drinks and laid out the plan of action. "I thought we would head over to the university after this. The library opens at 8 a.m. I texted Dr. Howard from the hotel and he has open office hours in the morning too. Ty and I will see Dr. Howard and you guys check out the library. Then Ty and I will go to the lake and see what some of the people in the area have to say. This investigation might be challenging because in San Antonio we had that town hall where people came to us. Now we just have to find them and see if they have or know of anyone who has seen Champ before," said Carson.

"I agree Dr. Howard will be a good source. Most of the students probably won't be too helpful because they are just here for a short time. Mid-week in the morning might not have a lot of traffic on the lake, but there could be some. You might have to find out where longtime locals hang out. That might give you more success. Maybe you can find the father of that girl who was attacked or some of the dog owners from the news?" suggested Kareem.

After they finished the coffee and determined the plan of action, they headed to the college. Carson found a visitor's parking lot off Main Street, and they walked to campus. Walking past the large red brick building on the right called the Dudley Davis Center, they continued to Bailey/Howe Library, directly behind it. Tegan and Kareem headed inside while Ty and Carson wandered the campus looking for the College of Arts and Science, finally locating Williams Hall. After additional searching inside the building, they found the office of Dr. Millard Howard.

Dr. Howard was not only a renowned scholar in the field but a researcher at the forefront of contemporary research in anthropology, especially paranthropology – the use of anthropological approaches to the paranormal. It was at an academic convention in Dallas, 2013 that Carson met Dr. Howard. Talking in the lobby between sessions they began discussing the paranormal, cryptozoology, and the intersection between those fields with the traditional areas of anthropology and psychology. After losing his teaching position Carson drifted away from most of his old contacts, but the meeting held a special place in the memory of both men, and Dr. Howard retained Carson's contact information over the years. When the news broke out in the summer regarding the chupacabra, Millard remembered his old friend and thought about reaching out, but had not yet found the time. When Maisie approached him after class by happenstance, he provided the contact information to her hoping it might lead to reconnecting. When Carson followed up yesterday, it was an excellent opportunity to get reacquainted and discuss the recent happenings in the lake. In addition to being an expert in the field, Millard Howard had lived in Burlington for more than thirty years and was an excellent local historian, especially in the area of unusual circumstances.

Dr. Howard did not have classes today but was in his office preparing lesson plans for the following week. He was wearing a checked UVM green button-down dress shirt, beige khaki pants, and a pair of brown Merrell hiking boots and drinking a cup of Green Mountain Coffee. An issue of Psychology Today, the academic journal *Paranthropology*, and the morning issue of Burlington Free Press were scattered across his desk. He was jotting notes in a moleskin journal when Carson and Ty walked in. He felt their presence, put the pen down, and stood to shake the hands of his visitors.

"Gentlemen! Nice of you to stop by. Carson, it's good to see you again. It looks like you fellows have had a busy couple of months," he said.

"It certainly has been. Very different than what I have been used to the last couple of years. Doc – this is my buddy, Tyson," he said jerking a thumb in Ty's direction.

"Nice to meet you, Tyson. So, you're the one who took the chupacabra bite if memory serves me."

"Yes, sir. It took me by surprise. It was fast and it was pissed. I'm probably lucky just to have made it out with a few stitches and sore ribs."

"Indeed. It looked like a real bugger from the photos I saw. Glad you guys helped those people out down there. What brings you up this way, into our neck of the woods?"

"Originally, we just came up here to get away from all the media attention from this summer. Thought it would be nice to come up to New England and relax a few days, but now it looks like we are back on it. We talked to one of your students last night, and she thinks something's going on here," said Carson.

"Yes, Maisie. She's a special girl - one of my brightest students, and she has an interest in some of the work I do in the paranthropolgy area. We spend a lot of time together, you know, discussing the concepts," said Dr. Howard.

"How's that going? I heard you're doing a lot of research and making some headlines yourself," asked Carson.

"It's good. I was just writing up some notes reflecting on a roundtable discussion back in July at the 58th Annual Parapsychological Association Conference where me and others in the field had the opportunity to introduce a larger audience to the subject. We might be conducting some investigations and experiments next year on the world's ten 'Vile Vortices' - sites of numerous unexplained disappearances and all happen to be located in a natural alignment around the globe," he said.

"Interesting research!" said Carson. "Doc, I know you've been in the area a long time. What do you know about Champ? Maisie seemed to believe the creature existed and said that normally it is peaceful. But she swears she saw it attack that young girl the other day," continued Carson.

"She's right. Champ is perhaps the country's oldest cryptid with sightings on record for as long as four hundred years. Native American tribes have even older legends of a creature in Lake Champlain," Dr. Howard explained. "Most reports have said Champ is about twenty feet long with a horse-like head and a serpentine body. The accounts and descriptions are very similar to what you have in Scotland with the Loch Ness Monster. And as far as believing it is real, the government even agrees. There are laws on the books the government has passed to protect the animals. Going back to the early exploration of the land, Samuel de Champlain was a French explorer for whom the lake is named. You can go back to his writings in the 17th Century and see his discussion of a large animal called by the natives *Chaousarou*, and it appears that over time evolved into reports saying he saw a creature that resembled a twenty-foot serpent thick as a barrel, and a head like a horse. Some theorize what he actually saw was a garfish, which is a fish with a needle nose that commonly is over six feet long and weighing upwards of a hundred pounds. But we also have reports from 1819 in Bulwagga Bay from Captain Crum who was onboard a scow and wrote that he saw a black monster about one hundred eighty-seven feet long with a flat head that resembled a seahorse. He went on to say this monster reared its head more than fifteen feet out of the water and was able to swim 'with the utmost velocity' while being chased by two large sturgeon and a bill-fish. Even though it was two hundred away he claimed he could see it had 'three teeth, large eyes the color of a peeled onion, a white star on its forehead, and a red band about its neck," reported Dr. Howard.

"Well, even though there may be some question on the accuracy of the details, that is some impressive history. Four hundred years of documented sightings, plus who knows how far the Native American legends go back," said Ty. "And the sightings continue? Has anyone attempted to find and study the creature?"

Dr. Howard updated the sightings and efforts. "Yes, the sightings continue through the present day. There are multiple active research teams on the lake running investigations and some of the other sightings, even documented by amateurs. One of the most revealing artifacts came from an amateur. The Mansi photograph is the most famous artifact with Champ. That came back in 1977 when Sandra Mansi, her fiancé, and kids were driving north along the shore of Lake Champlain near the town of St. Albans around noon. The stopped at a small bluff overlooking the lake. The kids got in the water and waded along the shore when she saw something. She thought it was a large school of fish or maybe a scuba diver, but then the head and neck broke the surface of the water. The parents were suddenly scared and called the kids out of the water. Sandra grabbed her camera and took the photo, but back then it was old Instamatic cameras that didn't have the clarity we have of today. The photo is a little grainy, and it is unclear what we are looking at, but it does show an object in the water. She said she then put the camera down and watched as the creature turned slightly and then disappeared again beneath the water's surface. All totaled it was a pretty long sighting - remarkably long – at about estimated from four to seven minutes per her account," he shared.

"Are they sure the photo is real? I know today there is always the risk someone has doctored the photo. That might have been more difficult in 1977, but not impossible," asked Carson.

"You are right. Several experts have examined the photo and the conclusion has been that there is absolutely no evidence of tampering with the picture," said Dr. Howard. "Historically, there are additional reports of the monster resurfacing in newspapers around 1873, and even P.T. Barnum offered a fifty thousand dollar reward for Champ, captured dead or alive," added Dr. Howard.

"And I take it no one claimed the money?" asked Ty.

"Correct, although a lot of people did try. But Champ's existence has never been either disproven or conclusively proven. The burden of proof does lie with those who claim that there is a monster in Lake Champlain. Science tells us it would be impossible to have just one Champ, if it existed. As I've said, these sightings go back hundreds of years, if not thousands. But no single creature has been proven to have a lifespan that lasts longer than a millennium. Second, except for single-celled life forms, no living animal can reproduce itself consistently. With that in mind, scientists speculate a herd of at least five hundred creatures would be necessary to maintain a healthy population over time. To this point, there has never been the sighting of a beached carcass or other biological traces of Champ or his

Champ and A Bit of Sunshine

predecessors recorded, and that is the key point those who claim he cannot exist hold to," said Dr. Howard.

"Kind of like the Bigfoot body argument," said Carson.

"One more question – how could an animal, or animals of this nature get into the lake?" asked Carson.

"Well, speculation is that the animals arrived during the last ice age. In this area was the Champlain Sea, which was created by the retreating glaciers and was a temporary inlet of the Atlantic Ocean. The sea covered land that is now part of the Canadian provinces of Quebec and Ontario, as well as parts of the states of New York and Vermont. At the end of the last ice age, while the rock was still depressed, the Saint Lawrence and Ottawa Rivers, as well as modern Lake Champlain, were below sea level and flooded with rising worldwide sea levels. Once the ice no longer prevented the ocean from flowing into the region. But eventually the land rose again, and the ocean receded to its present location," stated Dr. Howard.

"So, the lake is closed today? But how did the battle with the English take place in the lake?" asked Ty.

"No, not completely closed. You've heard of the Erie Canal? The Champlain Canal is a sixty-mile canal that connects the south end of Lake Champlain to the Hudson River in New York constructed at the same time as the Erie Canal. The canal was proposed in 1812 and construction authorized in 1817. By 1818, they had twelve miles already completed, and in 1819 the canal was opened from Fort Edward to Lake Champlain. The canal was officially opened in September 1823," Dr. Howard revealed. "There are a series of twelve locks throughout the canal, but it would be possible to access the ocean from the lake if that's what you are wondering."

"You would think if these creatures are coming in from the ocean, which would certainly be large enough for them to live and hide, someone would have sightings in the lock system as well as the lake," speculated Carson.

Carson looked at his watch, and the men stood up. "Thank you for your time, Dr. Howard, and for giving us some background on the history of Champ," Carson said.

"Anytime, gentleman. Good luck in your search, and feel free to stop by anytime. Maybe we will see each other at another conference sometime?" spoke Dr. Howard.

"Well if it is it will have to be a cryptozoology conference. I am not currently working in the education field," said Carson.

"So what's next for your search?" inquired the doctor.

"I think we are going to head to the news station and see if we can talk to that reporter. Maybe she can give us some more information," responded Ty.

"That's a good idea. Maybe some people who saw the news story called in saying they've seen something too," suggested Dr. Howard. The three exchanged handshakes, and Dr. Howard returned to his reading while Carson and Ty exited.

In the library, Kareem and Tegan were searching the computers for recent Champ sightings. "I am getting a lot of search results," said Tegan. "And some of these are as recent as just last fall. Multiple sightings in 2014 – one in Charlotte, Vermont and near Button Bay, and even evidence from two well-known Champ investigative teams. In one of them, the witness says he saw it at least three times over the summer."

"Wow, that's a lot of action for a cryptid in just a few months," said Kareem. "But, if all of these recent reports are in fact the animal too, then it would make sense there has been increased activity over the past few months."

"Maybe we should try to meet up with some of these researchers? This article says they have been on the water searching for years, and last year they picked up some rare vocalizations and echolocation readings that suggest something unknown or unexpected is out there," said Tegan. "Besides that one there was a report just on August 1st, and that witness took four photos that aren't clear but do show something in the water," she said.

"This article states that due to recently collected bits of evidence the number of believers in Champ is growing. It's as if people around here are fairly confident the creature is real," said Kareem.

"Yes, it seems that way to me too," said Tegan. "Those recordings that were recently captured aren't the only ones. They also recorded similar sounds in both 2002 and 2014, but didn't explain what they were," she concluded. "The search team's main goal was to protect the creatures, not discover if they existed. And it says that law protects Champ in Vermont and New York and any harassment or violent acts against the creature are prohibited. That doesn't sound like an unknown animal, but something they are confident exists," said Tegan.

"This will take a long time to research fully. Some of these findings appear that they are even on microfiche. I see records as early as 1819!" Kareem said. "We also have to look at the similarity of sightings hear to other places. I mean, Champ here, the Loch Ness Monster, Tessie in Lake Tahoe, and others in lakes and large bodies of water around the world. It cannot be a coincidence," said Tegan.

"We are going to be here a long time," said Kareem as he continued to see a seemingly endless list of hits online.

Carson pulled into the parking lot of the news station. "I searched for the story online, and the reporter was Veronica Esqueda. Let's see if she is in today and maybe she can help us find some witnesses that can help get to the bottom of this," suggested Carson.

A few minutes after checking in with the receptionist a young Hispanic lady in her late 20's approached. Her just-passed-shoulder-length black hair draped down the front of her antique pink-colored designer Ponte suit skirt.

"Good morning, gentlemen," she said extending a hand. "You had some questions regarding the story on the girl attacked in the lake?" Veronica asked.

"We were hoping for some more information," said Ty as he shook her hand.

"We also saw the story on the missing dogs, and we think the incidents are related," said Carson. "Do you think it is possible for us to get in contact with the girl's father or some of the dog owners from the story? Have you received any additional reports from others who saw the story?" he asked.

"We have had other people call in. Some more have reported missing dogs, and a call came in yesterday evening from someone who reported a large animal in the lake, but we have not investigated it or returned the call yet," she said.

"What about the possibility this is Champ?" Ty said attempting to gauge her reaction.

"Well, I've only lived in Burlington for two years. I'm aware of the Champ legend, but I always dismissed it as silly tales that are good for tourism," she said.

"Perhaps," said Carson, "But there seem to be sightings for hundreds of years. Much longer than tourism marketing departments have been around. Maybe there is something to it?" suggested Carson.

"The stories that I have heard when people see something are just that it is something unknown in the water. I have not heard anything about it eating people or animals, that's why I think it is just a draw to get people out to the lake," she said.

"But what if it's not? And what if now the creature is attacking? Shouldn't that be investigated? Maybe warning people of potential dangers?" asked Carson.

"We don't want to create an alarm if there is no basis, and at this point, there hasn't been a conclusive sighting. No body or other forms of evidence. It's just speculation. We would need more to go on before we reached that point," she said.

"We would appreciate if you could pass our contact information to some of the people from the news story," said Ty. "And if you get any more people calling about sightings, send them our way. We would love to meet with them and check it out," he said.

"Good luck in your search, and hey – if you find anything, give me a call first," she said.

"This is interesting," said Kareem as he searched through an article online. "This report claims that people witnessed seeing the creature on land. That's a unique report – everything else has been in water," he said.

"Wow, that is incredible. Most marine animals do not appear on land. Where did that report originate? Maybe we should check out that area?" said Tegan.

"Yes, I agree. I am taking notes of the locations in some of these more solid accounts, and when we get back with the guys, we should talk about visiting these places. I hope they are having luck with their search," said Kareem.

"Me too. Maybe we should check in with them. There is a ton of information here, but I think the most recent sightings are the ones that will help us the most. I am printing out a map of the lake area. Maybe you can draw the locations you found on here, and we can plan the next steps," suggested Tegan.

"That's a good idea. I will draw them in. Why don't you text Carson or Ty and see what's up?" responded Kareem.

Ty picked up his vibrating phone and began texting back. "Looks like Kareem and Tegan are ready to roll," he said to Carson. "It's about mid-day. Whaddaya say we go pick them up and stop for some lunch to discuss what they found? We can fill them in on what we learned and go from there?" suggested Carson.

Arriving back at the university, Kareem hitched a thumb and pulled his jeans leg up slightly while sticking one leg in the air. "Going our way?" he said jokingly.

"I don't know," replied Ty. "Might take a couple of drinks first."
"Speaking of drinks…and lunch, how about we hit up Zero Gravity just down the road and discuss what we found? It looks like it just opened a few months ago. Well at least the Pine Street brewery location," suggested Carson.

"Yes, we found a lot of things. Recent things," said Tegan.

Just opening at noon, they were the first to arrive. "Jesus, I hate being the first to arrive. Makes me feel desperate," said Ty. "But, whaddya gonna do?"

"Wow! This is a nice space," said Tegan. I love the white tile behind the bar, the large rows of wooden tables with plenty of space, and check out that mural on the wall!" she said as she pointed to a large painted of a bird perched upon a multi-colored, artistic tree branch. Gavin Knight was busy wiping down the bar counter and making his way to the tables to prepare for the day.

"Good afternoon, and welcome." He turned opening an arm as if presenting the offerings on the Showcase Showdown, "Sit anywhere you'd like."

"Hmm. Kinda hard to pick," Carson said sarcastically before deciding to take the first table inside the door. "This one will do I suppose."

Gavin was a young man, about twenty-three with a close, well-kept short red beard. He wore dark blue jeans, a partially buttoned green Henley, and a black flat cap.

"Here's the lunch menu, if you're hungry. Our beers on up there on the wall," he said pointing to a series of six placards on the wall; five named beers and one that read "Ask what's on cask." The group studied the offerings.

"Well…, and I'm sure you get this all the time," Carson began. "…what's on cask?"

"Glad you asked!" Gavin replied enthusiastically. "Our cask is Conehead with Mandarina Bavaria."

"Sounds pretty good. I will have that one," said Carson.

"The Green State Lager," said Kareem putting down his menu.

"What's the Bretthead?" asked Tegan.

"That's our Conehead with a twist – adding Citra and Brettanomyces wild yeast," replied Gavin.

"Hmm. Yeah, that one for me," she said.

"So either the Bob White witbier or the Little Wolf pale ale. I am trying to decide between those two…" said Ty. "Or better yet, how about a flight? Those two, plus the Conehead, and the Green State Lager."

"Sounds good. Need a little time to look at the food?" They talked amongst themselves for a minute.

"Can we have three chili dogs, a lamb & rosemary sausage, and Italian sausage?" asked Kareem. He looked up at the group, "Two of those chili dogs are for me," he said.

Gavin brought the pints and one flight to the table, "Your food should be out pretty quickly. Can I get you anything else until then?"

"We should be good," said Ty. "Just wondering about the space here. You've been open here just since spring?"

"Yes, so we've been in business for a few years. In 2012 we began distributing Zero Gravity for off-premise sales, but this Pine Street brewery we just opened in the spring. It's a thirty-barrel brewhouse, we have a full canning line, the tasting room, a small retail shop, and the beer garden is a nice spot when the weather is nice. We also are housing our barrel aging program here, so that gives us more flexibility to make styles that we previously did not have the space to attempt," Gavin said.

"It's nice. Lots of space, nice clean look, and the beers are good. I like this Conehead," said Carson.

"Thanks. That's our flagship beer, and you can see from the cask to the Bretthead that we use it in other variations. It's getting some good buzz," Gavin revealed. "Let me go check on those 'dogs," he said, returning to the kitchen.

"So what did you and Kareem find out?" Carson asked Tegan.

"There has been a lot of sightings over time. We didn't spend a lot of time on the older ones in great detail because we wanted to see what has been happening recently, and every year there are sightings. It seems to be a little more over the past couple of years. We found some in 2012, a few more last year, but already this year there have been multiple accounts with sometimes as many as five people seeing the creature at a sighting. So it's not just the word of one person who maybe isn't sure what they are seeing," she said.

"Well, you are right about a lot of sightings. We met with the professor and these sightings go back older than this country – back to the Native Americans who lived here before settlers, and even the first explorers of the area wrote about something in the lake," said Carson.

"We took some of the recent sightings that sounded most credible and plotted the location on this map," said Kareem. "As you can see, the sightings are around the lake. People often think of Burlington, and even the baseball team here is called the Lake Monsters, but it's all over the lake."

"We went to the news station to speak with Veronica, the reporter on the story we saw at the pub, and those reports of missing dogs happened as far up as Plattsburgh, New York, so we need to explore as much of the lake as we can," said Ty. "

Some of the sightings that we penciled in give us good coverage. One is not too far from here – the Auer Family/Charlie's Boathouse is a spot where people have claimed to see the creature on land. We should check that out. Button Bay State Park is another spot, and our most southern point is the Champlain Bridge Marina down in Addison. I think we should check out those for sure, and if you want to hit the New York side we can get over there from the bridge," suggested Kareem.

"Great!" said Carson, "And Veronica is going to pass our number along to some eyewitnesses that responded to seeing the news. Hopefully, we can meet with some of them as well and get some first-hand information on what people are seeing."

"Good work, guys. Maybe we should start up at Charlie's Boathouse since it is close – and the reports of seeing the animal on land are interesting," suggested Carson.

"What is Charlie's Boathouse? Do we know? Sounds like a residence?" asked Ty.

"We did some digging on that," said Tegan. It's called the Auer Family Boat House, but people also know it as 'Charlie's. It's been open since the 1920's and sits off the Burlington Bike Path right where the Winooski River meets Lake Champlain. It's a place where people can stop, sit for a bit, and watch the lake. They have kayak rentals, canoe rentals, and snacks – ice cream, burgers, and hot dogs. A pretty popular local spot that people associate with the city. Many people grew up stopping there to fish, hang out with the owners, and learn about life on the lake. It will be closed now – it closes for the season usually at the end of September, but we can check out the area. I read a report that the current owner had a Champ sighting years ago," she concluded.

"Even though it is closed there might be people in the area. Probably boating, fishing, or riding on the bike path," added Kareem.

"That's where we will start then," said Carson. They finished up the beer and lunch and checked out with Gavin.

Just over six miles later, they arrived close to the boathouse, found a parking spot, and walked the rest of the way. As Kareem suspected, the shop was closed, but there were a few people around. They approached one young man who was kneeling down and working on his bicycle chain. Carson asked him if he had ever seen Champ. The man was a freshman at Saint Michael's College and was new to the area. He had heard some stories from locals but hadn't seen anything himself.

"I really think the thing is fake and it's just a local urban legend to attract business," he said. "Everyone who has seen it and told me about it has been a townie. I don't know anyone from my classes or anyone who visited and just happened to see it. I mean, it's a big attraction, and it's good for business, so that's why they keep talking about it," he suggested.

"Well, you might have a point – but it's been seen for hundreds of years," said Kareem.

"Although it died down for many years until some article resurfaced it and got people talking. Then people started coming to look for it, and that helped business," the man replied. "He does have a point…" pondered Ty.

Thanking him, they continued walking around the area, but no one they approached revealed any experiences with the creature. Walking down near the shore of the lake they stopped near the dock to take in the view. A man in his late sixties with a gray beard that matched his still thick hair walked close by with a couple of fishing rods, a tackle box, and a small bait bucket. He set the bucket down, adjusted his bucket hat, dug through the bucket, and removed a minnow before attaching it to the hook.

"Whatcha fishing for?" asked Carson.

"Hopin' to get some walleye. Used to be pretty big in these parts, but this year I haven't caught too many of 'em," said Clarence Bowman. "I've been coming up here to the boathouse since I was a kid and always had pretty good luck around here."

"Are you catching other things if the walleye aren't biting?" asked Ty.

"Sometimes. Get some largemouth bass, some perch, northern pike, or some brown bullhead, but I'm getting less this year than last year," he said.

"So you spend a lot of time fishing up here?" Carson asked.

"Oh yeah, nearly every weekend and sometimes I get some mid-week fishing in when I can. The wife passed away a couple of years ago, so I come up here to reflect and enjoy the peace. The water keeps me company. Things have changed over the years, but it still reminds me of my childhood. Helps this old boathouse has been here the whole time, and the owners – they're good people," Clarence said.

"What about those stories about Champ?" asked Tegan. "Have you ever seen him?"

"Oh yeah. A time or two I've run into him. This here's a pretty good spot actually. A few years ago after they installed a new dock and underwater lighting here some came around," said Clarence matter-of-factly.

"Some?" repeated Tegan.

"Yeah, there's a group of them that live out here. You got a pretty good circle here from where the Winooski River comes here, across ta South Hero Island, and back over there on the New York side with the Ausable River. September to October is a pretty good time to spot them. That's when the fish start running, and it attracts them here," he said. "There were some sightings across the lake down in Port Henry from what I recall. 'Round 1980/81 I believe," he said.

Kareem pulled out his printed map and searched to locate Port Henry. "Hey, that's down by Addison where we were planning to go. That's the Champlain Bridge Marina area," he said.

"Yep, that's the area. If you plan on being' down there, check out Bulwagga Bay. That's another hotspot," said Clarence. "They travel this whole lake, so you find 'em all over."

"Wow, that's certainly helpful. Thanks for the information – and good luck with your fishing," said Carson.

"Yep. Good luck on your hunt too. Probably do better to get out on the water. Then you can cover more ground and spot 'em," suggested Clarence.

"Thank you for your time and information," Ty said extending his hand to Clarence.

As they left Clarence and walked around the back of the boathouse, they passed through trees and walked back to the bicycle trail. "Maybe we can see something along on the shore by the bridge?" suggested Kareem.

"Perhaps there are some tracks down there in the mud, you mean?" suggested Tegan.

133

"Exactly. Clarence suggested September and October are good times and that they hang out where the river joins the lake, and if that's where they have been spotted on land, maybe we will get lucky?" Kareem replied.

As the bike bath reached the bridge crossing over the river, the group walked off the trail onto the sloping hill leading down to the shore. There was some sand, but more rocks than they expected.

"This doesn't look like a very comfortable spot to rest on the land. Can we get down there under the bridge?" asked Carson. Ty went ahead of the group.

"Yes, it looks like there is enough of passage down here. It's sandier too," Ty observed. He walked on the thin strip of sand and to the other side of the bridge. "Hey guys, it curves around here and goes a little back inland. Looks like a small cove back there," he said.

"A cove? That would be a nice hiding spot," suggested Carson. The others soon caught up with Ty and explored the area.

Tegan bent down to the water's edge. "It is a little smooth here. I can't tell if it is from the water or if something. If you think about a large sea animal like walrus or elephant seals, they are large animals that are in the water and on land. When they are on land, they cannot walk, but slide with the help of their front fins. That leaves a smooth tracking mark where the body rests and marks in the sand where the fins push off. With Champ, you would expect it to be similar. Reports say it has fins instead of feet, so it shouldn't be able to walk. It should move like a walrus if it does come ashore," Tegan said.

"There are boats around here, but it's pretty quiet. And I am sure even more so at night," said Carson as he surveyed the area. "There is good tree cover here to hide even a large animal. Even if we saw a slide mark in the sound, we can't say it's an animal. Might be someone pushing a small kayak into the water from here," he said.

"Yeah, I think unless we see the animal here first-hand, we can't be for certain. And I don't see anything right now," Ty said.

"Yeah, let's roll and check out some of the other sights," suggested Carson.

"On the way down to Button Bay State Park, we should also look at Kingsland Bay State Park. That's on the way, just a little north of Button Bay, and that's where that girl we saw on the news was attacked," suggested Kareem.

"Oh yeah, that's a recent sighting so we should definitely see what's there. One thing I noticed is that people talk about Lake Champlain, but a lot of the sightings are in the bays and coves. Perhaps that can be a clue. From fishing, I know that the cove is a mini-version of the lake and if you found fish in the back of the coves, they will probably be concentrated in the river end of the lake, in shallow water. If you found fish half-way back in the cove, they I would concentrate on the middle section of the lake. If the animal lives in the lake, in the deepest waters because of its size, then it would likely be in the front end of the cove. A lot of fish congregate there, so maybe that is why it would be drawn to the coves more than seeing it in the open waters," said Carson.

Walking back to the car Tegan looked at the map. "We could also check out Malletts Bay. That's not far from here, and that's where one of the dog owners from the news reported his dog missing," she suggested.

"Oh yeah. I haven't received his contact information from Veronica, but we could check out the area," said Carson.

"Might as well if it's close," said Ty.

"It's about five miles," she said.

"Well if we are correct that the attack on the girl and the disappearance of the dogs are connected, then we have to check it out. If the dogs were attacked it means the animal was there," said Carson.

"And that's another cove," said Ty.

The cloud cover increased overhead, and the temperature dropped slightly as the group made their way over to Mallets Bay. "The report said the guy was renting a cabin there, and I'm pulling up the area on Google Maps – from Ledge Road, there is a large swath of land right up the peninsula that is uninhabited. Nothing but trees on the map, and right along the water. That might be a good spot for it to hide as well," suggest Kareem.

Mallets Bay was a large bay that also contained a small island, Coates Island. There was a road that extended all the way to Coates Island, but there was also an inlet and two coves that were further inland in the bay. "It looks like a lot of potential hiding spots here," said Kareem.

"This is beautiful country," said Tegan. "I don't know if I like the mountains and the fall colors more or if I like the lake area. I would love it in either place," she said.

They drove to the end of Ledge Road and pulled over in a dirt turnaround that overlooked the lake. It was the end of the road, but a path lead down to the beach. As on the other side, it was a very narrow beach that was sandy and rocky but also covered almost completely by the overhanging trees.

"If something lived over here, it would be very difficult to see it," said Carson. "These trees provide great coverage, and on the backside of this peninsula, there is likely very little traffic. Especially this time of year," he said.

While the area looked like a good hiding spot for a large animal, there was no sign of it at the moment.

"It will be difficult just to happen to find it. Many people live here their entire life and never see it. I doubt we just happen to run upon it," said Kareem.

"You are right," Ty said as he looked across the water. "Very unlikely."

"I think the best approach for right now is to talk to people. See if we can pinpoint some recent sightings. We know that guy lost his dog right around here about two weeks ago. We know the next spot is where the girl was attacked just Sunday. Maybe it migrates to different parts of the lake during different times of the year, and it was on its way from where it lives in the summer to maybe the more southern part of the lake in the fall and winter?" theorized Tegan.

"I think you're right, and there aren't many people here to talk to. The news story said that guy was just here for the weekend, so he is probably back wherever he lives, but there could be other dogs in the area," said Carson.

Once again they headed back to the car. This time slowly driving out of the neighborhood and paying attention to the people and sights around the street. There were very few people walking around, but one thing they did notice was the number of missing dog signs on the telephone poles.

Driving up Ledge Road, turning left on Marble Island Road, and left onto West Lakeshore Drive, Carson continued driving by the public boat ramp, general store, and restaurants. Throughout the area where a larger number of people might see them, signs were affixed to the telephone poles and small bulletin boards along the sidewalk. Not just one sign per pole, but each appeared to have dozens. Without getting out of the car they couldn't be sure, but they assumed it was multiple dogs. Why hang numerous posters for the same missing dog on the same pole?

"It might be far more missing animals than they reported on the news," said Carson. It reminded Carson of a scene out of Lost Boys and the number of missing children signs. People initially wrote those off as just separate random incidents, but as it turned out, they were all connected to a growing unseen threat in the area. Perhaps this was no different?

"It does seem odd that Champ has been relatively peaceful over the years and in just the past few weeks or months there has been an odd spike in small animal disappearances and the attack on the girl. It seems there must be a connection between those incidents," said Carson. "Kareem, did you guys find any prior sightings that mentioned it attacking people or animals," Carson asked.

"No, we did find a report from August 1873 where a small steamship loaded with tourists, allegedly struck the creature and nearly turned over, but it didn't attack the boat. The boat basically ran into it," Kareem said.

"The sightings were from all over the lake. I watched one video from a guy filming in 2009 at Oakledge Park, just south of Burlington. It was something in the lake, near sunset, and he did capture it moving, but it was hard to see exactly what it was. He took it with his cell phone so it was a little grainy and had limited zoom back then," said Kareem.

"Is this park worth checking out?" asked Ty.

"I don't know. It is along the way but also fits in with all of the other places. We could really stop anywhere and have a similar experience. That video was shot at the end of May, so the sightings are all year-round."

"Let's just head down to Kingsland Bay then," suggested Carson.

"What do we know about Kingsland Bay?" asked Ty. "That's where Otter Creek flows into the lake. Similar to how the Winooski River flows into the lake near the boathouse we just visited. There could be a connection with increased sightings near two bodies of water coming together. Actually the river comes right in between Kingsland and our other spot, Button Bay," said Tegan. "And there are small coves around the park like there are near the other spot," she added. "Another commonality is the point of the peninsula, MacDonough Point, is heavily wooded and uninhabited like Malletts Bay was," she concluded.

"And what about Button Bay?" asked Carson. "It has a lot of woods in the state park, but there are more open field and people than in some of the other places. One thing there is we have a couple of small islands, Ship Point and Button Island – so that could narrow some of the waterways and affect migration of the animal," Tegan responded.

"Since the two spots are close and similar in makeup, maybe we should just hit one. We still have to hit the southern part of the lake yet. I say we hit up Kingsland since the accident took place here and then check out Bulwagga Bay area," suggested Carson.

Carson found a parking spot in the main lot for the park. Being Tuesday afternoon there were not many other cars. As they walked along the dirt road, Kareem looked at a transcript of the news coverage on his phone.

"Says the dad was up near where we parked, and the kids were a little south. They were in the cove and near another…look, over there," he said pointing ahead. "There's another pier. That must be where they were rescued. It's not too far from the first one and the report does say the dad heard the screams and ran toward them, so it must be close," concluded Kareem.

"This is just at the inner part of the cove," said Ty as he looked around. "The animal could have been further out and been alerted to the girl by her kicking in the water," he said. "That would draw it further into the cove where it might not normally go."

Carson walked further down near the water, and searched for clues. There was a lot of debris that washed up onto the shore, but nothing significant. He found a small, but the somewhat long branch that had washed into the pile of leaves and plastic bottles. It was only about four or five inches thick but was over three feet in length. The perfect walking stick, or a stick to poke through the debris. He used the other end to clear away some of the algae, leaves, and random trash that appeared. Searching through the garbage, his stick poked against something solid. It wasn't too big, but it looked promising. Using the end of the stick to push the thing toward the shore, Kareem reached into the lake and pulled it out. It appeared to be a piece of a board, perhaps the girl's paddleboard? It was small, certainly the backend of the board, and maybe the cops took the larger portion when the girl was rescued. Kareem looked it over, running a hand along the edge.

"Look here!" he said. "It is jagged. Like teeth marks. We know from the report that something attacked the girl and that the board was broken. This appears to be the other piece to the paddleboard. I bet when the creature attacked it went to bite the girl, but missed and it broke the board in at least two. If it did catch the rear portion of the board that piece would have propelled behind while the top portion went forward. The report did mention the paddleboard piece, but it was likely just the one. This one probably floated out further into the lake and the waves brought it back over the last couple of days. And here it rests in the trash and debris that also washed up," he said.

"That makes sense," said Ty. "And looking at these marks, it has some sharp teeth." Carson looked over at the board as Ty held it. "Yes, certainly sharp enough to eat a little girl…or some small dogs," he said.

"This shows that there definitely was a creature. It couldn't have just been a wave or something like a log that turned up in her path and knocked her off the board. Something – with teeth – actually attempted to eat her," said Tegan said.

"We should probably keep this. Put it in the trunk for our investigation," suggested Carson. As they walked back toward the car, they saw a young man walking near the lake while looking down at his phone. He was in his early twenties, with medium-length floppy dark brown hair in a side part haircut that swept nonchalantly over his blue eyes. His thin long-sleeve red and blue plaid flannel shirt was rolled up to the elbows, unbuttoned at the top and untucked over the dark wash jeans he gave the appearance of casual and comfort. Staring intently at his phone as he walked he certainly didn't appear to be someone who was worried about being attacked by a monster in the lake that had allegedly done just that only a few days ago in this very location.

"Hello," Carson said as they walked near the man. He glanced up from his phone, said a quick "hey" then returned his attention to the device.

"Hey, do you come up here to the lake often?" asked Tegan. His finger gliding across the screen he spoke without looking up,

"Yeah. I come up here almost every day." He stopped staring at the phone and turned his attention to the group. "Sorry, I was trying to catch this Pokémon that I hadn't yet added to my Pokédex," said the young man.

"The what?" asked Carson. "Like the old card game from when I was in school?"

"Yeah, but now it's mobile. It just came out in July, and it's pretty popular. It gets kids out of the house and into enjoying outdoors. A lot of the monsters appear in parks or along the water like the lake. So people spend more time in those areas looking for hard to find monsters."

Ty looked at the group and then over at the young man. "Speaking of looking for hard to find monsters at the lake… have you ever seen anything around here? Not a Pokémon, but like a real monster?" asked Ty, then waited for his reaction.

"Oh, you mean Champ? Yeah, I have seen him – and just recently too," he said.

"Really? Where did you see it?" asked Tegan.

"Right here. Well, a little more south. More like Button Bay in Ferrisburg. But yeah. I saw a hump surface about three feet out of the water, and it was probably fifteen feet long. Just swimming along, then it submerged," reported the young man.

"Did that strike you as strange?" asked Kareem. The young man drew his lips in slightly and shook his head.

"No, not really. I've seen it once before, and everyone has stories about it, so I didn't think much about it," he said.

"So, it's real?" asked Kareem.

"Yes, it's real. A lot of people see him. The only thing that is strange is I heard it might have attacked someone here the other day, and that's unusual. I haven't known it to attack anyone or anything before," he said.

"It did seem unusual based on prior reports we've seen," said Ty. "Thanks for your information, and good luck chasing your monsters."

"No problem, and yeah, same to you!" the young man said.

141

"Actually that Pokémon game might be helpful for us," suggested Carson.

"You want to catch them all?" asked Ty jokingly.

"No, ass. I mean if it is bringing more people outside that could help our investigation because maybe more people saw something," he said.

"True – if they looked up from their phones long enough to notice there are real monsters around them," said Kareem.

Back at the car, Carson put the paddleboard in the trunk. "Let's go down and check out the Champlain Bridge. We're less than twenty miles to Port Henry, and Bulwagga Bay and the marina are just before that. Let's see who's there and what we can see. From the reports that I saw this is one of the main hot spots," said Carson.

"That part of the lake has fewer trees. Nothing like the coverage that we saw on the other points. The Champlain Bridge Marina, over to Chimney Point, the Lake Champlain Visitor's Center, Crown Point State Historic Site, and all-around Bulwagga Bay is open and flat. It isn't too population dense until you get around to Port Henry," said Kareem.

"The visitor's center might be a good source of information too," said Ty. "If this place is, in fact, a good sighting spot they will likely know something there."

The drive down VT-17E had very little traffic and worked through rural countryside with now empty fields on each side of the road. It appeared everyone in Vermont must know a farmer or was a farmer. Carson was beginning to think the cows outnumbered the people in this state. He pulled into the marina parking lot, taking one of the final parking spaces. The parking lot was close to the marina, and despite only a few parking spaces, there weren't many people walking around.

A small inlet of water near Crane's Point served as the water supply to the marina. Just down the street from the marina, within walking distance was Chimney Point. There a historical museum that sat showing the story of human habitation dating back as far as nine thousand years ago. It provided a detailed look at three early cultures in the Chimney Point area - Native American, French Colonial, and early American. It also provided a good look at Lake Champlain as it narrowed and the border changed from Vermont to New York.

Walking to a nearby boat with multiple fishing poles in hand was an elderly African-American man. In his early-sixties, about six foot one, and lanky, he stopped and knelt down to adjust the contents of his tackle box, adding a few new purchases from the marina store.

"Hey my man, do you have a minute?" asked Ty.

Standing up to address the visitor the man extended his hand to Ty, "What's up? What can I do for you?"

"Thank you for your time, sir. We were investigating the lake and were looking for people who visit frequently. Do you come up here a lot?" asked Carson.

The man extended his hand to Carson, "Sir? I'm Johnnie. Johnnie Jones. But most people here call me "Holiday" because I lived in New York City back in the late seventies, but I always vacationed here, or as they say 'holidayed' here," he said.

"So they call you Holiday Jones?" clarified Ty.

"That's right. Been comin' up here for over forty years now. Not just for holidays now. Moved up here in 2005," Holiday Jones said.

"Nice to meet you, Holiday. I'm Ty, that's Carson, Kareem, and Tegan."

Holiday Jones tipped his fishing cap at Tegan, "Ma'am."

"Since you are a regular here and seem to be a cool dude, let me get down to it," said Ty. "We have heard stories about a serpent in the lake that may be attacking people and dogs. We're trying to cut through the bullshit and see if it really exists and what is going on. If it does exist and it's attacking people, that has to be addressed," said Ty.

"Well, he…Champ…he does exist. Seen 'em myself a couple of times. First time back in either '74 or '75. I believe it was on Labor Day weekend," he said.

"That is certainly a long time ago. Did you tell anyone?" asked Carson. "Tell them what? I mentioned it, but everyone has seen him. It's not like a Bigfoot or something. He lives out here with us. Has been here for hundreds of years," Holiday Jones said.

"Hundreds of years? You think it's the same creature?" asked Kareem. "Of course not. There are dozens of them if not more. They live in the lake and travel up and down it throughout the year. It freezes in the winter sometimes and they move more south…although we have been getting fewer days where the lake freezes completely," he said.

"When you saw the creature, what did it look like?" asked Tegan.

"When I saw it the first time it was a little more north, up 'round South Hero Island and Ausable River outlet. And the best time is during the salmon run season. They like to wait just underwater like a bear would do for the salmon to try to get into the river inlet or when they come out," reported Holiday.

"We were up there earlier today," said Tegan.

"That's a good spot, but I think down here later in the year is better. Near the Champlain Bridge here is where the animals would have to go through a bottleneck at the point. You might have success high up on the mountains on the New York side of the lake 'cause you can see down in the water from that height. The lake has a channel on the New York side, and if you can find a spot where the channel would be about sixty feet deep or so, where the visibility to the channel is good from above, you can probably get lucky and see them. Look at a US Coast Guard map, and it shows the depths and how close it is to the mountains," Holiday said.

"How many times have you seen the animal?" asked Ty.

"Three times. That time in the seventies, then I saw the creature once in 1993, and it had a baby with it. It looked like a camel's head and snake-like body traveling through the water. That was down here and maybe more toward Bulwagga Bay. The third time was just over a year ago over by Port Henry. I think all three times I've seen it has been in the fall," he said as he reflected on his experiences.

As they were speaking another man walked up with his fishing gear, about to board one of the small boats in the marina. "I couldn't help but overhear you were talking about Champ," he said. The man was also in his late fifties to early sixties and had short grayish black hair and a mustache.

"You've seen him too?" asked Kareem.

"Yes, sir. I've seen him up in some of the parts your friend there described. I sighted one of the creatures just south of South Hero Island. It was displaying behavior of 'spinning' like you might see in crocodiles. They do that to disorientate and dismember the fish apart since they have no hands or claws to reach their mouth," the man said.

"Hey, I'm Carson," he said greeting the man.

"Nice to meet you. I'm Timothy Fisher."

"You don't seem startled by the creature being here, Timothy?" asked Carson.

"Nope. We've been sharing the lake with them for hundreds, maybe even thousands of years. They typically don't bother us, and we don't bother them. They even have a state law that says not to bother them, so we follow it," he said.

"You say he hasn't bothered anyone, but the thing is, recently there have been some sightings and some suggestions that say, that suggest, things have changed. A young girl was recently attacked, and it looks like her board was bitten by something in the lake, and her legs were cut up pretty bad. Then there are all of these stories of being losing their dogs. And while no one has confirmed it, seems like Champ might be to blame," said Carson.

"Well if that's true, then something has changed because ever since I've been here he hasn't hurt anyone," responded Timothy. "So what are you trying to do? Catch it? Kill it?" asked Timothy.

"We are trying to study it — first see if it exists, then attempt to find out what the change is that has caused the attacks. Once we know that we can attempt to correct it and return life on the lake back to normal. Until then, it seems like a dangerous situation," said Ty.

Timothy thought about it for a moment. "Then I would say the best way to spot them is with underwater cameras with infrared. I know there are also some groups out there that patrol the lake searching for Champ and they have had success recording them on audio. You can attract them with lights and sounds of distressed fish. But don't use active Sonar as they can actually hear it and it drives them away. Use passive sonar and listen for their echolocation signal. Sounds just like a beluga, dolphin, and orca whale chirp. You can tell they are close when you hear this," suggested Timothy.

"Sounds promising. How do you know that will work?" asked Tegan.

"That was proven by a doctor lady a few years ago when she tracked these sounds at the lake. She made a video of about an hour long and the chirps can be heard on the video. I think if you were to try to do it yourself you would need a good microphone in a waterproof container and a very good stereo amplifier capable of frequency response above 25 kHz up around 35 kHz. Adult humans have trouble hearing this high without special equipment but for some reason teenagers seem to be able to hear this high. It would be up around the frequency of a mosquito buzz. And that's the state bird of Vermont, so you might have trouble distinguishing that from actual mosquitos that are all over here," Timothy stated.

"It seems like everyone here has a story. It's as if everyone firmly believes this unknown creature is real," said Tegan. "Everyone else would say this was a myth, but no one here questions it."

"You're right," said Holiday Jones, "Don't dare tell a Vermonter that Champ doesn't exist. It's like telling a child that Santa isn't real. We've all seen him and know otherwise. We know more about it than the flatlanders that come here in the fall and summer," he said.

"Flatlander? What's that?" asked Carson.

"That's a fella that comes up here – tourists if you will. They create the only traffic we see because they are driving and unfolding maps, reading maps, and leaf-peepin'," interrupted Timothy.

"We were planning on doing more looking in Bulwagga Bay," said Carson.

"Well, it's a good place to look. Lots of sightings in the area, but I would look more over to Port Henry or up by South Hero Island. It's only about thirty feet deep in Bulwagga Bay. A little shallow for a creature that size. I think they prefer deeper water, but a lot of people have seen it around there. It is a small cove, so it's a good place to catch fish, and with the low water level it might make it easier to see the animal," suggested Timothy.

"Port Henry is definitely a spot we want to check out as well," said Carson.

"You might be able to check with one of the scientific research teams, maybe someone upta the ECHO, or someone at the university if you need some of that equipment," suggested Timothy.

"That's a good idea," said Ty. "Carson, maybe your friend Dr. Howard can help us with some equipment?"

"I am sure he can point us in the right direction at least. I will give him a call and see if we can get something for tomorrow morning."

"You guys have been a big help," Kareem said as they all exchanged handshakes and the group returned to the car.

"Let's hit up the visitor's center next, then go over to Bulwagga Bay. We will need to secure a boat for tomorrow if we want to get a good look at what's out there. Just sitting in one spot and looking likely isn't going to be too effective," said Ty.

It was a short drive to the visitor's center, and unlike the marina, it wasn't too busy. Walking inside they found only one person, and he was working. As soon as they walked in, he greeted them eagerly, glad for something to do.

"Hello, guys. Welcome to the Lake Champlain Visitor's Center, I am Ellery, and I am happy to answer any questions you have about the lake or give you a cancellation stamp for your Champlain Valley national heritage partnership passport if you have one" he said cheerfully.

Ellery was in his early forties and had dark brown hair cut in a simple low fade with thick, full waves on top. A slightly past five o'clock shadow graced his face. He wore black designer frames, a khaki button-up dress shirt with a dark olive tie and dark olive V-neck thin sweater. He had worked in the old New Hampshire Railroad toll collector's house that served as the Lake Champlain Visitor's Center at the foot of the Lake Champlain Bridge since 2005. He enjoyed being around the lake and introducing people to the beauty of the region.

"Questions?" asked Tegan. "Let's see...have you seen Champ?" she said playfully.

"As a matter of fact, we did have a sighting last evening just around civil twilight. We could just barely see him as the sun quickly faded," said Ellery.

"Seriously? I was just joking. We have heard sightings, but not that recent. We weren't sure that he really existed," she said.

"Yes, they exist. There are more than one of them, so "they", and this time of year they are frequently in this part of the lake. Twilight and from nautical dawn to just after sunrise are the best times to spot them, but occasionally people do see them in the daytime," Ellery reported.

"Right — we saw that story on the news about the girl getting attacked, and that was late afternoon," said Carson.

"Champ is normally not aggressive. I am not sure about that story. In all my years living around the lake I have not known Champ to attack anyone," he said.

"But there seem to be increased reports of missing animals and now people attacked. Do you know why they might think Champ is responsible?" asked Ty.

"No, I'm not sure. Typically they eat fish, mostly perch, salmon, and walleye. I don't think they would eat domestic animals or kids," Ellery said.

"We were planning on getting out on the lake tomorrow and have a look around," said Carson.

"That's the best way to spot them unless you just wanted to hang out here all day and hope," Ellery said. "From here over to Port Henry would be my first choice, and early in the morning or late in the evening," he suggested. "Good luck with your hunt. Here's a map that might help. Remember, they are protected so don't harass them or attempt to capture or hurt them," he reminded. They nodded in agreement as Tegan took the map and they exited back to the parking lot.

It was only an eight-mile drive from the visitor's center at the bridge to Port Henry. The road curved along Bulwagga Bay and Tegan, Kareem, and Ty watched the lake intently as Carson drove, although he too occasionally stole a few glances. As they rolled through the town it appeared to be a hotspot for Champ – there was the Champ trading post, the Port Henry Campgrounds & Champ Beach Park, and Champ Car Wash. A sign still hung on a window of a business on the street announcing Champ Day, held the first Saturday in August. Another flyer showed the Labor Day parade weekend festivities, in which Champ was also invited. They also saw a three-panel sign depicting Champ and the numerous sightings in the Bulwagga Bay area.

"Maybe we can get our name on that sign after this week," said Ty. Carson continued driving to Van Slooten Harbor Marina. "We need to find a boat for tomorrow. I know they had charters up by King Street, but they were closed for the season. Maybe we will have better luck here," said Carson.

Walking around the Van Slooten Harbor Marina, several boats appeared to be already docked for the season as no one was around them. A few people in the harbor on boats fishing, but not many people milling about the marina area. They walked around the inlet and looked for more than twenty minutes, but no one was around. As they experienced at other parts of the lake, the regular running boats were closed for the season.

"Now what?" asked Kareem. Carson ran his fingers through his hair and looked at the lake impatiently. "We need to get out on the water if we are going to investigate this creature," he said.

"I'm going to call the doc and see about that equipment. You guys see if you can find out where we can rent a boat for tomorrow morning," he said.

Carson walked off through the parking lot calling Dr. Howard and discussing the possibility of equipment for researching the lake. He asked about sonar equipment, thermal cameras, thermometers, and other scanning equipment they could borrow. "I believe the next step, not just in our investigation but other researchers, will be had out on the lake. As more scientific equipment becomes available and prices make it more affordable to the everyday person on the lake, that's when the amount of documented data will increase," suggested Ty.

Ten minutes later Carson returned and confirmed he secured equipment through the university. Dr. Howard would speak to a Champ search team that he was friends with and his fellow professor, Dr. Javan Thomas, would lend equipment for the search. "Now we just need a boat," said Carson.

"It's been a long morning. Let's find some lunch," suggested Kareem.

"Yeah, everything is clearer after lunch," suggested Tegan.

Back in the car, they headed back up New York 9N just a few blocks. Just down from the Mobile station sat a gray vinyl siding building with a delightful atrium. There were only a couple of cars in the driveway, but it appeared to be open. The Kettletop Café looked like a down-home comfort food restaurant that attracted mostly locals and at least on this day, a few visitors.

"Let's just try this place. It's close to the lake, and we can get back and try to find a boat after we eat," suggest Carson.

Champ and A Bit of Sunshine

"Right. No good having the equipment if we don't have a boat," replied Ty.

Inside the restaurant it was dark and the décor dated, but the smells were satisfying and reminded Carson of home. The smell of fried chicken and bread – like Southern-style biscuits type bread…and an undertone of candied yams hit Carson as soon as they opened the door.

"Damn, I don't know what they're serving, but this place gets my vote," said Ty.

A voice from the front said, "Seat yerself. Anywhere you like." They found a booth near the front door and sat awaiting the hostess. A young, college-aged light-skinned African-American lady approached the table with a handful of menus and a tray of waters. "Thanks for stopping by today. My name is Dishonne, and I will be your server today.

"Nice, you have a beer menu," said Ty as he looked at the options. "More than Coors Light. I'm happy to see that," he said with a smile. The young lady coyly returned the smile and lowered her eyes in a slightly embarrassed yet flirty reaction.

"Can I get the 14th Star Brewing Company Maple Breakfast Stout?" Ty asked.

"Yes – so that one is on draught and comes on nitro if that's ok," Dishonne responded.

"That's perfect. Even better," Ty returned.

"Well if we're going balls-out, can I get a get a Foolproof Brewing Company Peanut Butter Raincloud Porter?" asked Carson.

"Fer sure. That one's in a can if that's okay? I can bring a pint glass," she said.

"That'll do," he said.

"For you, hun?" she asked Kareem.

"How about The Shed Brewery Mountain Ale?"

"Yes, we have that one in a bottle. It's an unfiltered brown ale," she responded. Kareem nodded in agreement.

"And for you?" she asked Tegan.

"Do you have the Drop-In Brewing Company Six Holes In My Freezer?" she asked.

"Yes, we just received a mini keg of that one to try out," Dishonne added. "It's a wheat beer that tastes like key lime pie. I tried it myself. It's crazy good! – and I don't really like beer," she said with a smile.

"I'm game to try it," she said. "Cool – I'll come right back with the drinks and give you time to look over the food option.

As she left the group turned their attention to the menu. "Lots of options, and it all sounds good," said Carson. Tyson looked over the menu, then quickly laid it down on the table.

"Mama's fried chicken. Mac and cheese. Candied Yams. I'm done," he said.

"Wow, that was easy," said Tegan, still looking at the menu.

"Can we share an order of fried green tomatoes? Someone?" asked Kareem.

"You know I will help eat that too," said Ty.

"I want an order of the southern biscuits. They smell so good," said Tegan. "And the pot roast with creamy mushroom grits..." she added.

"Ah yes, the chicken and dumplings," Kareem said, finishing his order.

"Hmm. I think I will go with what appears to be local favorite comfort food. American chop suey," he said.

"Chop suey? I didn't see they had Chinese food on the menu," replied Kareem. "No, this apparently bears no resemblance to the chop suey found in Chinese restaurants," said Carson. With that Dishonne returned.

"American chop suey contains tomatoes, ground beef, elbow macaroni, vegetables, and cheese mixed in a large pot or pan and served in a bowl with additional shredded cheese on top," she said.

"Kind of like a big bowl of beefaroni with extra stuff?" asked Carson.

"Kind of. It's not soup but it's slightly juicier than a casserole," she added.

"When in Rome," he said placing his menu down on the table, then collecting them all to hand to Dishonne.

"Well now we have the beer and the food handled we just need to find a boat for tomorrow morning to get out there and look for Champ," said Ty.

Ty felt the booth move slightly as the man on the other side changed position, causing Ty to glance over his shoulder. The man soon got up, put some dollars on the table for his bill, and got ready to leave. As he started to walk out, he stopped in front of the group's booth.

"I couldn't help but overhear ya," the man said as he adjusted his red toboggan. He was in his mid-to-late-fifties with a tan, wrinkled face, wrinkly hands, and a short but scruffy gray beard. And eyebrows. Very bushy eyebrows. He wore a blue turtleneck and yellow raincoat pants with black suspenders and tall black rubber wader boots. He looked like a weathered version of the Gorton's Fisherman.

Ty looked up at him, hesitant at the man's appearance.

"Do you know what we did last summer?" he said.

"Huh? No, I heard that you said you needed a boat tomorrow," the fisherman said.

"Oh, yes. We have some equipment, and we want to go out and search the lake for Champ. But so far we haven't been successful," said Carson.

"All of the commercial charter boats are shacked up for the winter," he said. "But, I have a boat and can take you out for a reasonable price," he said.

"Really? That would be great. It might be for most of the day. I'm not sure," said Carson.

"What's your name?"

Trollinger

"I'm Captain Dandy," he said reaching into his pocket and retrieving a pipe he began to pack for his trip outside. "Or you can call me Jim," he added.

The group looked at each other. "You're Jim Dandy?" asked Kareem.

"Cap...Captain Jim Dandy. Yes. At your service," he said once again adjusting his red cap.

"Well Jim Da-...Captain Dandy, are you available tomorrow morning? We have to get the equipment from the college and then we can set sail," said Carson.

"Yes, I am up and on the water at first light," Captain Dandy said.

"Great!" Carson said as he motioned to Tegan who quickly handed him a pen from her purse. He wrote his number down on a napkin, and the Captain wrote his down for Carson.

"See you fellas tomorrow," he said as he walked out the door lighting his pipe. They all watched him leave then turned attention back to each other.

"Well, that's settled I guess," he said. He picked up the menu again and looked it over. "I suddenly want a large ice cream sundae with marshmallow, strawberry, and chocolate," said Carson.

The attempt at humor was broken up as Dishonne returned with the food.

13 SAILING (TAKES ME AWAY)

Thursday, October 8, 2015

Carson and the gang pulled into the Van Slooten Harbor Marina while the skyline was still into the deep azure haze of the Blue Hour. It was a short night after planning the details for their adventure on the lake and picking up the equipment from Dr. Javan Thomas at the university.

Dr. Thomas provided a variety of equipment that would be useful for the investigation. The acoustic investigation by sonar was a primary scientific method that was frequently used to measure depth and investigate geological conditions underwater; however, using this method also had been historically costly and usually required researchers to have specialized training. Specialized training that none of the T.I.M.E. team had. Instead, Dr. Thomas recommended a fish finder. He told Carson that the performance of leisure-use fish finders had improved considerably in recent years.

They provided high-quality depth measurements and high-resolution sonar images. Also, the data are recordable with simultaneous positional information, so a wide range of scientific data could be collected at a relatively low cost. Moreover, the equipment could be used on small boats because of their small size and light weight so using Captain Dandy's ship would be just fine. Carson initially seemed skeptical, but Dr. Thomas assured him these modern fishfinders had been used in a variety of research fields, including marine engineering, glaciology, marine biology, archeology, and geology. The fish finders used for providing sonar images, depth data and synchronized positioning information used a global navigation satellite system. The sonar images differed depending on acoustic sources. Dr. Thomas' provided equipment that operated at approximately 455 kHz. The tools provide not only traditional sonar images but also side-scan high-resolution sonar images with higher frequency acoustic sources. Dr. Thomas stated side-scan imaging was a technology that could be used to survey broad areas and could produce images of shape and dimensions.

Also, he included echolocation/bioacoustics equipment, a couple of trail cameras for any potential land sightings, a couple of GoPro cameras, an underwater camera with infrared capability, and one drone. They could also to play underwater sounds of distressed fish that they hoped might attract the animal. Additionally, they had a high-grade hydrophone in a waterproof container and an excellent stereo amplifier capable of frequency response above 25 kHz to around 35 kHz. With that Carson felt they would have enough for the initial investigation. Now Carson was dock-side with the gang helping Captain Dandy load the equipment into the boat.

"We should have a good day on the water," Captain Dandy said. "Temperatures between forty-eight and fifty-eight, visibility at about ten miles, winds between three and twelve miles per hour, and no precipitation."

Once everything was loaded, and they began to leave the dock, Ty asked Captain Dandy about prior investigations on the lake.

"I haven't been involved with any myself, but I have heard about others that have been out here. Champ is a popular attraction, and everybody is always looking for him. About ten or fifteen years ago, I heard of a scientific team working on the lake. They discovered a unique echolocation signature that was new to science and there was an excitement that this information might could help identify a new species of animal living in the lake. I heard it was sent to universities for analysis, but over the years that research was apparently set aside and we heard no more about it," he said.

"Have you ever seen it yourself?" asked Tegan.

"Yeah, I have seen him a time or two. It's kind of green color, sometimes they are a bit darker and liken to brown. They're usually fifteen to eighteen feet long, but I've heard some people say they can be up to thirty feet long. I never saw one that big though. That's just me," he said.

"I just don't know about this," said Carson. "I mean doesn't the lake freeze up in the winter?"

"In the past, it has though we have been seeing fewer days each winter where the lake freezes up. Must be getting warmer or that climate change malarkey might be something to it. And in the winter, if I had my guess I would say during the cold winter months they travel by the extensive cave system below and around the lake."

"There are caves at the bottom of the lake?" asked Ty.

"Sure are, but it's murky down there, and one person cannot go alone. I don't think they have really been explored to see where those tunnels go to," the Captain said.

The sun was still coming up, and the lake glowed with a beautiful orangish-red sunrise. "Wow, that's so beautiful out here on the water," said Tegan.

"Red sky at night, sailors' delight. Red sky at morning, sailors take warning," said Captain Dandy.

"I have heard that, but I don't even know what it means," Tegan responded.

"It means we might see rain after all," said Carson. "If the morning skies are red, it is because clear skies over the horizon to the east permit the sun to light the undersides of moisture-bearing clouds," he added.

"How deep is the lake?" asked Carson.

"It is hard to get clear readings," said Captain Dandy. "The density of rock in the area – it makes it hard to get accurate depth readings. But they estimate it averages about sixty-four feet, and the deepest point is about four hundred feet deep over between Charlotte, Vermont and Essex, New York."

"How do you think the idea for Champ first started up here? I know the early explorers supposedly saw something in the lake, but some stories I read said it was just a big fish like a gar or a sturgeon," said Kareem.

"Glaciers once covered Vermont during the last ice age, and some say the creature came in then and somehow survived. Actually, the oldest known fossil reef in the world was discovered in Lake Champlain, and it's between four hundred fifty and four hundred eighty million years old," the Captain added.

The waters were still calm as the boat sailed out of Bulwagga Bay and over to the Vermont side by the Champlain Bridge Marina.

"We can see nearly from coast to coast this morning," said Carson.

"Yes, visibility is good. The lake is only twelve miles at its widest point, so we should be able to see it all. Up to South Hero Island is about sixty miles on the land, but about fifty on the lake," said Captain Dandy.

"That's pretty long," said Carson.

"Yep, for a short time – about two weeks – the lake was the country's sixth Great Lake," the Captain said.

"Really? I never heard that," said Kareem.

"March 6, 1998, President Clinton signed it into law, but there was an uproar over it and March 24 the status was rescinded."

"How's the fishing out here?" asked Ty. "I enjoy hitting the lakes back in Texas," he said.

"The lake has eighty-one species of fish, and it's well-known for its bass fishing. They say Bassmaster lists it as number five in the United States. But ta me the past several months it's been fairly light. Not like the past few years when we come up here. We've seen more largemouth bass than before, but other fish is hard to come by. Used to come up here for walleye, and perch. Jesum crow there was some good fishin'," reported the Captain.

158

"Maybe it is Champ then?" said Ty. "I mean if you have a group of large mammals or whatever they are and they eat fish, wouldn't they deplete the lake?"

"Some say that," said the Captain. "Others think it may eat more like a snake or maybe an alligator and it doesn't have to eat all the time like a mammal. Like maybe they get a meal then sit for a long period before they need to eat again," he said.

The Captain continued to direct the boat north closer up the Vermont side of the lake. "There have been some sightings up near Button Bay. It seems to live the coves," said Carson.

"Yes, I think they go for perch, salmon, smelts, and walleye mostly and they run upon them in those shallow coves," said the Captain.

Carson turned his attention to the equipment. The fishfinder seemed to be working well and charting the lake walls and depth. They were recording echolocation readings and temperature of the lake water. "Maybe we can pull up in a cove or two and set the drone out to scout from above," he suggested.

The wind picked up more speed as they continued up the coast. It was just over ten miles per hour now.

"We might not have much luck right now," suggested Captain Dandy. "Most of the sightings have been with calm surface water and gentle wind," he continued. "Wind strength less than three is ideal. With the wind higher usually sightings are rare."

Carson looked over the lake, and the wind was causing more ripples on the surface. Frequently when the breeze was gentle, the lake's surface looked like glass allowing good visibility underwater.

"We've been at this a couple of hours already, and I haven't seen anything. Even just a few fish on the fish finder, but not anything big enough to be mistaken for a sea monster. And the clouds are rolling in now. I hope it doesn't turn up rain," said Ty.

In Spaulding Bay they approached the first of two small islands. The first one was Mud Island, and the further was Rock Island. Mud Island was mostly tree-covered with a small beachy area on the eastern side. Using the Captain's small handheld telescope Ty looked ahead. Rock Island also appeared to be mostly tree-covered with a rocky beach on the south side.

"Maybe one of those islands would be a good spot to anchor and get the drone up in the air?" asked Ty.

"We can do it. I need to hit the pisser anyway," he said. The Captain chose Rock Island as it was larger and might provide more surface for the creature to hide.

The water lapped against the boat as the Captain pulled into the cove. Captain Dandy set the engine into reverse to slow the forward momentum before killing the motor. Carson took the anchor and carefully lowered it into the lake, maintaining a slight tension in the line until it reached the bottom. The Captain maneuvered the boat backward slowly until Carson had the proper length of anchor line handed out. Carson fastened the line around the deck cleat while the anchor flukes dug in and caught. Ty used a compass and wrote down reference marks in the Captain's log.

"That should do it," said Carson as he turned and gave a thumbs up to Captain Dandy. The gestured was acknowledged and returned. With the boat secured, the Captain headed to the porta-potty in the cuddy cabin.

Tegan set the drone on the deck and prepared to take flight, checking the camera and ensuring everything was operational before launch. The wind speed had dropped since they entered the cove, making flying easier.

"Let's see what's out there," she said as she turned the power on the transmitter. With a quiet whirl, the drone's propellers came to life, and she slowly pushed the throttle upward. The quadcopter started to take off from the deck. She held it in position a few feet above the deck to get a feel for the controls on this model. After a few practice maneuvers, she pushed the throttle up again and ascended higher above the boat.

The drone's transmitter included a monitor allowing her to see everything the drone was seeing. She hit record as the drone began to

160

fly around the small island and check the harbor for any signs of aquatic life. The drone picked up what appeared to be a couple of small burrows constructed in the bank by a submerged tree. She concluded these belonged to otters which she soon verified when a couple of otters were spotted on the shore.

Some critics speculated the sightings of Champ were misidentified as otters swimming together and playing in the lakes and falsely appearing to be humps witnesses saw when describing the creature's appearance. The calmness of the wind and the glass-like display of the water allowed for clarity that enabled the drone to capture several feet below the lake's surface. Circling the island turned up nothing on the video except for the small group of otters and a few bass swimming near the in the cove.

"Finding anything?" asked Kareem.

"No, nothing of significance yet at least," replied Tegan.

The Captain returned to the deck to check for updates. Ty and Carson monitored the lake temperature using the Walker duo sense temperature and checking out the fish finder to locate any significant anomalies. The fish finder showed nothing except the bass Tegan picked up with the drone. Ty wrote down the temperature readings in the Captain's log. Tegan circled the island and along the shore another twenty minutes before bringing the drone back to the ship before the battery depleted.

"Well, it doesn't look like we're getting anything here," said Carson. "Can we head further up the lake?"

The Captain nodded and started the motor. He slowly maneuvered the boat forward releasing tension on the anchor line. Carson pulled in the length of the anchor line until the line was vertical. Pulling firmly, he lifted the anchor's shank and freed the flukes from the bottom. With the anchor clear, Carson motioned for to the Captain who proceeded north up the lake between Rock Island and the coast, passing Arnold Bay and reaching Button Bay.

"Let's keep out eyes peeled here as there have been sightings in this part of the lake," said Carson. The boat did not enter the Button

Bay cove, but stayed west of Button Island and slowly moved north across from the Basin Harbor Club Golf Course. The surface of the lake was calm with just a gentle wake as the boat slowly made its way further northeast as the lake took a bend in direction.

Captain Dandy pointed over to the New York side of the lake. "Over there is Split Rock Mountain, in Essex, New York," he said. "You see the rocks? Some think the natural rock structures resemble petrified snakes and maybe some of those old Native American stories about a horned serpent living in the lake may have been due to that mountain."

"I don't see the resemblance there, but maybe they could have thought that," said Carson.

"Another thing that people think Champ could be is just debris from the lake. It is long, deep, narrow and cold, just like Loch Ness over there in Scotland where people see that Nessie. Scientists have studied both and discovered that both bodies of water have an underwater wave phenomenon that they called a seiche. That throws debris from the bottom of the lake up to the surface, and they say that could explain many of the monster sightings. Then you have all of the various types of dinosaurs from zeuglodon to tanystropheids to plesiosaurs," the Captain said.

Across from Split Rock Mountain was Kingsland Bay State Park, where the young girl was attacked just days ago. "Do you think the girls saw the rocks across the bay and mistook it for Champ?" asked Kareem.

"It might be possible in appearance, based on what the Captain said about prior sightings, but something did break the paddleboard in two – and not just break like running on a rock. We saw the board. Those marks appeared to be teeth marks. No way mountains did that. There is something big with enormous teeth living in these waters," said Carson.

"The longnose gar is found in the lake and does have a long snout and numerous sharp teeth," said the Captain. "It is something else that some speculate Samuel de Champlain may have actually have seen when exploring the area. They have been around for nearly one hundred million years, and they can grow between two and four feet long, although there have been some spotted about six feet in length and weighing around fifty pounds."

"A six foot long, fifty pound fish with sharp teeth?" responded Ty. "NO THANK YOU!"

"The bowfin is also an old fish living in these waters. It's around sixty million years old and it also has pointed teeth, but they are a little smaller, usually about eighteen inches to two feet," replied the Captain. "A six-foot fish would truly be a 'monster,' and I could maybe see that as able to break a board if it weighed fifty pounds, but these two-foot fish? I don't think that's what we're dealing with," said Carson.

As they continued up the coast Carson and Ty seemed to grow disappointed in the lack of results. "We've been out here since daybreak and we haven't seen anything that could be what people think is a lake monster," said Ty.

"Yet hundreds of people have not only seen it, but they swear a monster is here. There is no doubt in their mind," added Carson. "Just a quiet day on the lake. Don't get me wrong, for any other purpose this would be awesome – just hanging out on the water, not too cold yet, but trying to get to the bottom of this case is really troubling. We have absolutely nothing to go on," said Carson.

They reached South Burlington and passed by some of the familiar sights from earlier in the vacation. The marina where they first stopped off King Street and eventually up to Charlie's Boathouse had minimal activity on the shore, with both of them closed for the season.

"As large as this lake is, it may be impossible to locate anything – if anything even exists," admitted Ty. Carson stared over the lake's surface and near the shore as they passed the boathouse.

"I don't know, man. Seems impossible and maybe it is just a drum up for tourism, but the chupacabra turned out to be a real animal, and it wasn't long ago that giant squids were considered to be more mythical beasts – but then they turned out to be real. So who can say? It's a big world, and it's filled with some crazy shit," said Carson. "When we get up to South Hero, I say we circle the small island, head over near Valcour Island, then turning back. We've covered a lot of ground, but doesn't seem like we're going to find anything, and it will take a couple of hours to get back," suggested Carson.

"We haven't even seen a lot of the fish on the fish finder," said Kareem.

"As I said, fishing has been down the past couple of years. There was a big fish kill in the winter of 2013-2014 that caused most of the game fish in the lake to be killed," said the Captain.

"Really, what happened?" asked Tegan.

"Well after investigation the fish and wildlife folks determined the most likely common cause was a reduction of the oxygen level in the water," he said.

"What causes that?" she asked. "Well, it maybe is due to many different factors like drought, algae bloom, overpopulation, or a sustained increase in water temperature. Infectious diseases and parasites can also lead to fish kill. Toxicity is a real but far less common cause of fish kill," he said.

Passing south of Schuyler Island and across from Port Douglas, Tegan noticed something on the sonar. "Hey guys, we just picked up sound waves from something in the area. Kinda faint, but it's there," said Tegan. The guys took notice of the news and gathered around Tegan to look at the data.

"Whales and dolphins use echolocation, but those animals wouldn't be in a freshwater lake," said Carson.

"Not anymore," said the Captain.

"What do you mean?" responded Carson.

"In the past when the lake was still directly connected to the sea there were whales. Researchers have unearthed more than thirty fossil specimens of belugas in the area around the lake," the Captain said. "But the strange thing is, for more than ten years, they have picked up unidentified animal audio on underwater hydrophones. The sounds resembled belugas."

"How're our hydrophones? Anything else?" asked Carson.

"No, just that one faint reading. I marked the location in the log, but whatever it was is gone now," Tegan said.

"Damn it," said Carson as he looked over the lake's surface hoping to detect whatever created the underwater sound visually. But there was nothing. As it had been all day the lake was quiet and the surface calm except for the small wake created by their vessel.

The clouds rolled in, and the wind picked up more as the fishing vessel continued heading south back toward the home marina. A long day on the lake had turned up very little evidence of a giant lake monster living in the waters. Carson told himself that while there have been hundreds of sightings of the creature over the past four hundred plus years, there were not sightings every day. Most people even those who are frequently on the lake have only seen it once or twice in a lifetime, so the thought that they would find it today did seem unlikely.

It was now about five in the afternoon, and the air was cooling down quickly. As they passed by Mullen Bay, the outline of businesses in nearby Port Henry was beginning to appear. The crew started to relax and lower their alertness to the area as they were coming down from their day-long lake adventure. Even though they didn't find what they were looking for, it was still tiring to be on high alert for so many hours. It was nice to come down a bit and think about what the next steps would be over the next couple of days.

As Ty bent down to gather some of the equipment in preparation for their arrival, he caught something out of the corner of his eye on the starboard side of the boat. Not quite in the bay, but heading toward it was an object. An objective that was moving.

"Hey, dude, what's that?" Ty asked Carson, who was also bent over gathering items. He paused and looked up to see the object also. It appeared to be a creature, pea-green in color quietly swimming. It didn't create waves or noise, just a graceful, quiet movement through the water.

"Guys!" Carson called out. Kareem and Tegan both turned around and saw it too. There were what appeared to be three humps behind the head of the creature, just like other eyewitness accounts. They just stared in disbelief for a moment when Tegan whispered: "Get the camera!" She wasn't sure why she whispered, but it felt like the thing to do at the moment. Kareem slowly reached into a crate on the deck and removed the D-SLR camera and began taking photos. Even with the zoom fully engaged it was challenging to get a good photo, and the further he zoomed the grainer the picture.

"Can we move the boat toward it?" Ty asked the Captain. The Captain reduced speed and turned the wheel to guide the boat closer to the bay, but then the head dipped below water and was gone. Ty ran over to the equipment still capturing readings. The hydrophones did detect sound, and a large object was spotted on the fish finder moving quickly below the boat.

And like that, it was gone. But something was there. What it was they were uncertain. It left as quietly as it must have arrived. There were no waves, no commotion from ducks closer to the shore, and no sound, at least above water.

"Kareem, did you get anything?" asked Carson. Kareem looked at the back of the camera and scrolled through the nearly one dozen photos he snapped in those few seconds.

"I can tell there is something there, but it's not clear, and if I zoom in more on the photo it's just a grainy mass."

As the board pulled back into Van Slooten Marina, the energy was more optimistic than before the sighting in Mullen Bay. They were glad to be back on land and were eager for dinner, but the conversation focused on the unknown thing spotted in the water. Something that wasn't there on the trip up, but was in the late afternoon hours heading back.

"We need to wrap our heads around this thing, but I think we need to come out and do a full investigation. What do you think?" Carson asked the rest of the group.

"For sure. I say we sleep on it and get back out here tomorrow," suggested Ty.

"Right, maybe late afternoon because that's when it seems to be the best chance historically for sightings, and we saw it ourselves in the late afternoon," suggested Tegan.

"Captain, are you available tomorrow afternoon?" asked Carson.

"Yep, I can do'er," he said.

"Great, then let's meet you back here tomorrow about 5 p.m.?" suggested Carson.

"I'll be here," he confirmed.

"See you then," Carson said with a handshake. "Thank you for everything today. It's a beautiful lake, and I am stoked we finally saw something there at the end. Can we do some diving tomorrow night?"

"Yes, I have a couple of suits at home that might fit you and Ty. I will bring them with me," said Captain Dandy.

"Great!" Carson said. "Let's grab something to eat," he said turning to the others.

14 BACK ON LAND

Friday, October 9, 2015

Around 4 p.m. Carson and the gang parked along the road off Canal Street in Winooski for a late lunch and a drink before heading to the lake for a nighttime investigation. Ty had read good things online about a brewery that opened last year and had been called "one of the best little breweries you've never heard of" by Food and Wine.

They were surprised at the how warm the day was, in comparison the earlier days of the trip. It was cloudy and spots of rain, but sixty-one degrees in October? The surprising temperature caused them to have to stop by a souvenir store and purchase t-shirts. Carson selected one with a large maple tree and the words "I'd tap that" underneath.

Four Quarters Brewery was located in a green aluminum siding building with glass windows and a big white garage door as well as a few picnic tables for seating outside. Inside the taproom was small — just enough room for a wooden bar. An expansive chalkboard behind the bar revealed a few beers on tap and an offering of bottles. Jayden Tanner, a tall twenty-three-year-old athletic African-American man with a trimmed goatee, greeted them.

"Hey guys, first time here?"

"Yes, just visiting for a few days and thought we'd stop by," said Carson.

"Nice – well, welcome. We have a food truck that should be here soon, we have two taps, but we also have some bottles available for on-site consumption," he said.

"If you want you can hang out here or if you want to sit down, we have the picnic tables outside," he said.

"Outside is fine. That will give you little more time to finish opening up. We didn't realize you didn't open until 5 p.m.," said Carson.

"Not a problem," said Jayden. As they sat down and looked at the chalkboard menu and headed outside to wait, Carson brought up yesterday's outing on the lake.

"I've been thinking about what we saw yesterday," he began. The others looked over the menu but listened. "I'm not sure what we saw was a lake monster," he said.

"We were out there all day and didn't see anything. It was only as the sun started to go down," said Ty. "I saw the movement and the shape, and I think I got excited wanting to see something," he said.

"But it wasn't there when we got closer – and there was something on the fish finder," replied Kareem

"Yes, it was probably just a log from the seiche Captain Dandy told us about," said Carson.

"Moving logs up from the bottom of the lake, we saw it, and then it sank back town as we headed over there," added Ty.

"No, we did see something. All of us saw it," said Tegan. Ty thought about it and shook his head.

"No, we thought we saw something. It's probably pareidolia – you know, where your mind perceives something recognizable that isn't really there.

"Like seeing the face of Tim Tebow in a piece of toast?" asked Carson.

"Right. Looking back, we never saw definitive proof of an animal, just an object that was no longer there when we approached. Maybe we saw it because we wanted to see it?" Ty said.

"Maybe you're are probably right," said Kareem. "We were out there all day, we were caught up in the stories, and since we found the chupacabra, we probably wanted to solve this mystery too. We bought into the local legends and saw what we wanted to see."

"Maybe you guys are right, but I am still holding out from definitively writing it off. Not every one of those accounts could be in on some mass tourism plot," said Tegan.

"Well, either way, I think we should go back out tonight with Captain Dandy and have a look. If we don't find anything, then we write it off as an urban legend and move on," said Ty. "But there is still the issue of those missing dogs," he added. "Something is causing that."

"Yeah, and the girl was attacked," reminded Tegan.

Jayden walked outside with some water, "Did you have a chance to decide what you wanted yet?" he asked.

"Oh, no…sorry. We were wrapped up in talking. Hey, what do you think about this Champ?" asked Ty.

"Champ? I've never seen it, and I have been around the lake for about five years since moving here from St. Louis. I've always just thought it was some local folklore myself, but that's just me. I've talked to several people who have seen it…or think they have seen it and come in here," he said.

"Before or after drinks?" asked Kareem. The table chuckled collectively increasing the perception that the animal did not exist. The discussion paused as The French Quarter food truck arrived.

"We better hurry up and order so we can get out to the Captain," reminded Tegan.

"Good point. Let me get the Horn of the Moon Witbier," said Kareem. Carson ordered the Sundog Imperial IPA, Tegan the Misery Sour, and Ty with the Darkest Heart Maple Liqueur Barrel Aged.

"What's been the best beer here?" asked Carson.

Champ and A Bit of Sunshine

"We canned the Sundog recently, and that was really popular. Most recently was a different release of the Opus Dei aged in rum barrels with golden raisins, red currants, and lemon zest," he said. The group turned their attention to the food truck.

"Mmm, Cajun and Creole!" said Ty. The menu offered savory hand pies stuffed with Cajun beef and tasso, crawfish-and-shrimp etouffee, a po'boy made with house-made tasso, andouille sausage, and smoked pork tenderloin, and even a dessert roll of ripe peaches with bourbon and maple cream in a puff pastry crust.

"Damn, everything sounds good. Let's try it all," suggested Kareem. Each ordered one of the items, and they shared the dessert.

The maple liqueur with roasted malt had hints of anise, dried dark berry, and oak paired well with the spicy crawfish-and-shrimp etouffee, thought Ty. Kareem felt equally impressed with the po-boy and the notes of coriander and dried orange in the Horn of the Moon. Tegan's sour provided a nice tartness with undertones of yeast, passion fruit, berries, and lighter apricot that she found very refreshing. Carson enjoyed the Citra and Amarillo hops with the house Belgian yeast, giving it a sweet orange and grapefruit taste.

Jayden returned to check on the table.

"Everything good? Can I get you another round?"

"No, we have to get going to meet up with a friend, but thank you for everything," said Carson.

"Thanks for stopping in. I hope you have a good rest of your vacation. Watch out for Champ!" Jayden said, getting another laugh from the group.

"Actually we are on our way to look for him, so that's good advice," said Ty.

Carson looked down at his cellphone. "It's okay that we are running late because Captain Dandy sent a text saying he was running late too," he told the group.

"We've got about forty-five miles to get back over to Van Slooten. We better get to scootin' down the road," said Carson.

The sun was already setting as they headed down the US-7. Carson's phone vibrated again. He passed it over to Ty and asked him to read it after he saw it was from Captain Dandy.

"He said to meet him at Crown Point," Ty read aloud. "He said we could park at the site and there is a winter fishing access area on the western site just south of the ruins. There's a trail where we can take down to the lake."

"Sounds good. That's a shorter distance than going all the way over to Van Slooten," said Carson. "That site is right at the mouth of Bulwagga Bay, and that's where our focus is going to be." Another twenty minutes and they arrived at the site.

They parked and began walking down the trail, finding the signage easy to follow. Carson texted the Captain as they walked. The response indicated he was still not there yet, but was on the water and heading to the pickup point. They passed the old gray remnants of the French Fort St. Frederic and the ruins of the barracks and walls of the British Crown Point fortress that defended Lake Champlain and played an essential role in the attack by Ethan Allen and the Green Mountain Boys to get cannons from Fort Ticonderoga. Although the buildings were in ruins, they were still an impressive sight and still commanded their place on the lake.

In the distance, they saw some barns and a nineteenth-century quarry. From behind the Crown Point fort ruins, a strange light appeared - bright enough in the dark sky to cause them to stop and look in its direction. The mysterious illumination disappeared, and they stared into the darkness attempting to determine what caused the lighting.

"That was weird. Now there's nothing," said Carson. They continued to stare, but only darkness remained. Deciding whatever it was must have moved on, they turned back toward the path to proceed to the fishing access point.

As they turned back around, they once again stopped, slightly startled to see a figure in the near darkness. The light from a nearby street lamp along the trail partially shone on the form, allowing them to know that it was a man – a strange looking man standing near a closed fence along the path toward the lake.

"Jesus Christ!" said Ty aloud while the others thought the same thing internally. Still startled by the sudden appearance, the group stood their ground. Looking at the man, they noticed he was about six feet tall, very lanky - approximately one hundred eighty-five pounds, and wore a metallic green suit. He had a dark complexion with small, beady eyes set wide on his face. He had dark black hair that was slicked back, and he appeared to be in his late thirties or early forties. Another feature that stood out was what seemed to be a tremendous, almost inhuman grin.

Once the man noticed them, he started to move slowly toward the group. The man assured Carson that he and the others would not be harmed, but they needed to remain calm. However, instead of speaking, the communication took place telepathically, causing the group to be surprised, nervous, and frozen with shock. The conversation continued telepathically as the man introduced himself as Indrid Cold, a visitor not from this country, but here to learn about the human race. Indrid continued to communicate with the group but kept his hands tucked firmly under his armpits as if to hide something. Carson nor anyone in the group could muster the words to speak and continued to stare in disbelief.

Staring at the group and slowly bending his head left and right, reminding Carson of a dog hearing an odd noise (and Ty of Jason in Friday the 13th), the man continued to grin widely and eerily.

"I am here to study humans. You are here to study the creature called Champ," he said telepathically. "You do not have to prove Champ is real. He, or rather they, are real and they exist not only in this body of water, but many others around the world: Okanagan, Tahoe, Raystown, Loch Ness, Kariba, Gloucester, Tianchi, Phaya Nak, Casco Bay, and many others. These animals have been here for millions of years and have lived mostly out of sight from human eyes," he said.

The telepathic words, as well as the constant wide inhuman grin, sent chills down the spines of each investigator. Carson took a large, slow gulp while remaining fixated on the "man", or rather an apparent being.

Indrid continued, "The mystery to solve is not that they exist, but why has their diet changed? They remained hidden for millennia because humans are predators and represent a danger. Apparently even in shadow, humans have proven to be a threat, causing the creatures' environment to change. Look to the water for your answers."

Still grinning, the being stepped backward, where now an open gate stood behind him. He continued to stare and smile as he stepped back without looking until he disappeared into a small wooded area. A light reappeared as a flash, then darkness once again. The man was no longer there. Carson and the group stared into the woods, turned looking in each direction, then up to the sky, but saw nothing.

What seemed to be an extended period passed.

Kareem broke the silence, "What the actual eff did we just see?!" he asked. Tegan was uncertain.

"He-he looked like a man, but like the Joker…but I don't think it was a man," she said as she searched the sky above.

"You all heard him too?" asked Ty. Carson turned toward the others. "He said his name was Indrid Cold…Ty, you remember I was into aliens when we were in school?…Indrid Cold was a being that appeared multiple times in the mid to late sixties. Sightings in New Jersey, but more famously in West Virginia just before the Mothman sightings and the incident of the Silver Bridge in Point Pleasant," Carson revealed. "And it wasn't just one guy who reported the contact. It was multiple people, and the stories were all very similar — this was years before the internet so it would be hard for people in different locations who apparently do not know each other to corroborate a story. Not like it is today," he said.

"So what was this being?" asked Ty. "He claimed to be a visitor from a planet called Lanulos. A planet that was just over fourteen light years away from Earth in a galaxy called Ganymede," said Carson.

"Aliens? Can the Men in Black be far behind?" asked Kareem.

"MIBs? Cool, I love Will Smith…make your neck work," said Ty as he stood and bobbed his head forward. The uneasiness was broken up by the vibration of Carson's cellphone. He looked down at the message, then back up at the group.

"The Captain is here. Time to go," he said.

15 NIGHTSWIM

Friday, October 9, 2015

They continued the rest of the way to the fishing access area walking in silence, still uncertain as to what just happened. To Tegan and Kareem the days of early June felt like a lifetime away. Back then neither thought of strange creatures in the night, but now just five short months later, short in calendar days at least, their whole world had changed. They had an encounter with a chupacabra and in just this week alone have searched a lake for a giant sea serpent and had a visit from an alien being. The paradigm shift was massive and gave them an uneasy feeling as they wondered what other things lurked in the dark?

They came to a small overlook where the trail headed down to the shore. Carson saw Captain Dandy's boat already there and waiting for them. While the afternoon was pleasant and unseasonably warm, the temperature now dropped into the low forties, and a light rain began to fall.

"Why is it always raining on these night investigations?" wondered Carson internally, trying to get his mind off of the visit from Indrid Cold.

The Captain waved to the group as he saw them descend the hill along the path. "Good evening! Are you ready to do a little hunting?" As they approached the boat the Captain greeting them and welcomed them aboard.

"How's your evening?" he asked.

"Out of this world," replied Ty.

"So what's the plan, Captain?" asked Carson.

"Well, I figured we would start the search in Bulwagga Bay, out where the bay first forms. The water is a little shallow around the visitor's center, but it deepens once past that. That is where many of the sightings occurred and where we thought we saw the creature the other day. Maybe they come out more in the evening, the camouflage of night you know? I have scuba gear for Ty and Carson. I think getting under the surface may be our best chance. Kareem and Tegan can operate the underwater mics, the fish finder, and the thermometers," Captain Dandy said.

"There is another option. There have been a lot of sightings here near Bulwagga Bay, going back to Captain Crumb's 1819 sighting. But up near Thompson's Point in Charlotte, the area between there and Essex, New York is the deepest part of Lake Champlain at over four hundred feet," he said.

"Last night I spent time online in the hotel room looking at some of the research conducted on Champ," said Carson. "I saw a few videos that were interesting, one video aired on ABC News in 2006 and showed a creature swimming alongside a boat. But for me, the audio research was the most compelling. There was evidence shown on Discovery Channel in 2003, last July there was a recording up around Scotch Bonnet near Button Bay, and there have been other research teams that have documented audio recordings. Back in 1993, a Japanese team searched the entire lake with fifteen boats and multiple helicopters. They came back with a sonar report of a huge object, about twenty feet long, passing under them," said Carson.

"All of those things suggest something is out there. It may not be what people think of as Champ, but it is something substantial. Captain Dandy laid the scuba gear on a bench on the deck of the boat.

"You guys need to be careful when you are diving tonight. I mentioned before the lake has deep channels that create seiches. With that, it can take you by surprise. The weather temperature changes in the spring and fall affect the shallow areas of these long lakes more rapidly than they affect the deep channels, causing the deep water to slosh back and forth, between the lake's boundaries. At the surface, the seiche in Lake Champlain may be barely a ripple while below the surface it can be about thirty feet high and at times may grow to a height of three hundred feet. If it's strong tonight you could get swept away without us being able to help or maybe even knowing you're in trouble," the Captain warned.

"There are also shipwrecks under there. More than three hundred confirmed shipwrecks in the lake. Easy to get caught in because the water may not be that clear under the surface. There is a lot of algae that reduces visibility. Small seiches less than a foot high are an everyday occurrence on the lake. Hopefully, we will be in business and able to dive. If the seiches are too big, it can clash ships together in harbors, snap mooring lines, and swamp fishing boats. That could be what happened with some of those boats now resting under the water. The conditions, the winds, and pressure differences are present to make them fairly common. But most of them are insignificant. We'll take some readings before you attempt to go in," he continued.

The equipment began collecting data on the lake conditions: temperature, depth, and wave activity were among the essential data for Carson and Ty. The underwater microphones detected no movement, and the fishfinder remained predominately inactive. After searching the bay for nearly an hour, the Captain determined the area was dead and suggested they move to the other location. Carson and Ty agreed and headed into the cabin as the rainfall began to intensify slightly.

It was after 10 p.m. when the boat arrived at Thompson's Point. Carson liked the location of this search because of the closeness to Split Rock Mountain, where many prior sightings occurred in the past, and some felt the shape of the rocks potentially gave some explanation to the sightings. Additionally, it was close to Kingsland Bay State Park where the young girl was attacked. It would seem this triangle could provide excellent opportunity to find the animal, given not only the sightings but the depth of the lake in this area.

Kareem and Tegan monitored the size of the underwater currents and turned toward Ty and Carson giving a thumbs up. The rain had was no more than a light drizzle here and did not provide a hindrance to working on the deck. After completing a final equipment check, Carson and Ty nodded to each other and prepared to begin the underwater search. Carson clicked a button on his head-mounted GoPro to start recording, and each man grabbed a dive light. They sat on the edge of the boat, and when the Captain gave the signal, they rolled backward into the cold water of the lake.

Slowly getting acclimated to the water, they were able to gradually swim down past one hundred feet to cruise along a ledge that dropped deeper into the lake. It was pretty dark at that depth and visibility was minimal, but the bright light from the dive lights helped illuminate the way.

As they went along with their dive lights, they started to find old bottles strewn along the bottom. The Captain said there were a lot of shipwrecks in the lake and there were undoubtedly many other objects under the water. Even though some ships had been underwater for over a hundred years, most were remarkably well-preserved. The cold fresh waters of Lake Champlain served to preserve the old wooden ships, unlike the ocean where currents and living creatures would quickly eat their way through a wooden vessel.

As Carson and Ty continued to search under the lake's surface for any signs of the animal, they only found the wreckage of an old wooden ship - a schooner-rigged canal boat. That was a sailing cargo boat designed to fit through the canals and locks to bring cargo up and down the Hudson River from as far away as New York City into Lake Champlain.

The size of the locks determined the size of the boats and because of this archeologists were able to identify the age of the ship from its size. As time went on, the locks grew bigger to bring through larger ships laden with cargo. This particular boat reportedly went down in a storm in 1895 carrying a heavy load of bricks and tiles. The light from the dive light shone across the wreckage, illuminating it in a golden glow. The ship's wheel and aft cabin hatch cover were still intact as the boat became visible, as well as tiles, bricks, bottles, and other artifacts.

Despite the relatively mild underwater current, they discovered good buoyancy control was mandatory to avoid running into and damaging the fragile structures on the boat as well as preventing touching the bottom and kicking up a cloud of silt. At their depth, some light still filtered down from above, but the flashlight was needed to identify and take in the details of the submerged ship. Carson felt this would be an enjoyable dive if they were still there for vacation and the sake of enjoying the activity, but they were not. They were searching for an underwater creature that had recently acted out of character and began allegedly attacking those who entered the water.

Ty pointed to the back of the ship, communicating through hand signals that he was going to explore the end of the wreck. Carson responded with a thumbs up and examined the front of the vessel. Nothing unusual was found except an unexpectedly low number of fish in the area. Carson and Ty met up on the other side of the boat, and Carson gave a signal pointing up to return to the surface.

On the deck of the boat, Kareem and Tegan continued to monitor data. All was quiet above the surface. Just as peaceful as the search was yesterday. Kareem looked over the equipment as the data continued to record. The underwater wave activity had increased slightly but was still relatively natural. A pod of fish appeared on the fish finder; a small school, but more fish than they had spotted so far in the lake.

Carson and Ty bobbed on the surface of the lake, removing their masks to catch a good breathe and talk to each other about the next plan in their quest. They looked around in darkness at the lake. Captain Dandy and the boat were not too far from their location, and they were able to signal to each other and give a thumbs up. Carson and Ty decided to return to the shipwreck below then travel south to some of the deepest parts of the lake, and where underwater caverns were speculated to exist in those deep valleys. Caverns that had not yet been explored, per Captain Dandy's earlier accounts.

As the duo descended back to the ship, the school of fish Kareem spotted on the finder passed. Carson thought it was exciting to encounter fish and get a glimpse of an entire underwater world that most people never experience. He also enjoyed the sighting because as much as the lake had been a favorite fishing destination until now, they had not encountered a group of fish that surpassed five or six in number. This group was only about ten to twelve bass, but it was a sizeable increase from what they had been observing. Back on the boat, Kareem noticed a large object on the fish finder moving quickly behind the school of fish he previously saw.

"Hey, Tegan. Come check this out. That's weird, huh? It seems to be a living creature and moving quickly. What could be that size down there?" he asked.

"Wow, I don't know. That is big. Looks to be about fifteen or twenty feet on the device. The currents are steady, so I don't think it's a log or other debris that churned up," she said as she continued to stare at the display.

Carson turned around to watch the fish swim by unaware that the object Kareem and Tegan were watching on the monitor was rapidly approaching from behind. Ty was about twenty yards away when he caught movement from the corner of his eye. A large object moved passed quickly and silently, but it was big enough and powerful enough that the waves rippled underwater as it moved. Waves that pushed back on Ty enough to propel him closer to the hull of the shipwreck. Ty attempted to motion to Carson, but his back was turned, and he did not notice.

After the fish disappeared into the darkness, Carson happened to turn around slowly as the object drew closer. It appeared to be a dark gray color underwater with a large head that resembled a giant turtle or dragon and a long neck. Rapidly approaching him, the creature opened its mouth and let out a high-pitched sound, almost like an underwater roar. With only a split second to react Carson screamed out of sheer surprise seeing the creature directly in front of him, jaws wide. He spun to the left, narrowly avoiding the large open mouth. He saw its large body pass by, appearing to have multiple spikey humps, and four flippers. It was difficult to get a good glimpse because of the speed of the creature and the surprise leaving Carson little time to shine the flashlight on it.

Sensing a disturbance in the water, the fish in the pod turned and swam back toward the wreckage. As Carson turned to right himself in the water, he looked up to see the large underwater animal swimming back toward him. His eyes widened, and he panicked as he felt the giant beast prepare for another attempted attack. He knew that he would be unable to outswim the creature and he was doomed to an attack. He shone the light at the monster and once again saw its large mouth open swimming toward him. The light gave a better view of the creature, its giant head, large sharp teeth, and spikes that Carson imagined would be quite painful. It appeared to be a sizeable snake-like creature and very agile for its size.

Just as Carson thought he was about to become its next victim, the animal dipped below Carson and passed him over, but close enough to knock him out of the way and to feel the force of the massive spikes on its back. Just as he imagined, the spikes were hard and cut into his upper leg and hip as the creature attempted to avoid the underwater diver. Carson screamed in pain as the wound opened and a stream of black blood began to spill into the lake. Ty headed over quickly to his friend, secured him in his embrace, and headed to the surface. The creature disappeared into the darkness as suddenly as it had appeared.

Ty and Carson reached the surface, and both immediately removed their mask and gasped for air. Carson winced as his leg continued to bleed. The colder temperatures, adrenalin rush from the encounter, and the injury to his leg left Carson fatigued. Ty was able to signal the Captain to their location. The Captained turned the spotlight on Ty while he swam toward the boat, dragged Carson with him as he continued to bleed. "Good thing this isn't where they filmed Jaws," Ty said. Kareem, Tegan, and the Captain helped get Carson aboard the boat and laid him on the deck. His suit ripped by the animal's spiked back. The wound was open, and his hip was red with blood. The Captain had a medical kit onboard that Tegan frantically grabbed while the guys attended to Carson.

"What the hell happened down there?" asked the Captain excitedly. Ty told him about the creature, even though he only got a quick glimpse as it passed by and headed toward Carson.

"We've got to get the bleeding stopped and get him to a hospital," said Kareem. Tegan washed the wound thoroughly with clean, fresh water, let it air, and repeated the process. Then she dried the wound with a towel from the cabin, applied antibiotic cream, and wrapped it in gauze. As they headed toward the shore, Kareem called to the paramedics for transport to University of Vermont Medical Center in Burlington. It was just over sixteen miles away, but the closest option for medical attention.

Everyone was surprised that Carson had survived the creature's attack. An animal of that size with the ability to move stealthfully at rapid speeds underwater would easily defeat a man, especially one who didn't know he was under attack until it was too late. Carson struggled to speak as the pain increased now that he was on land and the lake's temperature was not keeping the throbbing and pain to a reduced level.

"You're right," he said painfully. "But I don't think it was trying to attack me." He took a deep breath and thought back on the incident. "That thing could have easily done more to me than scrape my leg. It was hungry alright, but it was after those fish that passed by. It was pursuing them, and I just happened to be in the way, then when they turned and headed back to the boat, it circled back. I thought it was attacking me, missed, and then was coming back to finish the job, but it was just trying to catch the fish, and I was again in the line of fire," he said.

The paramedics were already waiting at the Point Bay Marina when the boat arrived. They quickly embarked and secured Carson to a stretcher. They praised the group for acting swiftly and dressing the wound to help reduce the risk of infection.

"He will probably need some stitches and another good cleaning, but he will be okay," said one of the paramedics. They removed him from the boat. Tegan went with him to the hospital while Kareem and Ty stayed with the Captain.

"Well...I guess we know he's real. Whatcha say?" said Captain Dandy.

"That Indrid Cole did tell us it was real," said Ty. "I just didn't expect to find out like that."

The Captain reached down and removed the SD card from the computer.

"Here's the data the equipment collected. I don't know if it will do you any good since you saw the creature, but just in case. What are you going to do now?" asked the Captain. Ty took the card from the Captain and put it in his pocket.

"Now? I don't know. We know there is a creature. We don't know exactly what that creature is and we don't know why it is attacking dogs and children. So I guess that is the next piece of the puzzle. We will look at the data and the videos to see if it helps answer those questions," replied Ty. He reached into his wallet and removed four one hundred dollar bills for the Captain. "Well, thanks for the ride...," Ty said. "We'll catch a ride down to the car."

The Captain prepared the boat for the return to his home marina while Ty used his phone to order an Uber for the ride back to Crown Point.

"Shit," he said a few seconds later as he hit cancel on the app.

"What's wrong?" asked Kareem. He gave Kareem a mystified look,

"Carson's got the keys." He returned to the app, changed the drop off location to the University Medical Center, and waited.

16 AN INCONVENIENT TRUTH

Saturday, October 10, 2015

Just after 5:30 a.m. when Carson was released from the hospital. Ty and Kareem arrived at the hospital, received the keys from Tegan, and took an Uber back to the car. Now they were back and ready to pick up their friend. It was a long night that continued into the next day, with no sleep for anyone thanks to the encounter with the creature in the lake the night before.

"How you feelin', Hoss?" asked Ty.

"Not as bad as you'd think. The doc cleaned me up, stitched me up pretty good, and gave me some pain pills to keep my mind off it," Carson said in a voice groggy from fatigue.

"So, how'd the night turn out?" asked Carson.

"We received the data from Captain Dandy. We are going to drop it off at the university this morning with Dr. Thomas and Dr. Howard. Maybe they can run some analysis on it and see what's happening there in the lake," said Ty. "Let's blow this popsicle stand," he said.

"We can stop by the university on the way back to the hotel. I texted Dr. Howard already and he said he will be there around 8 a.m. and should be able to look at the data today. I also have the SD card from your GoPro. Maybe your camera captured the animal."

"Let's hope so. I didn't get a good look at it in the heat of the moment," said Carson. "One good thing is the university is right across the street so that we can drop off the cards at Dr. Howard's office. He said he has a drop box right outside his office. We can leave it there, and he will jump on it as soon as he gets in this morning. Being a local historian he is really excited to see what we captured," replied Ty.

Carson stood up, slipped his jeans on under his hospital gown, and then removed the gown.

"Hand me my shirt?" he asked Kareem. He reached for the t-shirt and slipped it on, tossing the gown on the bed. "Let's roll. After we drop off the cards, maybe we can get breakfast. Fighting with a lake monster worked up my appetite," Carson said.

"If we picked up some decent footage on the GoPro maybe we can submit it to When Vacations Attack…" Ty responded.

It was a short walk from the university and Dr. Howard's office, but even that distance caused the pain in Carson's leg to increase. He was able to walk, but at a much slower than usual pace and with a noticeable limp. He was glad when they made it to the office and to find Dr. Howard had a small plastic chair sitting outside his door.

"I need a few minutes, guys," he said as he bent over, took hold of the armrest, and slowly sat down. As Carson sat, Ty found a blank piece of paper in the doctor's drop box and borrowed a pen from Tegan to write a note and leave his number. He wrapped the paper around the two SD cards and dropped it in the box. "That should do it," he said. "Let's eat!"

"Why don't you wait here, Carson, and I will bring the car around?" said Kareem. "There are a few breakfast places close by, but too far for you to walk with that hip."

"I won't argue with that," said Carson. Kareem left the science building and jogged over to the parking lot to get the car. Moments later he was back in front of the medical center. Carson, Tegan, and Ty had moved outside to await his arrival.

"There's a place just over off Main Street called The Skinny Pancake. They open at 8 a.m., but it's a popular place that draws a big line so we can get there now and be among the first," suggested Kareem.

A parking lot just off University Heights led to the building housing The Skinny Pancake. Not quite open, there were already a couple of people waiting.

"I hope Dr. Howard can determine why Champ has been increasingly aggressive," said Tegan. "If word gets circulating that it has become dangerous, that will be a huge hit for the local economy."

"Not only why, but what can be done to stop it," added Ty.

"Just think we were this close to writing it off as fantasy," Carson said as he reached down and rubbed his hip as the throbbing increased at the mention of the animal. Moments later the restaurant door unlocked and a young lady stepped out to welcome those waiting. Carson slowly pushed himself up from an outside chair and hobbled inside with the others.

A young woman in her mid-twenties with her blonde hair pulled back in ponytail sat them at a table near the door.

"Is this okay? Being up here in the front? We also have plenty of seating outside" asked Shelby North.

"Yes, this will be fine," replied Carson as he winced from pain due to the recent walk.

"Ooh, are you okay? What happened?" she asked.

"Uh…minor fishing accident," replied Carson.

"Well, I hope it's not too bad. You guys place your order at the cashier. It should be out in a jiffy since we are just opening," Shelby said.

The menu was written on the giant chalkboard over the register and offered a large variety of breakfast options including hash browns, bagels, English muffin sandwiches, but the house specialty were the crepes. Carson looked over the menu, then quickly made his selection.

"That was easy," he said. He was quickly at the front of the line and placed his order with the cashier. "I am going with the Sassquash." He turned back toward his friends, "How can I pass that up? A savory crepe with locally roasted squash puree, Vermont apples, spinach and Vermont chevre."

"Hmm. Sounds good, brother. But I will one-up you," said Ty. He stepped up to the register and ordered The Crepedilla. "That sounds like a monster - black beans, pico de gallo, and Cabot cheddar wrapped in a scallion crepe and served with a side of chipotle Cabot sour cream. Almost sounds like a bit of Texas," replied Ty.

"Speaking of monster, that Veggie Monster sounds good with the fresh spinach, roasted red peppers, caramelized onions, basil-sunflower pesto and Cabot cheddar," Kareem said to the cashier as well as his friends. Following his order, Tegan stepped up.

"And a Jonny Crepe for me," said Tegan; a slow braised local pulled pork with sweet maple barbeque sauce, caramelized onions and Cabot cheddar with a side of local root vegetable slaw.

With the orders completed, they returned to the table.

"After breakfast, we should head back to the hotel and try to get some sleep," suggested Tegan. "It's been a long time for all of us. Some more than others," she said looking at Carson and trying to estimate his level of pain.

About fifteen minutes later the air suddenly smelled of bacon, pulled pork, cooked batter, and eggs as Shelby brought the food to their table and other nearby tables also began receiving their orders. The smells created a comfortable, homey feeling that eased the pain in Carson's hip.

"Enjoy," she said with a smile."

"Oh my God, this is so good," said Carson. Tegan agreed as she picked up the Johnny Crepe and dipped it in the maple barbeque sauce, her eyes widened with enjoyment at the first savory bite.

"I feel like I would move here just for these crepes," she said with a mouthful. "Jesus, they have a beer bar with Heady and a nice overall assortment of Vermont craft beers here too," said Ty. "I might move with you!"

After finishing their meal, the group didn't stay long. The line stretched beyond the front door provided some intimidation that their seats were already eagerly anticipated and in high demand.

"Now that my belly is full, I am ready to go back to the hotel, take a pain pill, and catch some Z's," said Carson. Kareem offered to drive and let Carson rest in the back seat. "Later we should start gathering our shit. We are supposed to fly back to Texas late tomorrow night," said Carson.

Arriving back at the hotel Carson beat Ty into the room. He took a swig of water from a plastic bottle on the nightstand, took a pill, and climbed under the sheets by the time Ty was just entering the room.

"Good night, John-Boy," Carson called out as he closed his eyes and rolled over. The prescription kicked in and almost immediately Carson was asleep. It wouldn't take long for the others to also fall asleep without the aid of medication. The sheer rush of excitement and lack of sleep from the day before did the job well enough.

Their slumber was cut to about four hours when the silence was broken up by the ring of Ty's phone. It was Dr. Howard calling with the results of his analysis of the data.

"Uh...hello?" Ty answered faintly, his consciousness still somewhere between the dream realm and reality.

"Good afternoon, Ty. It's Dr. Howard. I worked with Dr. Thomas this morning on the data you dropped off. He was very interested as well. Say, do you have time to meet up and go over the findings?"

"Uh, yeah – Yes...we can meet up," said Ty, his senses slowly coming back to him as he sat up in bed.

"Great! What do you say about 2:00 over in my library?" asked Dr. Howard.

"Yes, that will be fine. Is it the same as the main library on campus?" asked Ty.

"No, this one is in the science building. Kind of our own personal library; Dr. Thomas and I. It's on the same floor as our office," he said.

"Sure. We can find it. See you in a few minutes, Doc," replied Ty.

He moved to the edge of the bed, still sitting up. He flexed his shoulders back and rubbed the sleep from his eyes, then passed his hand across the top of his head. He stood up, walked over to Carson who had just rolled over on his side, and gave him a hard slap on his shoulder.

"You're lucky you're hurt. That was going to be your ass," he said.

"Five more minutes, Mom," Carson talked into the pillow still half asleep.

Arriving at the campus, the group made its way through the science building, down the hall past the faculty offices, and to a door marked "Employees Only," which per Dr. Howard's text, was the correct room. Ty opened the door and looked around as they entered.

"Seems to be the place," he said. "Dr. Howard said they are inside waiting for us."

The thick smell of aging paper filled the narrow spaces between each bookcase filled with books, some vertical and some horizontally placed on the shelves. A large table with a computer, stacks of more books and newspapers, and other cluttered remnants of academia lay on the table. There they found Dr. Howard and Dr. Tanner looking at readings in front of the computer monitor.

Dr. Howard looked up, "Welcome to our private lair as it were," he said.

"Quite the place you've got here," said Carson.

"We find it is a nice place to disappear into our research. Mostly quiet back here. The sign on the door keeps most people out." He looked over the group.

191

"Glad to see you all again. I see you made it out in one piece...mostly," he said as he focused on Carson whose injury was apparent even through the jeans.

"Just a run in with one of the locals," said Carson.

"We were excited to look at the data you dropped off, Ty. Some solid evidence on here, both analytically and video. Safe to say we can answer the question 'Is Champ real?'" he said.

"Check," said Carson as he motioned an invisible checkmark in the air.

"Right. So now that we know it's a real animal, one question is what is it? Another question is if the historical sightings are accurate, and there haven't been previous attacks on people or other land animals, why has that changed. Carson, do you think the animal was attacking you?" asked Dr. Howard.

"It happened very fast, and it was dark down there. I turned around and just saw a big mouth and sharp teeth coming at me...but later thinking about it I don't think it was me that it was after. There were some fish in the area, and I think it was hungry," replied Carson.

"We do think fish are its primary diet," said Dr. Tanner. "One interesting thing we noted in the data from the fishfinder is there were a very low number of fish spotted in the lake during the whole trip up the lake. And that would make sense. There were reports of a winter-kill situation last year that left the lake depleted of many varieties of fish."

"What is a kill situation?" asked Tegan.

"Fish kills are natural occurrences that happen for a variety of reasons. Infectious diseases and parasites can also lead to fish kill. Toxicity is a real but far less common cause of fish kill. But fish kills are often the first visible signs of environmental stress. They are usually investigated as a matter of urgency by environmental agencies to determine the cause of the kill, and I haven't seen any reports on conclusive investigations into ours yet," said Dr. Howard.

"Environmental stress? Like what?" asked Kareem.

"Many fish species have a relatively low tolerance of variations in environmental conditions and their death is often a potent indicator of problems in their environment that may be affecting other animals and plants and may have a direct impact on other uses of the water such as for drinking water production. Pollution events may affect fish species and fish age classes in different ways. If it is a cold-related fish kill, juvenile fish or species that are not cold-tolerant may be selectively affected. If toxicity is the cause, species are more generally affected, and the event may include amphibians and shellfish as well. A reduction in dissolved oxygen may affect larger specimens more than smaller fish as these may be able to access oxygen richer water at the surface, at least for a short time," replied Dr. Tanner.

"But we were able to pick get some other data from your research. We measured the analyzed the temperature of the lake and compared it to prior measurements, not only in Lake Champlain, but we tapped into some other research being conducted around the world," Dr. Tanner explained.

"Yes, when we talk about environmental stress, temperature exerts a major influence on biological activity and growth. Temperature governs the kinds of organisms that can live in rivers and lakes. Fish, insects, zooplankton, phytoplankton, and other aquatic species all have a preferred temperature range. As temperatures get too far above or below this preferred range, the number of individuals of the species decreases until finally there are none. Temperature is also important because of its influence on water chemistry," said Dr. Howard.

"What does the water chemistry have to do with the lake and its inhabitants?" asked Carson.

"One such effect is the displacement of cold-water species. As air temperatures rise, water temperatures also do—particularly in shallow stretches of rivers and surface waters of lakes. Streams and lakes may become unsuitable for cold-water fish but support species that thrive in warmer waters. It can also create dead zones. In a warming climate, a warmer upper layer in deep lakes slows down air exchange—a process that normally adds oxygen to the water. This, in turn, often creates large dead zones—those are areas depleted of oxygen and unable to support life. Persistent dead zones can produce toxic algal blooms, foul-smelling drinking water, and massive fish kills," Dr. Howard replied.

"Freshwater ecosystems have been critical to sustaining life and establishing civilizations throughout history. Humans rely on freshwater systems not only for drinking water, but also for agriculture, transportation, energy production, industrial processes, waste disposal, and the extraction of fish and other products. Those are big things here in Vermont especially. As a result of this dependence, human settlements worldwide are concentrated near freshwater ecosystems, with over half of the world's population living within twenty miles of a permanent river," said Dr. Tanner.

"There have been several studies on the impact of rising temperatures on bodies of water, and freshwater lakes such as Lake Champlain provide a good testing ground. Just last week the Lake Champlain Basin Program and New England Interstate Water Pollution Control Commission released their final report regarding the study of climate change and stormwater management in the Lake Champlain Basin. The study stated the effects of a changing climate have been and continue to be observed in the Lake Champlain Basin. And since the 1970s, there have been notable increases in air and lake temperatures, with the rate of increase progressing more quickly over time. Human activities within the last century have led to a dramatic rise in atmospheric concentrations of carbon dioxide and other gases that contribute to the greenhouse effect. Within the next century, carbon dioxide concentrations are expected to rise to levels at least twice as high as those present in pre-industrial times, and global climate is expected to change in some ways as a result. This climate change will primarily affect freshwater ecosystems through changes in water temperature, quantity, and quality. The fishing industry is important here not only for local consumption, but it is part of the tourism industry as people travel here specifically to book those charter fishing trips. A loss of fish can bring that to a halt," said Dr. Tanner. "Lake ecology can be extremely temperature-sensitive. A small change in temperature can have quite a dramatic effect."

"What's interesting is that while humans rely on freshwater systems, they are also responsible for damaging that system. There is widespread consensus that the greenhouse effect will lead to a global rise in air temperature," replied Dr. Tanner.

"You mean global warming and climate change?" asked Kareem.

"Yes. Scientists estimate changes in the mean surface temperatures are increasing 1.5 to 5.8 degrees Celsius by the year 2100. The temperature increases are expected to vary based on factors such as latitude and lake depth. Temperatures are expected to increase more at higher latitudes, and in many of these regions, the effects of global warming have already been documented. In Canada for example, mean air temperatures, water temperatures, and evaporation have all increased in the past twenty to thirty years, and ice cover durations over lakes and rivers have decreased over the entire northern hemisphere by almost twenty days since the mid-1800's. Here we have seen fewer days below freezing, and it has taken longer into the winter for the lake to freeze over, and when it does, it thaws earlier in the spring than I remember from even my childhood," said Dr. Howard.

"The number of days that Vermont experiences freezing temperatures are down twenty percent since the 1940s. This is not surprising, since nine out of ten of the warmest years on record in the Vermont and Quebec portions of the basin were between 1990 and 2012, with 2012 recorded as the warmest year on record."

"We looked at some global trends and compared your lake findings to what has been seen elsewhere. One interesting study used satellite measurements provide a broad view of lake temperatures over the entire globe, but there are limitations. They only measure surface temperature, while ground measurements can detect temperature changes throughout a lake. Also, while satellite measurements go back thirty years, some lake measurements go back more than a century. But combining the ground and satellite measurements provides the most comprehensive view of how lake temperatures are changing around the world," Dr. Tanner said.

"Using satellite data, the findings indicated many lake temperatures were warming faster than air temperature and that the greatest warming was observed at high latitudes. Your new research confirmed those observations, with average warming rates of 1.3 degrees Fahrenheit compared to prior numbers collected in the lake over the past several decades," said Dr. Howard. "These results suggest that large changes in our lakes are not only unavoidable but are probably already happening," added Dr. Tanner. "When temperatures swing quickly and widely from the norm, life forms in a lake can change dramatically and even disappear," he continued.

"And that decline in life forms, er fish…is due to increased water temperature? Captain Dandy said there were less fish that he saw on his fishing expeditions, and we didn't see many when we were in the lake," said Ty.

"Yes – and as we mentioned, fish is the primary diet of the animal. It seems Champ has become more aggressive due to diet. Global warming is impacting the temperature of the lake and killing off fish that it normally eats. Therefore he has to find something else to eat," replied Dr. Howard.

"This isn't just something happening here at Lake Champlain," added Dr. Tanner. "Globally, observations show that many lakes are heating up. In eastern Africa, Lake Tanganyika is warming relatively slowly, but its fish populations are plummeting, leaving people with less to eat. In the U.S. Upper Midwest, quicker-warming lakes are experiencing shifts in the relative abundance of fish species that support a billion-dollar-plus recreational industry."

The group looked at each other and tried to take in all of the information.

"That is a big economic hit. It's something we don't think about unless we are watching those shows like The Biggest Catch, but fishing is a vital commercial industry, not to mention the recreational appeal and tourism dollars it brings in," said Ty.

"By some estimates, cold-water fish in North America — salmon and trout, for example — could lose as much as half their suitable habitat if average global temperatures increase by eight degrees Fahrenheit," responded Dr. Tanner.

"We can look at it simply as the hotter the air above a lake, the hotter the waters get, and the effect that alone has on the fish population, but it's more than that. As warming rates increase over the next century, some estimates as much as twenty percent in lakes, algae blooms, which can rob water of oxygen. Algae blooms that are toxic to fish and animals are expected to increase by five percent. Emissions of methane, a greenhouse gas twenty-five times more powerful than carbon dioxide on one hundred-year time scales, will increase four percent over the next decade if these measured rates continue," added Dr. Howard.

"Have there been other lakes where the impact on the fish has been observed and studied?" asked Tegan.

"Yes, one similar to Vermont was conducted in Wisconsin. They have a large recreational freshwater fishing industry of more than one point five billion dollars annually. Back in 2000, fishermen and biologists began reporting that walleye numbers seemed to be dropping – much like we are seeing here now," said Dr. Tanner. "Researchers analyzed water temperatures in more than twenty-one-hundred Wisconsin lakes from 1989 to 2014 hoping to figure out why the walleye were disappearing. Some of these lakes had seen populations of walleye drop but also indicated populations of largemouth bass increased. Largemouth bass are also popular catches, although not as popular as walleye," he added.

"What did they find with the walleye study?" asked Carson.

"The scientists simulated how lake temperatures would probably rise through the year 2089 and how that might affect walleye survival in the state's lakes. The team used a measure that describes whether walleye could spawn and their young can survive in a particular environment, compared with the relative abundance of largemouth bass. Up to seventy-five percent of the lakes studied would no longer be able to support young walleye by 2089, while the number of lakes that could support bass could increase by sixty percent. Bass and walleye seem to be responding to the same temperature threshold but in opposite directions," Dr. Tanner reported.

"Okay, so we know Champ is real, and we know the lake temperature has been rising and may be responsible for the fish kill which has reduced the fish population normally in Champ's diet. Because food is scarce, he is hungry, and he is eating whatever he can find. Dogs, kids, me…" said Carson.

"Correct," said Dr. Howard.

"So in our list of earlier questions, how do we stop it?" asked Ty.

"What if they could find other types of fish that could live in the warmer waters? Introduce them to the lake, and he can go back to eating the fish," suggested Tegan.

The doctors looked at each other and considered the question. "Climate change is beginning to impact cold-water fish. Cold-water fish kills in Minnesota lakes have been reported in the summer of 2006 and again in 2012. As the water in the lakes warms, living space for cold-water fish is lost. Fish respond to water temperature change differently, depending on whether they are adapted to cold, cool, or warm water. So, that might work as a short-term solution. Obviously, longer-term options such as policy changes and reversing damage to the lake will require more drastic measures. Observations of temperature in the Lake Champlain Basin and the surrounding region indicate that air temperatures have been rising for more than a century. Meteorological data from the Global Historical Climatology Network indicates that average temperature in the Vermont and Quebec portion of the basin has been increasing by approximately 0.34 degrees Fahrenheit per decade since 1958. Their analysis suggests that temperature is warming faster in recent years: from 1990 to 2012 the average lowland temperature increased by one and a half degrees Fahrenheit per decade, while the average highland temperature increased by one point eight degrees per decade. But in the meantime, adding more fish that can survive in warmer temperatures could stop the animal from attacking things typically not in its diet. As you said, Carson, the animal attacked you not because it was attempting to eat you, but because you were in the way and there were fish in the area. It probably hadn't seen that many fish together for some time, and that's why it aggressively pursued. Otherwise, it wouldn't have attacked you, because from the video, at that range, it certainly could have if it wanted to do so," said Dr. Howard.

"Sounds like it all makes sense, but where do we get fish? It's not as simple as restocking a local fishing pond. Lake Champlain is a huge area to repopulate," said Ty.

"The Lake Champlain Fisheries Technical Committee, a sub-committee of the Lake Champlain Fish and Wildlife Management Cooperative is the official body that would have to come up with a new strategic plan for Lake Champlain Fisheries," said Dr. Howard.

"This new plan would have to highlight goals for the fish community and the Lake Champlain fishery, including a framework to develop and guide fishery management programs for the Lake and its tributaries. Also, the new plan should review the history of fishery management in the basin, guiding principles, and develop management actions and information priorities to help management agencies achieve these goals. The actions of the management team would have to be careful with the introduction of new species to the lake. It isn't as simple as adding new fish, and it's all good. They have to work to prevent new introductions of invasive species and suppress current populations of nuisance species. Otherwise, that could have continued negative effects on the fish population," warned Dr. Tanner.

"Specifically where to get fish, there are five fish hatcheries or fish culture stations that operate in the Lake Champlain Basin. These operations help to rehabilitate fish populations and expand the range of desirable fish. New York DEC, Vermont Fish and Wildlife

Department, and the US Fish and Wildlife Service all maintain fish stocking programs in Lake Champlain and its tributaries, including rainbow trout, lake trout, brown trout, and landlocked Atlantic salmon. Several of the hatcheries are open to the public. Based on the results of that walleye study in Wisconsin, largemouth bass might be the best option. There are already a lot of bass in the lake, and the Wisconsin research showed they thrived as water temperatures increased," suggested Dr. Howard.

"I would suggest contacting some of the fisheries and seeing what the options are. I have a contact you can speak to at Essex County Fish Hatchery," said Dr. Tanner.

"Stop by? How are we going to order fish for the lake? We don't have that type of ability," asked Carson.

"The University has funding available for research. Dr. Tanner and I can use this as a study to add to the existing body of knowledge. Not only from a climate change perspective, but the local economic impact, and of course the acknowledgment of Champ, bringing it out of the realm of cryptozoology and into an identified scientific study," said Dr. Howard.

"I have a connection to the governor's office and can make that call," said Dr. Tanner.

"The published study will generate the needed attention that will help bring long-term change. Of course, we will also name you guys as contributors to the study. Can you believe that? First the chupacabra and now Champ? You guys will soon be in high demand," added Dr. Howard.

"Great...we are already busy with the attention from San Antonio," said Ty.

"Okay, we can stop by and talk to your guy at the fish hatchery. But there's one more question – what is Champ? Can you determine that from the video?" asked Carson.

"From the video alone, no," Dr. Howard said. "But when Ty first contacted me and told me what happened, I reached out to the medical center to see if the doctor could collect any DNA from the wound. He was able to get some skin samples and fragments from the spine – Champ's, not yours. He sent that over to me this morning. We still have to complete the analysis on that. Those results are not ready yet, but we should have an idea soon. The video was quite compelling, and we were able to get good physical features from watching that. I have printed off some still shots if you want to take a look," said Dr. Howard.

"Of course, I'm interested," said Carson.

"Yeah, we are too – we didn't get to see it like he did," said Tegan.

Dr. Howard handed Carson two photos that were printed off from paused video from the GoPro footage. The images were dark, but Carson's flashlight illuminated the creature enough to show the animal's head, teeth, and body. The body was thinner than some prior sightings that reported it to be more barrel-shaped. This looked more serpent-like with large bumps or spikes along the spine. They were surprised at the image on the photos.

"That's incredible. Those are very clear shots despite how quickly you said it happened," said Kareem.

"There's more – if you want to hear an audio clip," said Dr. Tanner. He clicked the mouse and an audio clip that Dr. Tanner had cleaned up and removed some of the distortion played. They heard a high-pitched noise and what sounded like an underwater growl.

"Jesus!" said Ty. "That high-pitched noise may have been Carson screaming, but the other sound is definitely something previously unheard," said Dr. Howard.

"That's amazing," said Tegan. "Thanks for going over all of this with us."

Dr. Howard wrote down a name and number on a sheet of paper and handed it to Carson. "Here. Call Rafferty McCallum over at Essex County. This is his cell phone because he won't be in the office on Saturday. Tell him I sent you. He can get things started. Take care of that hip."

They exchanged handshakes and headed back to the parking lot. "Well, that's some interesting shit, ain't it?" Carson asked.

"Yes, but it sounds like our collected data fit in well with what scientists have been studying already in recent years. Climate change is definitely happening and the numbers back that up. We can see first-hand now what effect that has on the ecosystem right down to a local level and how that impacts many aspects of human life, from the water we drink to the food we eat and even the economic impact," said Ty.

"Yes, we can get a good first-hand feel of that," said Carson as he rubbed his once again throbbing hip.

17 FISHES

Saturday, October 10, 2015

After leaving the university, Kareem drove down to Crown Point where one of the fish hatcheries Dr. Howard provided was located. Rafferty McCallum was the manager of the program and a long-time friend of Dr. Howard. Carson sent him a text as they left Dr. Howard's office. Rafferty wasn't working today but agreed to meet them at the hatchery to discuss the options and give them a tour of the facilities. Living nearby, he was there when they arrived.

"Good morning. Rafferty? I'm Carson – Dr. Howard sent us down to talk to you about a research idea in the lake?" he said.

"Yes, he phoned me and discussed the problem at hand. It's worth exploring, although it sounds like a short-term solution. But we're glad to help any way we can," Rafferty said. They walked with him down a gravel path toward the main offices.

" This is a big place you have here," said Ty. "How long has it been operational?"

"Essex County assumed ownership of the state fish hatchery in Crown Point back in 1982 and has already been providing a program where it stocked yearling brook, brown, and rainbow trout in roughly sixty-five bodies of water in Essex County," Rafferty explained. "Then in 1990, the program transitioned from yearling trout averaging approximately eight inches in length to one that included two-year-old trout typically between twelve and fourteen inches in length. Now we release approximately thirty thousand two-year-old and twenty thousand yearling trout annually," Rafferty said. "But trout won't do well if the water is warming. Studies in California showed rainbow trout in the Stanislaus River, which is one of the country's largest rainbow trout populations declined by seventy-five percent from an average of twenty thousand over the previous six years to just about five thousand fish this year. Increased water temperatures and severe drought in California were factors that led to the decline," he added.

"What are the other options? The rainbow trout will likely face the same fate here that they do in California", said Carson.

"The fisheries in Vermont typically specialize in trout, usually three varieties. There are others that have walleye and salmon, but those are cold-water fish that would have the same issues. The closest place specializing in largemouth bass is Hickling's Fish Farm down in Edmeston, New York. They are the largest bass rearing facility in the northeast. It's about a three-hour drive, but I think they can make the delivery. That can get us started until we can start building a production more locally. If this is going to be an on-going need, that would be the most cost-effective option. We have space here to add capacity for largemouth, smallmouth, and rock bass," Rafferty said.

"We agree this would only be a short-term solution. The leadership in the region will have to determine a better on-going solution," said Carson.

"Ultimately any management strategy for dealing with global climate change will simply buy time until either rapid, anthropogenic climate change ceases or species are no longer able to adapt, and massive extinctions result. Management strategies can only provide long-term protection of freshwater ecosystems if the root causes of climate change are addressed and solutions are enacted on a global scale," Rafferty explained.

As they walked around the grounds of the hatchery, Rafferty noticed Kareem wearing a gray t-shirt with a blue owl logo, reading "Blue Owl Brewing." "Where's that from?" he asked.

"That's a new brewery that just opened in Austin, Texas," replied Kareem.

"Oh yeah? Is that where you all are from?" responded Rafferty.

"Yes, we were just up here to get away and have a peaceful and relaxing trip to Vermont to enjoy the leaves and beer," said Carson.

"How's that workin' out for ya?" Rafferty replied.

"Not as planned," replied Carson.

"When are ya headin' back to Texas?"

"Late tomorrow evening," said Carson.

"Well, if you all like local beer I am having a small get together tonight with some friends. Probably watch the National League late game between the Dodgers and Mets. Give you a chance to enjoy some local favorites. Nothing big. Just a few of us, some pizza, some wings, and lots of good Vermont beer," offered Rafferty.

"That sounds pretty good. A lot better send off than Champ gave me," countered Carson.

"I will text you the address. Come whenever you want. We probably won't get started until after seven, but you are welcome anytime," he said.

"That sounds good. We'll see ya there," said Ty.

They walked back to the car happy to at least put the plan in motion to address the situation with Champ, and eagerly anticipated the bottle share later in the evening.

"We can head back to the hotel. I need to clean up the wound, and I wouldn't mind another rest," said Carson.

"Yeah, and we can hit up one of those packies near the hotel and bring some beer to the party," suggested Tegan.

18 DOWN SELLA

Saturday, October 10, 2015

Rafferty McCallum was recently divorced and lived alone in a beautiful house off Lake Road in Crown Point, New York. It was a massive four-bedroom, five-bath raised ranch-style home sitting on nearly eight acres. Rafferty was an outdoorsy, rugged man in his mid-forties, with close-cut sandy-brown hair, a short maintained beard, broad shoulders, and a husky frame.

Working with the Essex County Fish Hatchery for more than five years, and before that the Vermont Fish and Wildlife Department, Rafferty did enjoy the outdoors and working on a farm. His house sat on three parcels of agricultural land and had separate buildings for horse stalls, chicken coops, a barn, horse/cow stalls, and a pole barn. It also surprised many visitors with its indoor lighted batting cage, fitness center, driving range and putting green. The property included a tranquil pond and raised bed gardens, making it the perfect home for those with horses, chickens and any livestock.

The house was built in 1988, and he worked hard to transform it since he purchased it in 2005, customizing the interior with cedar throughout the home, as well as energy efficient thermopane windows. It indeed was luxury living in the country at a gentleman's farm in the Adirondacks. The finished walkout basement with hot tub added to the luxury of a real man cave that was more than sufficient for the occasional bottle share with friends.

Noticing the time and seeing the first guests arrive, Rafferty had a quick scurryfunge before the doorbell rang. Kareem and the others did not anticipate arriving with the first visitors, but they did. Carson felt somewhat relieved at their time though, as walking in with others would make them stand out a little less than showing up after everyone was already there and in full-swing with the bottle share. Rafferty was happy to see them as he ushered them into the lounging area of the basement and pointed them to two large couches placed in an L-shape around a wooden coffee table. He quickly picked up and moved an old Spider-Man 2099 comic book from the table and replaced it with some paper beer coasters.

"Here you go, make yourself at home, guys," he said. "These are two of my friends, Saige Davenport and Blake Ford. Saige is a blood bank laboratory technologist with the American Red Cross in Burlington, and Blake is a motion study technician with VHB in South Burlington," Rafferty introduced.

"What's VHB?" asked Kareem.

"It stands for Vanasse Hangen Brustlin, Inc. It's a transportation planning, engineering, and design company," Blake said.

Blake was a tall, slender African-American woman with a toasted brown complexion and hair worn in a natural short afro underneath a faded New York Mets baseball cap, her lips dressed with MAC Flat out Fabulous, a purple with a hint of berry color. Saige was an average height full-figured woman with radiant blue eyes, her past shoulder-length hair falling across her shoulders, glowing with mozzarella undertones.

As the introductions were completed, there was a knock at the door. Ellery Hoàng arrived with bottles in hand.

"Greetings! I come bearing excellent beers!" he said joyfully. He hosted the last bottle share event among the friends and was eager for another round. Ellery was a young Vietnamese male about five foot two with a small frame was what some described as a merman, a modern style trend involving guys with dyed hair and beards. A thick, dark black beard with a Pompadour haircut parted just off center; the most extended part dyed white and the shorter piece, yellow.

He wore a small silver hoop earring in each ear. It was apparent that he was innovative and stood out from the crowd, traits that made him successful when after dropping out of college he opened his own ski company and not only designed but hand-crafted customized fiberglass skis for his clients.

"That should keep you very busy here with all of the ski resorts in the winter," said Ty.

"Yes, but not just that. It's all year round. We get into water skis as well, and there are some local tournaments on the lake as well as recreational water skiing," replied Ellery.

Moments later another knock on the door. Two men and a woman stood outside with bottles and one small cardboard box opened from the top.

"Look who we found outside," said Gavin Knight, an athletic clean-shaven handsome man who looked like he walked off the cast of Friends. The white ring of his undershirt visible underneath the sky-blue cashmere sweater that clung to his muscular arms and chest. He soon drew the attention of Tegan as she was mesmerized by his fine, tall-person, handsome features, and his crust of a Shepherd's pie complexion.

Joining him on the front porch was Orson Fletcher, a skinny, mid-forties man who had short black hair, glasses, and a bookish appearance. He was a Terrazzo floor installer and part-time equestrian events judge. Finally, Everleigh Le Mesurier was about five foot six, with long layered ash blonde ombre hair that fell to the middle of her back. She had expressive blue-green eyes, a dimpled smile, and an Estuary English accent.

"Everleigh here is an escalator service mechanic…hell, she's about the best mechanic of anything around here. I take my car to her when I need something fixed on it," said Rafferty.

"She's a cool girl," said Orson. "Brilliant and funny, adores football and soccer, plays poker, tells and enjoys dirty jokes, can hang in a burping contest, plays video games, and drinks craft beer," he added.

"Wow, I'm sold," said Carson extending his hand. She smiled and returned the handshake, her hands small but rough and callused from her line of work.

"I haven't seen you guys at other shares. How do you all know Rafferty?" she asked.

"Actually, we just met earlier today," said Ty. "A mutual friend at the University introduced us to work on a...uh, research project," he added.

"Research project? That sounds pretty cool," Everleigh said.

Meanwhile, Tegan was interested in getting to know Gavin. She smiled and introduced herself.

"Nice to meet you, Tegan," Gavin said with a flirtatious smile. His eyes and warm smile instantly turned her into a giglet. "So, what are you drinking?" he asked.

"Um, nothing yet. You?" she returned.

"I brought a nice selection of Vermont beers. Some of my favorites. What is your style preference?" he asked.

"Normally I prefer Berliner Weisse, but we came here to enjoy the New-England-style IPAs," she said.

"We have some good IPAs. Have you been to The Vermont Pub?" he asked.

"Yes, we just stopped there the other day," she replied.

"Those hazy IPAs are popular right now, but The Vermont Pub was doing hazy IPA as far back as the mid-1990s," he said.

"Wow. I just really started hearing about hazy IPAs recently. The four of us, she said as she pointed to the guys she was with, are from Texas, and my friend Kareem there happened to get some in a trade. So good," she said. "So different than regular IPAs too."

"Yes, they get that from the brewing process," Gavin said. "Some brewers get haze from yeast strains that don't readily fall out of suspension, leaving a ghostly aura. Other breweries say they're using higher-protein malt plus late hop additions, in some wizard-like fashion that keeps hop polyphenols in suspension."

Impressed with his brewing knowledge, her eyes brightened and fluttered, again she uncontrollably smiled, 'You don't say?"

"What are you two doing condiddled over here in the corner?" asked Ty.

"Just discussing hazy IPAs. Are you ready for one?" Gavin asked. "Here, try this beer," he said handing a can to Ty.

"This is from a brewery just down the road in Brandon, Vermont." Ty looked at the white can with the branch of hops printed as the artwork.

"Prospect by Foley Brothers Double IPA? Sounds like something I would like," Ty said as he opened the can. Gavin handed him a snifter, and Ty poured it slowly at an angle. "Looks like you're a pro at that," Gavin said.

"I've had a few in my day," he replied. "I will go enjoy this over there with the others. Let you get back to your discussion," Ty said as he walked away.

Ty walked over and joined Saige and Blake.

"I see you found one of our down the road favorites," said Saige.

"Yes, Gavin hooked me up. It's really smooth. Nice hops, nice tropical fruit – like pineapple," Ty said.

"Yes, that's one of my favorite breweries," said Blake.

"So…Met's fan, huh?" he asked.

"Yes," said Blake. "I grew up watching them and love them. Nice to see them in the playoffs. This is their year I think!"

Rafferty was organizing the food table and making sure everyone had a drink and was enjoying themselves. The groups were intermingling well and seemed like it was time for him to relax and join in the fun now. He grabbed a Lost Galaxy IPA from Lost Nation Brewing and poured it into his glass. He joined Orson and Kareem over by a corner bookshelf.

"Hey, Rafferty. I meant to ask you, what are these things in this small tank on your bookshelf? Some kind of fish from the hatchery?" asked Kareem.

"No, those are brine shrimp, or you might know them as sea monkeys."

"Sea monkeys? I didn't know those were still a thing. I used to see them in comic book ads when I was a kid, but haven't thought about them for years," Kareem replied.

"I've always been interested in them. They are cool creatures. These shrimp live in salt lakes or salt flats, and when the water of the salt lake evaporates, the shrimp go into this state of suspended animation called cryptobiosis. They remain in this protective cyst-like casing until water is added," said Rafferty. "Back when we were little and reading comic books, although I do still read comics, there was this kind of idea that you could sell science to kids or sell them lifeforms that would entertain them from which they could learn about nature. It looked like a pack of powder but turned into something living. I guess it worked because I had them as a kid and I have worked with fish and wildlife my whole adult life," he added.

Kareem drank a double IPA from the can.

"Wow, this Mastermind by Fiddlehead Brewing Company is so juicy. That's what I wanted to experience up here. When Carson said he was coming to New England for a week I immediately wanted to come up even just for the beer," he said.

"Fiddlehead is doing some good things. Their Fiddlehead IPA is great, Second Fiddle, and if you want a lightly tart, refreshing beer I think the Brett On The Dancefloor is an excellent beer," said Rafferty. Orson agreed with the recommendation of Fiddlehead.

"This is another brewery I like, but not from Vermont. I brought it back from a recent trip to Maine," he said. "Baxter Brewing in Lewiston, Maine was a great find on that trip. I brought a few cans with me if you want to try some later. The Stowaway IPA is good, and if you like darker beer I suggest trying the Window Seat Porter or the Phantom Punch Winter Stout."

"Hey everyone, I hope you are enjoying yourselves. Glad to see everyone mingling and enjoying the beers. The pizza is over here on the table, along with some wings. They came from a new place in town called Rockyard Pizza. We've got a collection of beers from around the area in the coolers under the table. We'll pop some of the bottles here in a bit too and pass around so everyone can share. I just went down to Warren recently, so I came back with a bunch of beer from Lawson's. That's probably my absolute favorite right now. It looks like the game is going well with the Mets up 2-0. A couple of home runs in the second inning. Let's go, Mets!" Rafferty said exuberantly.

Saige and Ty walked over to the table to look at the selection of cans. "You have some great beers not only in the region but even locally," said Ty.

"Yes, we do, and it's always growing," she said. The table contained multiple cans of Heady Topper and Focal Banger from The Alchemist. "Everyone now is familiar with these two," she said pointing to the cans, "but they have some other excellent beer too. Like, this one for example," she said as she picked up a can of The Crusher, another citrusy Double IPA with pineapple and grapefruit notes or if you want a mixture of fruity notes butting up with hoppiness dank, their Rapture is another great Imperial IPA," she said.

"I've liked trying the IPAs and saisons up here. I drink those back home, but I am more of a Rauchbier fan, foremost," he said.

"Really? Well, you, my friend, may be in luck," she said." She dug around in the icy waters of a red Igloo cooler under the table and fished out a Crowler of Rauchbier from Liquid Riot Bottling Company in Portland, Maine.

"Here, Blake and I recently went to Portland and brought back some beers. I had this one at the brewery, and it was pretty good, but I am not sure I could do a whole thirty-two ounces. I brought it thinking it would be perfect for a bottle share," she said happily presenting the crowler as if she were 4-H'er presenting a prized show pig.

"What else do we have in that cooler?" asked Gavin as he and Tegan joined up with Ty and Saige.

"Some Substance and some Swish from Bissell Brothers, Maple Brown Ale and Fair Maiden Double IPA by Foley Brothers, some Queen City Brewery Landlady Ale…"

Everleigh immediately walked over and grabbed a bottle of Landlady Ale from the cooler, "That'll be mine, thanks," she said. "Do you know how hard it is to be a good ESB in these parts?" she asked rhetorically.

Saige continued, "There is also a Yorkshire Porter, too"

Everleigh reached for that one as well, "Mine! I can double fist them," she said.

"Alrighty then," said Saige as Ace Ventura… "We also have a lot from Lawson's Finest Liquids." Orson walked up to the group.

"I love what Lawson's is doing. What do we have from them?" he asked Saige.

"Looks like Hopzilla Double IPA, Super Session IPA #2, and of course Sip of Sunshine IPA," she said. Rafferty walked up to the group and presented another offering.

"We also have from Lawson's Finest Liquids, a couple of bottles of this bourbon barrel aged Fayston Maple Imperial Stout. It was aged in Pappy Van Winkle barrels and bottled July 2014. I was saving them for one of these get-togethers," he said happily.

"Wow! That's a nice gem," said Blake. "What else are you hiding back there in your vault?"

"Well, I do have another that I have been saving, and with our new friends here visiting from Texas and bringing a huge opportunity for the fish hatchery, it might be a good time to open it," Rafferty said while everyone wondered in anticipation what it might be. He walked to a small, secluded beer fridge in the far corner of the room. "That's where I keep the good stuff," he said. "I have two bottles of this, vintage 2011. It's a New England craft beer legend, and I've

213

heard from a friend who recently drank a 2008 bottle and said it was still excellent. From our neighbors to the east, New Hampshire, I present Portsmouth Brewery's Kate The Great, a Russian Imperial Stout."

Carson's eyes light up like a Christmas tree hearing the words Russian Imperial Stout.

"I have some five-ounce glasses that will be perfect for sharing these bombers," Rafferty said as he disappeared into the kitchen to retrieve the glassware.

Rafferty brought ten small glasses, used his bottle opener to pop the top on the two bottles, and slowly poured a sample for each person. "Ten of us, we will have to do about four ounces each...so just enough for everyone," he said.

The beer poured a super pitch black with a mixture of beige and cherry cola colored head on top. "You might want to let this warm up a bit. I should have taken it out earlier to warm up. It's still a little cool," he said. He sat the tray of samplers down on the table and cleaned up two empty pizza boxes and a Styrofoam box from one order of the wings.

Carson picked up a glass and took a sniff. A strong sweet smell with waves of chocolate, hints of dark fruits, maybe leather, and a more distant undertone of booze greeted him. His eyes were still gleaming from the anticipation. Unable to wait any longer he took a small, deliberate sip. Molasses, chocolate, and malt with a surprisingly creamy taste it was unbelievable! Very robust flavors of molasses vanilla and some barrel were present. It felt big, velvety, and slick with just a soft level of carbonation.

As he tasted it, he found it effectively masked the alcohol, and there was no hint of the twelve percent ABV. He had to make a conscious effort to slow down on drinking this one so that he can savor it. He took a spot on the couch next to Blake to enjoy the beer and watch the game.

"Holy mother of marmalade!" he said. "This is good. Makes me almost forget about my hip."

"I thought it looked like you were hobbling a little," said Blake.

"What happened?" Carson finished off the sampler and looked at Blake.

"You know Champ?" he said waiting for her reaction.

"Yes, I've heard about it. Never seen it," she said.

"It's real. I have the wound to prove it. I'd show you, but we just met. That would be awkward," he said.

She laughed softly.

"This beer is fantastic! So dark you could probably hold it up to the sun and couldn't see through it. Seriously, like the back of my phone," said Orson. "Sorry I was grumpy earlier," he said to Gavin. "I didn't eat anything all day. Like a plum, really that's it. Just a plum. I am better now after the pizza and beer."

"No, worries. How's the game going?" he asked Orson.

"Looks like the Mets are still up 2-1 in the sixth inning."

Ellery, Kareem, and Everleigh checked out the offerings on the table and in the cooler.

"Ellery picked up a Summer Session #2, while Everleigh was nearing the end of the Yorkshire Porter from earlier. Kareem reached into the cooler and pulled out a Magic Hat #9.

"Nice, it's been a long time since I've had one of these," he said.

"That's a pretty good beer. Nice place they have. Really great tour and spot to fill growlers," responded Everleigh.

"Magic Hat Brewery has been a staple of the Burlington beer scene since 1994," said Ellery.

"Speaking from my own experience, for many, the Magic Hat #9 was an introduction and somewhat of a pioneer in the craft beer scene across the country. I think it was one of the earliest brews to have a wide distribution," Kareem replied.

Everyone's attention suddenly turned to the game as a controversial play occurred, affecting the score. Down 2-1 in the seventh inning with one out and runners at the corners, a ground ball up the middle by Howie Kendrick turned into a force play at second base. Any chance of a double play ended when shortstop Ruben

Tejada got turned around while accepting the feed from the second baseman Daniel Murphy. Chase Utley executed a hard, late takeout slide, undercutting the fielder as the tying run scored.

Utley had no chance at touching second base, which could have resulted in an inning-ending double play awarded by the umpires, negating the tying run. Instead, the play was reviewed, and Tejada was ruled to have not touched second base, so Utley, who walked off the field, was ruled safe.

"Are you kidding me?!" yelled Rafferty at the television screen. The group continued to watch in disbelief as Tejada could not walk off the field on his own power. He was ultimately carted off, having suffered a broken right fibula on the play. That was the opening the Dodgers needed to change momentum in the game. Adrian Gonzalez delivered the tie-breaking double into the right-field corner to score two runs, and moments later Justin Turner followed with another double, his second straight multi-hit game against his former team, for a four-run inning and a 5-2 Dodgers lead. As the game moved into the eighth inning, the group hoped for a late-inning rally, but it was not to come.

The group's attention moved back to the beer offerings, with Carson and Blake each having a Sip of Sunshine from Lawson's. Carson really enjoyed Kate The Great earlier, but it wasn't a beer that one would consume multiples of in one sitting. This Sip of Sunshine offered an incredible taste in a more approachable level.

"This is one of the original New England IPAs," Blake said as they both enjoyed sipping directly from the can.

"Wow – the aroma is magical in this – even still in the can. It comes through. Like a tropical vacation," Carson said. "This may be my favorite beer of the trip," he said after taking another sip. He leaned back into the sofa and hollered for Ty and Kareem.

"Hey guys, you've got to try this one," he recommended.

"This is exactly what I was hoping to find up here," said Kareem. "This is what an IPA should be, all the time!"

"I have to agree with you, brother. Sweet and bitter. Lots of tropical and citrus. I could get used to drinking this often," said Ty. Gavin and Tegan joined them. Gavin always enjoyed Sip of Sunshine and said he was fortunate to be able to enjoy it regularly.

"This one is a beer that is always in my fridge," he said. "Drinkability is off-the-charts great." Ellery grabbed a can as well.

"One of my all-time favorites, a true heavy hop IPA," he said. "Rafferty, you've outdone yourself with this party," continued Ellery.

The game ended with the Dodgers holding on to the victory. The group remained and finished off the pizza, wings, and most of the beer.

"I really appreciate you opening your home up to us," said Ty to Rafferty.

"I enjoyed it. It was nice getting to know you guys, and I appreciate the opportunity to contract with the university. I will touch base with Dr. Howard in the morning and continue working out the details. You guys sure you're okay to drive back? You can stay here tonight. Some of these guys will probably stay," Rafferty said.

"We appreciate it, but we will be fine. Tegan was doing more flirting than drinking, so she's going to drive. We have to get back to the hotel and pack our crap. We head back to the airport tomorrow. It's a late flight back to Texas, but we will need to get up early to get on the road," said Carson.

They stood up and exchanged pleasantries with all of the others. Blake wrote her number down on a scrap of paper and handed it to Carson.

"Look me up next time you are up this way," she said with a smile. Gavin and Tegan were saying goodbyes in the corner as Kareem, Ty, and Carson looked on waiting for her.

"Don't worry about Gavin," said Orson. "He lives in a world of fribbledom." The guys looked at him uncertain what that meant. "He says he's really into a lady, but just won't commit," Orson explained.

"Well we're not worried about that," said Ty.

Tegan glanced over, and Ty gave her the motion to wrap it up. Gavin gave her a kiss that she felt throughout her entire body, down to her toes. She turned around, eyes extra wide and a mouthed rounded grin, and grabbed the keys from Carson.

19 BRATTLEBORO

Sunday, October 11, 2015

It was 7 a.m., and Carson was fully dressed and loading the trunk of the car. Ty came down with a final bag as Carson struggled fitting everything in the vehicle. Ty looked at the bags in the parking lot still to fit, and watched his friend strain for a few more moments. Finally, he stepped in.

"Bro, give it up. You have zero spatial reasoning skills. Let me do this," he said. Ty removed everything from the trunk and placed it in the parking lot. Looking at the space available and confirming with Carson that Tegan and Kareem already had everything down there he proceeded to pack the car properly. In less than five minutes everything was inside the trunk with a few spare inches remaining. "Now let's roll, he said as he closed the trunk."

Tegan and Kareem were inside checking out at the office and returned each with two cups of luke-warm motel lobby coffee, one for each passenger.

"Thanks," said Carson as he took the cup from Kareem. "It's early, but we have a good drive ahead of us to make it back to the airport. We can hit the road and stop for brunch later, but there is also a place I was to visit on the way back. The town of Warren isn't too much of a detour on the way to the airport, and that Sip of Sunshine from last night has me wanting more. Rafferty said the brewery wasn't open for visitors, but there are places in town where we can probably find some.

With everything loaded they set off, leaving Burlington and Champ behind. Taking I-89S to VT-100S, it was a quiet forty-five-mile drive down to Warren. The leaves were still exhibiting all of their magical fall colors, and the temperature was in the mid-50's, making it an enjoyable autumn afternoon. Once they arrived in Warren, Carson turned onto Main Street looking for a place to hopefully purchase the beer.

"Ty, you might have to reorganize the trunk depending on what we find," Carson said.

He pulled off the road and in front of a large white building

"This looks like a promising place," he said. The Warren Store was a charming country store with wooden floors, a deli, and an eclectic assortment of wares. The upstairs contained a boutique style clothing shop with some more gifts. The creaky wood floors with wide, uneven planks made them feel as if they'd been transported to a day a hundred years ago. Carson walked up to the front counter,

"Can you tell me where Lawson's is?" he asked. A young lady pointed toward the back of the store.

"We have some on the floor in front of the coolers and some in the coolers," she said. They walked toward the deli and in the middle of the floor were stacks of cases of Sip of Sunshine. As the young lady indicated, there were also multiple packs in the cooler. The Warren Store had a large selection, not only of Sip of Sunshine but many other local Vermont beers.

Carson was excited at the opportunity to stock up, but then remembered the limited space remaining in the car, and the realization they would somehow have to get it back through the airport. "Well, maybe one case," he said. They checked out and headed back to the car, giving the beer to Ty to figure out how to fit it in the trunk.

Driving back to connect once again with the I-89S, it would be another two hours before they reached Brattleboro, Vermont. Carson suggested it would be a good time for an early lunch.

"There's a place called The Marina Restaurant we should stop. I saw it on Rachael Ray once," Carson suggested.

Carson almost missed the turn into the restaurant. It was a little hard to see and was a sharp turn in the lot. Pulling up, they were impressed with the view. An enclosed dining area provided excellent views of the West River where it fed into a body of water called the Meadows, and then into the Connecticut River. The server found them a table with a good view of the river.

"I will leave these menus with you. Do you know what you would like to drink?" she asked. Quickly glancing over the beverage page of the menu, Carson ordered an Otter Creek Fresh Slice, a White IPA from a microbrewery in Middlebury, Vermont. Kareem ordered the Queen City South End Lager, Ty a Dead Horse IPA from McNeill's Brewery in Brattleboro, and Tegan an Equinox Pilsner, a Czech Pilsner produced by Northshire Brewery in Bennington, Vermont.

While the server left to get the drinks, they reviewed the meu.

"It says seafood and burgers, so that must be the best options," said Kareem. "I think since we are on our way home, I will go with the seafood. I imagine it is really fresh here, plus I can get a burger anywhere, right?" he continued.

While perusing the menu, they could not help but be distracted by the smells of puff pastry and buttery mushroom sauce from the lobster and scallop pie ordered by a nearby table.

"That smells amazing," said Tegan. "I don't know if I could eat a whole one or not. I will probably go with the lobster and shrimp bow tie pasta."

Ty ordered the New England Haddock with roasted potatoes and green beans and Kareem the swordfish and roasted red peppers sandwich. Carson finally decided fish and chips.

"This is probably our final New England meal," said Tegan.

"Everything has been great – the fresh seafood is fantastic here, said Kareem.

The food quickly arrived and was as good as they anticipated. They savored each bite while taking in the beauty of the river.

"We might have to walk around a little bit before we get back in the car," suggested Carson. After finishing the meal and paying the bill, they decided to walk around the parking lot a little before the final leg of the journey back to the airport.

As they walked around something caught Ty's eye. "Hey, is that your friend?" he said to Carson. Visible from the left side of the restaurant and in the waters of the river was a large, half-surfaced metal sculpture of Champ. The sizeable dragon-like head, bright green coils, with dark green spikes on the hump took Carson back to his encounter in the lake just a couple of days ago. It appeared that each part of the creature was anchored separately, allowing the thing to move around as if it were swimming. It made Carson also remember his hip, and suddenly the throbbing in the wound was more noticeable. He rubbed it as they continued walking.

Just then Carson's cell phone rang. He looked down to see it was Dr. Howard calling.

"Good afternoon, Dr. Howard," Carson answered.

"Yes, we are on the road heading back to the airport. We just stopped down in Brattleboro to get some lunch on the way. How's everything?" Dr. Howard thanked him for all of the hard work he and his friends did researching Champ.

"Your findings will help the University in getting more grant money for research. I also checked in with Rafferty this morning, and he said everything is set up for the initial delivery of bass and we will work on establishing a long-term contract until even longer policy changes can be enacted. The mayor and governor are on board, and we will get this moving quickly," said Dr. Howard.

"That's really great to hear. I am glad we could help, and we were discussing once the information on Champ is released that will further increase the tourism in the area as everyone will want to see these animals for themselves," said Carson.

"Exactly. Speaking of these animals, you might be interested to know that we were able to get information back on the tests we ran. We were able to collect enough DNA from your wound to get results on the lab tests and attempt to identify what the creature is," said Dr. Howard.

"What did you find out, Doctor?" asked an intrigued Carson.

"As you know, people have speculated for years trying to guess what Champ is. Some have thought it was a tanystropheus, which was a reptile, but not a dinosaur, from Europe typically last seen two hundred thirty million years ago. Some have even suggested it is a leviathan, which is a snake-like animal with wings and a bump where the legs used to be," he continued.

"Leviathan? Isn't that a Biblical creature?" asked Carson.

"Yes, The Leviathan of the Book of Job is a reflection of the older Canaanite Lotan. It parallels mythology to other cultures as well, such as such as Indra slaying Vrtra or Thor slaying Jörmungandr. We can also see sea serpents in Old-World writings such as Beowulf. Ryujin is the dragon king, sea god, and master of serpents in Japanese mythology. So stories of these creatures have existed for thousands of years," Dr. Howard said.

"Other cryptozoologists have theorized Champ is a Basilosaurus, which is a primitive whale that had a long snake-like body. Some fossils of this extinct dinosaur were discovered near Charlotte, Vermont, which gives the basis for the speculation. The shape of these creatures as well as the similarly sized thoracic, lumbar, sacral, and caudal vertebrae imply that it moved in a very odd, horizontal anguilliform fashion to some degree, something completely unknown in modern cetaceans. Judging from what we know in the skeletal analysis, from the relatively weak axial musculature and the thick bones in the limbs, Basilosaurus is not believed to have been capable of sustained swimming or deep diving, or terrestrial locomotion. Others have suggested that Champ is a plesiosaur. And from the DNA it turns out to be an elasmosaurus, a type of pleasiour. The video footage showed the attack in good detail and helped confirm the similarities. The elasmosaurus was a long plesiosaur at about thirty-four feet in length. These animals were top carnivores in their respective environment. They were pursuit predators or ambush predators of various sized prey and opportunistic feeders. Their teeth could be used to pierce soft-bodied prey, especially fish. Their heads and teeth were very large, suited to grab and rip apart large animals. Their morphology allowed for high swimming speed. They too hunted visually," Dr. Howard said.

"I thought plesiosaurs had a large round body," said Carson. "This didn't exactly look like that."

"Plesiosaurs showed two main body types. Some species, with the plesiosauromorph build, sometimes had extremely long necks and small heads. The elasmosaurus is the first recognized member of this group of long-necked plesiosaurs. These were relatively slow and caught small sea animals. But there were other species, some of them reaching a length of more than fifty feet had the pliosauromorph build with a short neck and a large head. These were apex predators, fast hunters of large prey. These elasmosaurus are from the genus of plesiosaur and would have had a streamlined body with paddle-like limbs, a short tail, a small head, and an extremely long neck. The neck alone was around twenty long," he reported.

"So Champ isn't the apex predator, and instead it mostly lived on fish?" asked Carson.

"Yes, that's why they didn't attack people before, but when their diet was greatly reduced, and they were hungry, they turned to eating small animals for survival. That's why we saw the dogs disappearing. Likely they were in the water, and the animals ate them," Dr. Howard said.

"Well, this sculpture in the river in Brattleboro looks pretty much like him. I am glad you were able to get information from the tests and identify the creature," said Carson.

"I appreciate all of your help this week. You guys have a safe trip back to the airport and Texas. I will be in touch as we work on the academic publication of this research. I will also reach out to some contacts here about getting you guys on a speaking tour as we talked about earlier. With another successful investigation I am sure you guys won't have any trouble finding speaking engagements in the future," said Dr. Howard.

After ending the phone call Carson and the others returned to the car and headed back on the road for the final two-hour drive to the Logan Airport Rental Car Center.

20 BACK TO AUSTIN

Sunday, October 11, 2015

Late evening Carson pulled into the rental car return lot with about two hours to go before their flight. "We should have plenty of time to check in and make it through security. I never like to risk it because there can always be something unexpected," he said.

"Yeah, and it's been a great trip, but I am kind of ready to get back to Texas. Especially with the weather getting cooler up here. Send me back to the warmth," Ty said.

Dropping off the keys with the attendant they grabbed a cart by the check-in booth for all of their luggage, which they could have carried except for the extra bags full of beer Kareem managed to pack up.

"It may be getting colder, but the beer is awesome and fresh. I will enjoy drinking it back in Texas and trading it with others...but we may have to come back up when it runs out," Kareem said.

Carson put his hand in his jean pocket and brushed up against the paper with Blake's phone number written on it. He thought about the fun conversation from the night before, even without looking at the paper. "Fine with me. I'm ready to come back anytime," Carson responded.

Tegan, thinking of her time with Gavin and that kiss said, "Me too."

The line through security was surprisingly easy to maneuver through, and they each found themselves on the other side with plenty of time before they were due to board the flight.

"Time for a bite to eat and the last drink in New England?" Carson asked the group. They all nodded in agreement and stopped at a sports bar just down from their gate. They sat at the bar and immediately the server asked if they knew what they wanted. Without looking at the menu Ty suggested a couple of orders of nachos and a round of beer, "something local," he said.

"Works for me," said Kareem.

The server put the orders of nachos in with the kitchen. "Anything in particular locally?"

"Your choice," replied Carson. "We've had a lot of good beer up here, and I don't think we can go wrong with anything."

"Same thing for everyone?" she asked.

"Mix it up," replied Tegan. She turned her back for a moment, put four empty glasses on the bar, and then turned around again. She pulled out four cans and sat them in the middle, letting each person chose their fate.

"These are some of my favorites right now," she said. The offering included Melcher Street IPA by Trillium Brewing Company, Vicinity, a Double IPA also by Trillium, Tree House Alter Ego IPA, and Tree House Julius IPA.

"Looks great. We love the IPAs up here," said Ty.

Carson picked up his can and held it in front of him.

"Well, gang here's to a successful vacation. We came for the beer, for the leaves, and to get away from it all. We didn't expect being thrown into another cryptid mystery, but we were, we solved the case, and we lived to tell about it!"

Each member of the group hoisted their can to meet his, "Here! Here!" they said.

"The project with the university will be a big success for everyone I think," said Ty. "The university gets the academic reputation boost from the research conducted. The finding that Champ does in fact exist, the towns around the lake will benefit from an increase in tourism now that people know for sure there is a creature in the lake. They will want to see it, especially with its appetite appeased, the state will also see benefit in the large contact with Rafferty's fishery, and we will likely see a bump too with our names associated with the discovery." They all nodded thinking about the possibilities.

"If we see a bump to what we have already been seeing after the chupacabra, we might need another vacation," said Kareem.

The order of nachos arrived piping hot and loaded with cheese, jalapenos, tomatoes, sour cream, black beans – the works. Carson and Ty looked up from their nachos and watched a bit of the Astros and Royals playing in game three of the American League Division Series.

"I love the World Series," said Ty.

"Me, too. I hope the Astros make it this year," said Carson. He took a bite of the nachos and a drink from the can of Julius. "Thinking about vacations…what do you think about checking out spring training?" he asked.

To be continued

Beer List

14th Star Brewing Company Maple Breakfast Stout

Alchemist Crusher Imperial IPA

Alchemist Focal Banger India Pale Ale (IPA)

Alchemist Heady Topper Imperial IPA

Alchemist Rapture Imperial IPA

Allagash Brewing Company 20th anniversary Fluxus Belgian Strong Pale Ale

Allagash Brewing Company Black Belgian Strong Dark Ale

Allagash Brewing Company Confluence Ale Belgian Strong Pale Ale

Allagash Brewing Company Farm To Face American Wild Ale

Allagash Brewing Company Ghoulschip American Wild Ale

Allagash Brewing Company Haunted House Belgian Dark Ale

Allagash Brewing Company James Bean Belgian Strong Pale Ale

Allagash Brewing Company Uncommon Crow American Wild Ale

Allagash Brewing Company White Witbier

Barreled Souls Brewing Company ABCs American Brown Ale

Barreled Souls Brewing Company Cookie Monster American Porter

Barreled Souls Brewing Company Dark Matter American Strong Ale

Barreled Souls Brewing Company Eat A Peach Berliner Weissbier

Barreled Souls Brewing Company El Dorado American Pale Ale (APA)

Barreled Souls Brewing Company Golden Cucumber Belgian Pale Ale

Barreled Souls Brewing Company Half Nelson American Pale Ale (APA)

Barreled Souls Brewing Company Mocha Grande American Brown Ale

Barreled Souls Brewing Company Quaker State American Stout

Barreled Souls Brewing Company Rosalita American Blonde Ale

Barreled Souls Brewing Company Spring Tonic American Pale Wheat Ale

Barreled Souls Brewing Company Stay Puft American Imperial Stout

Barreled Souls Brewing Company Teotihuacán American Imperial Stout

Barreled Souls Brewing Company Paper Planes Double IPA

Baxter Brewing Company Phantom Punch Winter Stout Foreign / Export Stout

Baxter Brewing Company Stowaway IPA American IPA India Pale Ale

(IPA)

Baxter Brewing Company Window Seat American Porter

Bunker Brewing Company Beast Coast IPA

Bunker Brewing Company Machine Czech Pilz

Bunker Brewing Company Ty the Cypher Pale Lager

Bunker Brewing Company Weekend At Burniez

Drop-In Brewing Company Six Holes In My Freezer

Fiddlehead Brewing Company Brett On The Dance Floor American
    Wild Ale

Fiddlehead Brewing Company Fiddlehead IPA American IPA India
Pale Ale (IPA)

Fiddlehead Brewing Company Mastermind American Double /
Imperial
    IPA

Fiddlehead Brewing Company Second Fiddle American Double /
    Imperial IPA

Foley Brothers Brewing American Double / Imperial IPA

Foley Brothers Brewing Maple American Brown Ale

Foley Brothers Prospect IPA - American Double / Imperial IPA

Foolproof Brewing Company Peanut Butter Raincloud Porter

Four Quarters Brewing Company Darkest Heart Maple Liquer Barrel
    Aged Imperial Stout

Four Quarters Brewing Company Horn of the Moon Witbier

Four Quarters Brewing Company Misery Sour Sour/Wild Ale

Four Quarters Brewing Company Opus Dei with Orange Zest and
    Chamomile Belgian Ale

Four Quarters Brewing Company Sundog Imperial IPA

Grassroots Brewing Legitimacy India Pale Ale (IPA)

Grassroots Brewing Brother Soigné Saison

Hill Farmstead Brewery Abner Imperial Pale Ale

Hill Farmstead Brewery Anna Saison

Hill Farmstead Brewery Civil Disobedience #5 Sour/Wild Ale

Hill Farmstead Brewery Clara Traditional Ale

Hill Farmstead Brewery Dorothy 2015 Saison

Hill Farmstead Brewery Edward American Pale Ale

Hill Farmstead Brewery Society & Solitude #4 Imperial IPA

Champ and A Bit of Sunshine

Hill Farmstead Brewery Susan India Pale Ale (IPA)

Hill Farmstead Brewery Vera Mae Saison

Hill Farmstead Brewery/ Kissmeyer Beer & Brewing / Cambridge Brewing
Company Nordic Saison

Lawson's Finest Liquids Bourbon Barrel Aged Fayston Maple Imperial
Stout (Pappy Van Winkle) American Double / Imperial Stout

Lawson's Finest Liquids Hopzilla American Double / Imperial IPA

Lawson's Finest Liquids Sip of Sunshine IPA American Double / Imperial
IPA

Lawson's Finest Liquids Super Session #2 American IPA

Liquid Riot Bottling Company Rauchbier

Lost Nation Brewing Lost Galaxy IPA

McNeill's Brewery Dead Horse IPA

Magic HatBrewing Company #9 Fruit Beer

Maine Beer Company A Tiny Beautiful Something

Maine Beer Company King Titus American Porter

Maine Beer Company Lunch DIPA

Maine Beer Company Mean Old Tom American Stout

Maine Beer Company Peeper Ale

Northshire Brewery Equinox Pilsner – Czech Pilsner

Notch Brewing Dog and Pony Wheat Ale

Notch Brewing Hootenanny Berliner Weisse

Notch Brewing Left of the Dial IPA

Notch Brewing The Mule Corn Lager

Otter Creek Fresh Slice India Pale Ale (IPA) White

Portsmouth Brewery Kate The Great Russian Imperial Stout

Queen City Brewery Landlady Ale Extra Special / Strong Bitter (ESB)

Queen City South End Lager

Queen City Brewery Yorkshire Porter English Porter

Salem Beerworks Blue Fruit Beer

Salem Beerworks REDeemer Imperial Red Ale

Salem Beerworks Salem Pale Ale

Salem Beerworks Watermelon Ale Golden Ale

Sebago Brewing Company Bourbon Barrel Aged Lake Trout Stout

Sebago Brewing Company Hefeweizen

Sebago Brewing Company Royal Tar Imperial Stout

Sebago Brewing Company Saddleback Ale

Squam Brewing Halcyon Steamer Stout

Squam Brewing Ice Harvester Porter

Squam Brewing Imperial Loon Stout

Squam Brewing Golden IPA

Squam Brewing Moose Ale

Squam Brewing Rattlesnake Rye-PA

Squam Brewing The Camp Barleywine

Sublime Brewing Company Blonde Ale

Sublime Brewing Company Double IPA

Sublime Brewing Company Grissette

Sublime Brewing Company The Plymouth Pale Ale

Switchback Brewing Ale

Switchback Brewing Citra-Pils Killer Bier

Switchback Brewing Export Stout

Switchback Brewing Märzen

Switchback Brewing Thai Lime Gose

The Shed Brewery Mountain Ale

Tree House Brewing Company Alter Ego American IPA

Tree House Brewing Company Julius American IPA

Trillium Brewing Company Melcher Street IPA American IPA

Trillium Brewing Company Vicinity American Double / Imperial IPA

Vermont Pub Handsome Micks Irish Stout

Vermont Pub Lake Champlain Chocolate Stout

Vermont Pub Maple Lager

Vermont Pub Smoked Porter

von Trapp Brewing Bohemian Pilsner Czech Pilsner

von Trapp Brewing Dunkel Lager Dunkel

von Trapp Brewing Golden Helles Lager Dortmunder/Helles

von Trapp Brewing Oktoberfest Oktoberfest/Märzen

von Trapp Brewing Vienna Amber Lager/Vienna

Zero Gravity Craft Brewery Bob White Witbier

Zero Gravity Craft Brewery Brett Head India Pale Ale (IPA)

Zero Gravity Craft Brewery Conehead with Mandarina Bavaria IPA

India Pale Ale (IPA)

Zero Gravity Craft Brewery Green State Lager Pilsener

Zero Gravity Craft Brewery Little Wolf American Pale Ale

AN AUTHOR'S TALE

FRIDAY, APRIL 14, 2017

It was late one Friday night in mid-April. Our author sat in the corner of his bedroom at a cluttered desk attempting to complete grading on the prior week's assignments in his online marketing class. Only seven papers left to grade, but the progress was slow. The television was off, he was all alone in the room, and expected to complete the work in less than one hour. It was quiet, but his mind wandered. He found distraction by looking at the walls, looking at the blinds, and walking around the room. "Why can't I focus?" he wondered. His mind raced from topic to topic instead of looking at the paper in front of him.

He thought about the chupacabra, he thought about the marketing campaign of offering a free e-book of his first story, then back to the paper on his screen. A couple of paragraphs read then his mind shifted to audiobooks. Yes, he needed an audiobook for the chupacabra. That would boost sales! But who would do the narration? He minimized the papers and searched for samples at ACX.com. There were a few that stood out to him quickly, but how much would that cost? He sighed as he saw the computer logged him out of the online classroom and he would have to log back in again once he finished this current paper.

Not ten minutes later his mind again wandered. This time it was Champ and the current book he was writing. Then projects he hadn't even started yet. A memoir? Who would want to read that? What had he really accomplished? What would he tell? And would anyone care? Maybe a one-shot short story of Carson, Ty, Tegan, or Kareem in a solo adventure? He had a whole document saved on the computer with ideas for novels as well as short films.

"That's right – I need to get working on that CDFL short film and gather a cast," he thought. But what of these papers? It was taking too long to read the current paper, and it wasn't even poorly written. But his mind was not focused. He then thought of brain fog, which he frequently had. More so in the past, but it was coming back. Just yesterday his doctor told him his lab work came back high in nearly every category and now his sugar was high too and in the diabetes range. Maybe that is why he was tired, and his brain was often foggy and forgetful. Okay, whatever. Back to the papers.

He managed to complete the one in front of him and surprisingly the next one. Now he was down to five. He checked out some videos on YouTube. But an audiobook would be cool, right? He got up from the desk and walked into the kitchen. A beer will do the trick. That's what his characters would do. He pulled a nice blue can with a balancing elephant from the refrigerator. Equilibrium Extra Special Bitter from Nickel Brook Brewing Company in Burlington, Ontario. He opened it and took a sip as he walked back to the bedroom.

"Hmm. Nice bitter taste. Strong malt up front," he thought. "I wonder if there are any creatures in Ontario I could write about," he wondered as he sat back in the chair and studied the can.

The drink worked for a few minutes. He was able to finish the next paper and another. "That's what I'm talkin' about!" he said as he opened the next paper. "Now we're cookin' with gas!" But again the progress was short-lived. He looked down at the phone, checked email, logged into Pokémon Go, looked at Facebook, and then realized he was doing it again. He knew the feedback on the papers wasn't due until Sunday, but he wanted to complete it before the weekend. True, most people considered Friday night the weekend, but for our author, Friday typically meant grading papers and watching paranormal shows from the DVR in the background.

Maybe he needed a break. Even though it was night, it looked nice outside. It wasn't too hot in Phoenix yet – probably another couple of weeks until it was hot even after the sun went down. Maybe it would do him good and clear his mind if he got outside and went for a walk. A quick check on the kids and the dogs proved everyone was fine. "I'm going to go out for a quick walk quick," he told the kids. "Probably just around the block," he said. The kids returned a surprised look at him because that wasn't a sentence they typically associated with him.

Leaving the house, he walked toward Arizona Avenue, then right on the street. He could walk a mile down to the QuikTrip. Maybe a soda and two taquitos would do the trick? But with the recent doctor news that wouldn't go over well at home, he realized. He started walking and thinking. Thinking about all of the projects he wanted to tackle. "A cover with a photograph of the characters!" he thought. "That will be nice. It would allow readers to connect with them more. Maybe a group shot and some individual photos. What about multiple alternative covers? That was a nice trick when he collected comics. Alternative covers were always a draw," he thought.

He continued to walk in the pleasant night air, oblivious to the traffic passing him by or his present location. He had already passed QuikTrip and was halfway to the next street when he noticed. "I might as well keep going," he deduced. "Arizona Wilderness Brewing is just another mile or so down the road."

It was one of his favorite local breweries, named a few years ago as the world's best new brewery. How fortunate it was just three miles down the road. A perfect place to stop for a beer – and they tapped something new every Thursday, so it created something to look forward to every week. Plus the food menu was incredible. A good selection of continually offered products, but also a daily special that featured fresh, local ingredients.

The brewery had great patios – both in front of and behind the store. The brewery itself was large with ample seating, but he always preferred the tasting room. It was smaller but comfortable. The bar was large enough for several people and there were tables, but he liked the taproom because it had less traffic. He especially enjoyed brewing days as the air inside was filled with the smell of the malts, yeasts, and hops. He imagined how nice it would be to work there on those days.

The final bit of the journey made him realize how far three miles truly was. Even though technically he classified himself as a runner and was in the Fifty State Half Marathon Club, he was lazy. He ran a half marathon at the beginning of February in San Diego, and just two weeks ago in Hollywood, but nothing in between. Not even treadmill workouts at the gym. That is why his running time and health risks all increased over the last five years. The next run was in mid-May, but then he realized that was just about three weeks away. The doctor told him he needed to get back in shape through diet and exercise. Walking to the brewery was exercise so that should be good for today, he thought.

He finally arrived at Arizona Wilderness around 10 p.m. Even though he was tired from the walk, there weren't any parking spaces, so he was glad he didn't drive. He had been a somewhat regular at the brewery since they opened, and there had not been many beers over those visits that he did not like. Even though he wasn't a huge fan of sours, the brewery did frequently have new sours in the lineup, and he would usually give in just to try it. "Only time for one or two," he thought, "then time to get home and back to work." A newly tapped beer was Pelton Pale Ale, brewed with Nelson hops. He really enjoyed Nelson hops. He also liked the straw color with the small white head.

"How's the book coming?" asked a man walking toward the bar and taking a seat next to him. Jeff was in his mid-30's, short brown hair, and a medium-length well-trimmed beard.

"I'm slowly starting," said Mark. "I finished chapter one, but I may rearrange it. Still forming the story in my head, but I am distracted by other ideas and some writer's block. I thought it would be nice to get out and take in some fresh air to unclog the block," he said.

"And of course a beer," said Jeff.

"Well of course. I mean it's research, right? I can't write about characters drinking all of these various beers and style of beers if I don't put in the work myself," he said with a smile.

"How is that Pelton?" Jeff asked.

"I like it. It's a pale ale, so it's clean, hoppy, and a little grassy. A very pleasant drink," he said. "It's good for starters, but I think my next one I am going to kick it up a notch. I kind of want to try that new collab with Jester King – the Stuffing. And that Hibiscus Tea Gose is wonderful. My wife and I were here the other day and she tried it. Every beer I have ever had her taste she stuck her tongue out and said 'I don't like beer'. Even though they are different styles and flavors she only tastes 'beer' and dislikes it. But this time she took not one, but two sips and said "Mmm, I like that one." She liked the smell more than the taste, but she didn't mind the taste either," Mark replied.

"That's a start I suppose," Jeff said. "Maybe you can find something else for her sometime."

"Nah, she's not really interested. But I am interested in this Chocolate Bunny. I am glad it is still on – one of my favorites. I bought a pint and a growler last week and I am down to have another pint tonight. Awesome chocolatey taste in a porter. I enjoy it every time," commented Mark.

"Maybe you'll have to write about that in one of your stories. Any creatures in Phoenix?" Jeff asked.

"I don't know. I don't recall coming across any in my reading other than the Mogollon Monster up around the Grand Canyon. Plus, I am still working on the ones in Vermont," Mark replied.

The server checked on Mark and Jeff.

"Do you guys want any food this evening before the kitchen closes?" he asked. "I am sure the doctor and my wife would kill me, but I want the peanut butter and jalapeno jelly burger with the house chips," said Mark. "I know it sounds weird, but I had it once, and it was amazing. I heard it's even better when they have it as a special on Taco Tuesday night. I have yet to have the peanut butter tacos, but I hope to find them one day," he said.

"They are as elusive as those crazy monsters you write about," prodded Jeff.

"Maybe so," replied Mark, "but I have a strong eyewitness claiming to not only have seen them, but he has ordered them before. Like the truth on the X-Files, it's out there," quipped Mark.

The burger arrived, and Mark took a bite and enjoyed the mixture of flavors. As odd as it sounded, perhaps just a little bit more peanut butter would make it even better. The jelly was slightly spicy but was a good balance to the meal. The chocolate from the Chocolate Bunny and the peanut butter from the burger reminded him of the old Reese's Peanut Butter cup commercial; Your peanut butter is in my chocolate. Your chocolate is in my peanut butter. Either way, it was good.

"I would say I shouldn't eat it all this late at night, but I will get my ass kicked if I bring a burger home," Mark revealed.

"Are you heading home when you finish?" inquired Jeff.

"Maybe. I don't feel that I am up to writing or grading yet, but I am walking so it will take a while. Maybe by that time, I will regain my focus," said Mark.

"Well, if you still want to be out, I am heading down the street to the Perch after this. They are open until 1 a.m., and the upstairs patio is awesome this time of night," offered Jeff.

"That's cool. I like the Perch also, and it's even closer to my house. A short walk back from there," Mark replied.

Mark finished the burger and the Bunny as Jeff cashed out. Mark's check arrived soon, and he paid the bill in cash.

"It is a very pleasant night," said Mark. "My friends back east don't really get it that it can be a high temperature and still feel nice. Like right now, approaching 11 p.m. and it's seventy degrees. That's more than the daytime high in many places."

"Hey, anything under one-oh-five I will take," Jeff said only half-jokingly.

"Ready when you are," said Mark.

The pair of friends exited the front patio and entered Jeff's red 1998 Toyota Tacoma pickup just outside the wooden fenced walls. Godsmack's Voodoo played as Jeff turned on the truck. While Mark was not necessarily a fan or regular listener of the group, he liked that song. His mind drifted back to 2000 when he first watched MTV's Fear, a show which drew him into the paranormal world and also used Voodoo as the show's opening music. It was just a few miles from Arizona Wilderness down to the Perch. They could easily park in the lot off of Arizona Avenue and Chicago Street, then walk the short distance down Wall Street. As they drove down a quiet Arizona Avenue, Voodoo ended and Amorphis' Black Winter Day played. Jeff was definitely hardcore. Mark wondered if the roars coming from the lead singer resembled what a chupacabra sounded like when it attacked? The drinks from Arizona Wilderness helped him begin to relax, and the menu at the Perch would certainly finish off the last of the resistance.

They walked the less than a block walk down Wall Street to the front of the Perch. Mark always liked the entrance, the heavily wooded dining area, the multiple cages of birds, and the layout of the tables created a charming, almost Southern atmosphere. He could see this dining area like a courtyard in Savannah or New Orleans, but it always felt somewhat surreal being just outside of Phoenix.

The outdoor dining, a large indoor bar, and the rooftop bar offered many options for diners as well as drinkers to have a good time. The hostess directed them toward the stairs leading to the upstairs bar. As they walked past the cages, the birds began to hop around and speak. There was Pinky the Moluccan Cockatoo, Bubba the Hyacinth Macaw, Mango the Sun Conure, Bebe the Nanday Conure, Jazz the Umbrella Cockatoo, Bogey the Green Wing Macaw, and many more. There were more than a dozen birds in total. The night air was filled with the songs and sounds of the birds. As they walked by Jazz called out "Night Night," but the duo continued walking. Bogey gave a cat call and kissing sounds as they walked up the steps to the rooftop bar.

Mark was thinking about just having a pint, but there were so many on tap right now that sounded good he felt like he had to go with a flight. The flight came in a nice round tree trunk and offered five individual four-ounce beers. Mark looked over the menu. So many to choose from he wasn't sure what to select. The Saison de Beaver by Belching Beaver was just tapped, that would be one.

Desert Cider House offered the Desert Dragon. Since his fantasy football team was named the dragons, he picked that as well. He pondered for a moment. Based on his football team and his geography, he thought he was The Desert Dragon. Then he realized after his doctor's analysis of his blood work he must be the dessert dragon. "Diabeetus," he internalized in a Wilfred Brimley voice. Some of the others on the menu he previously tried and decided to pass on this time even though they were good. He still liked trying new beers, even though there was no more World of Beer points to earn for new beers. There were others that sounded good, but he thought to fill out the rest with beers brewed by the Perch, so he selected the L'Phiddy Shades IPA, Luna Loves Simcoe Pale Ale, and Sprechen Sie Dunkel Dunkelweizen. Enough were remaining on the list to get a second flight if he felt up to it.

He and Jeff talked and drank beers from their flights. The conversation was a little about beer, a little about writing and monsters, and a bit about football. The NFL draft was less than a week away. Although living in Phoenix for the past thirteen seasons, Mark was not a Cardinals fan. Well, he was a David Johnson fan because he helped his fantasy team make it to the Shaker Bowl championship game last year. However, he could not keep him this season and having finished second overall in the league, David Johnson likely would not be available to him at pick eleven.

His favorite team used to be the Cincinnati Bengals, but when the team dumped Chad "Ocho Cinco" Johnson and Dhani Jones the same year, Mark dumped the Bengals and replaced them with the Detroit Lions.

Now a new team moved up the charts and was becoming Mark's not-quite-official second team; his side chick if you will. The Cleveland Browns. Yes, they hadn't won in years, but he thought they could be close.

"The Browns better not screw up and pick anyone other than Myles Garrett with the first pick," he told Jeff. "I will be pissed if they take Mitchell Trubisky at one. I wouldn't even take him at twelve. They need defense and some pass-catchers. Like Malik Hooker. That's a better twelve," he continued.

"Well my Cardinals need a quarterback," said Jeff. "Carson is getting older, and I like Patrick Mahomes as a building block for the future," he said.

The moon continued to rise in the night sky and was a lovely sight against the Chandler city line backdrop. Not a full moon, but a definitely a waxing gibbous phase, the phase when the moon is more than fifty percent illuminated but not yet a full moon. Mark thought about taking a photo with his camera, but knew he would be disappointed when it turned out to be just a speck of light as it always was his on his phone.

"Well," Jeff said as he stood up and put some cash down on the bar, "I think I'm going to head out since it's after midnight. Want a lift?" he inquired.

"No, I'm good. I will have one more flight then walk home from here to enjoy the weather a bit more. But thanks for the ride here," Mark said.

"Good luck on that book. Can't wait to read it," said Jeff. The two shook hands, and Jeff departed down the stairway.

Mark was almost alone on the roof now and looked over the menu once more. The server asked what next.

"One last flight," he said. "Touchdown for the Bear Red Ale, PaleYEAH! 2.0 Pale Ale, Choose the Ryeght Rye Beer, Wak-A-Mole IPA, and let's end with the Perch S'Wheat 2.0," he ordered. The flight arrived quickly, and Mark drank while enjoying the quietness of the rooftop. He could occasionally hear the birds from downstairs talking to passersby. He wondered if he would be able to write when he got home or if he would just go to bed. He had always heard the phrase "Write drunk, edit sober," to whom the internet had credited to Ernest Hemingway.

While it could sound like something he might say, it was not verified to the best of Mark's knowledge. Still, it seemed like good advice. He remembered writing Troll's Canterbury Tales in college for English Literature class in college. Uncertain what to write Mark drank a fifth of Jack Daniels and wrote the story. It did earn an A for the assignment and admiration from friends, but looking back now the story wasn't as good as the rave reviews his friends gave it or as he remembered it himself. Maybe he didn't edit sober?

Mark finished up the final flight glass, paid the tab, and confirmed he had his debit card in his wallet, his keys, and his phone. During that routine process, he frequently heard Austin Powers in his mind repeating "Spectacles, testicles, wallet, and watch."

Time to walk back to the house. At just over a mile, maybe a mile and a half he imagined it would take about twenty minutes. "Well, maybe thirty minutes after these beers," he thought. He turned to leave, held on to the handrail, and slowly made his way down the steps. Most of the birds were now asleep, and only the staff remained in the bar. Everyone else apparently called it an evening long ago.

By the time Mark reached the front entrance, the lights from the rooftop bar had turned off, signaling the server was finished and ready to go home for the evening. The hostess walked Mark to the entrance and locked the door as he exited. He stood there in the parking lot looking around, checking out the moon and stars, and marveling at how nice it still was at this early hour. He turned to walk back home when he suddenly felt the urge to use the restroom. Those flights were kicking in now. He turned back toward the Perch, but the door was locked, and the lights were slowly turning off throughout the facility.

"Good luck getting someone's attention now," he thought. Then he remembered two things – there was an alley behind the building, and he was a guy. "It's empty out here, so no one will find out," he thought.

He walked around the side of the building and to a back alley where he was confident no one would see. "Besides, it will only be a minute," he thought. In front of the brewery, the alley stretched in both directions. One direction led into an area behind the ImprovMANIA Comedy Club and Gangplank. He could see a painted mural wall in that direction, but there were also several street lamps lighting the alley. The other route seemed like there would be more people, but it was quiet. Chicago 55 sat on one side, a dumpster and Pirates Fish & Chips on the other. He decided to go that direction and was surprised to see how empty it was. Looking around there wasn't a good way to get behind the Perch. It seemed like the dumpster would have to do. He walked close to the dumpster and, standing in front of it he unzipped his pants.

Just then he heard a loud noise. It sounded like rustling in the trees from inside the brewery. The other birds were completely quiet despite the disturbance. In the wild that might symbolize a predator or larger animal in the area, but here? Who knew? It was probably nothing. Mark turned toward the brewery to see if he could see anything but did not detect the source of the disturbance. All he was certain of was that he was now unable to begin the process of relieving himself. All of a sudden, the rustling of leaves grew louder, and moments later a creature burst from the canopy! It landed on roof peak just above the brewery's sign.

Mark stared at the animal in utter surprise, his eyes widened, and his jaw dropped. Suddenly, the process of liquid elimination involuntarily began. The animal was a large bird-like creature and looked to be around eight to nine feet in height. The Perch's wooden entrance sign was wide, and this bird matched its width. From his dumpster vantage point, Mark estimated about forty inches wide.

"What the hell is that?" he said aloud. The monster-bird unleashed a loud, ear-piercing scream that did not resemble any bird he knew. The animal had a bird-like head with a large beak, similar to a pterodactyl or crane, but the head was not shaped like the prehistoric pterodactyl. The head was attached to an elongated neck and an extensive body with a tail that stood out like a peacock. It had long muscular legs that looked like they could snatch up large prey, possibly the size of a large dog or even a human. Hopefully not a burly-sized author.

The animal stayed perched atop the brewery's sign looking around its surroundings and down the alley where Mark stood. He searched his mind of all of the large birds he had researched in the past. It was not a big bird like a heron or crane. California condors were the largest known living birds but became extinct in the wild in 1987 when all remaining birds were captured. Once breeding programs proved successful, condors began being released in 1991, but this did not look like a condor. Despite the condor being the largest known bird, this creature appeared larger than the biggest condor recorded.

Mark's mind began running through legend for an answer. Perhaps Native American legend? A well-known legend was the Thunderbird, but those cryptids were said to have lizard features and resemble the extinct pteranodon. They were believed to have wingspans of between twelve and eighteen feet. It was known that the Tombstone Epitaph newspaper printed a story about the capture of a large, unusual winged creature on April 26, 1890. It was a creature that was shot in Arizona and described as having smooth skin, featherless wings like a bat, and a face that resembled an alligator. But this animal did not match that description. It was something else.

This land used to belong to the Hohokam, Mark remembered. Perhaps besides the Thunderbird, there was another large animal that hunted these lands. After all, there were drawings from the Hohokam on rocks on South Mountain. The Hohokam were known to have created rock art for more than a thousand years, before the tribe's sudden and still mysterious disappearance around 1500 AD. If this creature was the same as the large bird depicted in their rock art, perhaps it had something to do with the tribe's disappearance?

Thinking of the potential of that theory, and looking at the size of the legs and talons on the creature, Mark began to worry and started to walk down the alley further away from the brewery slowly. As he began to move, the animal took notice and let out another shrill, then suddenly shot straight up in the air.

In the air, it was easy to see the bird's wingspan, nearly eclipsing the moon. The creature glided effortlessly in the night air, circled, then flew toward Mark. He froze briefly with fear, but then began running. Not the slow, plodding half marathon pace he usually displayed, but one with more purpose. Across Chicago Street he cut through the now abandoned gravel lot, the bird-creature still following. The animal made a sudden move, diving down toward Mark, but he luckily slipped on the loose gravel and hit the ground just out of the creature's grasp.

While the bird flew back up and circled for another approach, Mark crossed over Arizona Avenue and ran along the sidewalk between the City Hall and under cover of trees. Mark passed by Serranos and continued to the corner where Modern Margarita and La Bocca located, but already closed for the night. Now he had to cross the intersection, and the danger increased as the trees opened up leaving him in the clearing.

The bird was following and ready for another attempt, but Mark managed to make it across the street and back under cover of trees before it had the chance to attack. He left the sidewalk and ran on the grass close to the trees. It was a long stretch, but well-covered to prevent the bird from getting too close. Further down the sidewalk, the terracotta cement pavilion of the downtown Chandler district provided the necessary coverage to remain out of range. As Mark ran from the pavilion toward the next set of trees, the creature swooped again, and again come up short. Here the trees were sparse. Mark's best hope was to stay under the largest tree and wait the animal out. As Mark ran to the tree and hugged the trunk. The bird circled the area high above the trees unable to get its prey. Suddenly, it swooped down and landed on top of a stone structure resembling a Mayan pyramid in front of the Chandler Administration building. The bird and man continued closely watching the other, each awaiting an opportunity for the advantage.

Mark watched the beast perched upon the pyramid for more than fifteen minutes. The standoff finally ended when the creature heard another noise in the far-off distance and suddenly took flight. It climbed high into the night sky and quickly out of sight as it investigated the noise, hoping to find easier prey. Even though Mark stood underneath the tree for several minutes, he was still breathing hard and unsure of the events that just took place. What was that thing? Where did it come from? Where was it going next? All answers the author would not find. This was like something out of his books – an unexplained creature right here in Chandler, Arizona.

He remained under the tree and phoned the police department. An officer responded within a few minutes and found Mark sitting on a park bench beside the large tree. Mark attempted to explain what he saw, but his description could not possibly do the event justice. The officer took notes but looked on with disbelief. Mark and the officer walked past the trees and into the lot where the pyramid stood. There they found three large feathers left by the unknown creature. The two men looked on with astonishment at seeing the size of the feathers. The officer did not appear to believe Mark's story, but the size of the feathers did leave him with uncertainty. He called forensics, and they arrived to collect the specimen. The officer offered to drive Mark home while forensics remained on the scene and finished data collection.

The report of the sighting made its way into the Arizona Republic within days. Given the location of the final conflict just across from San Tan Brewery, reporters dubbed the creature the Santanimal. No other sightings of the creature have been recorded. The creature remains at large.

ABOUT THE AUTHOR

Mark Trollinger is a fan of cryptozoology and craft beer. He grew up in Yellow Springs, OH and attended the University of Rio Grande in Rio Grande, OH, majoring in marketing. He completed a MBA in Global Management, a Master of Science in the Administration of Justice and Security, and all of the course work in a Ph.D. of Higher Education Administration (ABD). He currently is taking classes in screenwriting at Grand Canyon University in Phoenix, AZ.

He has authored articles for CDFL*Insider*, is co-host of the higher education podcast *Teaching Tips*, and the author of the upcoming dissertation *A Quantitative Study of the Factors Considered During Undergraduate Program of Study Selection*.

He is the author of *The Chupacabra and the Bat Rastard*, the first book in the cryptozoology series. He is also the author of *Corre*.

Champ and a Bit of Sunshine is the second book in the cryptozoology series.

Made in the USA
San Bernardino, CA
18 October 2018